Worth It

SISTERS AND SERENDIPITY
BOOK ONE

LADY MARIE

Cover design by Lady Marie

Editing by A.K. Edits

Formatting by Lady Marie

Contents

To Janice, the original Lady (J) Marie. You were always my best friend and you always will be.

To Sadie, because the love has always there and I'll never forget that.

I love you both and I couldn't ask for better grandmothers.

Author's Note

I started writing this book during the Covid-19 pandemic after a burst of inspiration, but in truth, this has been a long time coming. This project has been challenging, scary, exhilarating, and an all-around emotional rollercoaster (and if you know me, you know I do NOT do roller coasters in any capacity). Still, I can't help but feel as though all of that hard work and emotional labor has finally paid off. The dream that middle school me had of one day finally seeing her words in print has finally come true and that, more than anything else, makes everything worth it. So while the last couple of years gave me plenty of reasons to say they were cursed, they also gave me at least one blessing. For that, I will be forever grateful.

Content Warning

This book contains on-page explicit sexual content, familial pressure and conflict, as well as brief mentions terminal illness and death, specifically colon cancer.

CHAPTER 1

Makayla

"Kendall, please. What is it? I don't have time for your bullshit right now." Makayla Michaels didn't even attempt to keep her irritation out of her voice.

Her phone had been ringing nonstop for the last thirty minutes. She wanted to ignore it, and not just because she was on a deadline or because she was on her way to a meeting. As much as she loved her older sister Kendall, these days the other woman was the last person Makayla wanted to talk to. Damn near every conversation they'd been having for the better part of six months was either uncomfortable or the start of an argument. She didn't have time for either today.

"Uh-uh, watch your tone with me, little girl!" Kendall said on the other end of the line.

Makayla rolled her eyes. "Sorry to be the one to tell you this, Kennie, but I haven't actually been a little girl in at least two decades."

"And yet I'm still the oldest, so watch your tone," her sister responded.

Makayla took a deep breath and made a concentrated effort

not to snap the pencil in her hand. After quickly and quietly counting down from ten, she exhaled. The sooner she figured out why her sister was blowing up her phone, the sooner she could get back to work.

"Hi, Kendall. Can whatever this is wait? I'm going into a meeting soon to go over some things with the next issue, and I promised I would get my assistant these revisions before then."

"I swear you're always working. Weren't you supposed to be off today? It's no wonder you can't keep a man with that schedule. You really need to get you a whole life before you keel over in that damn office of yours," her sister said.

This was Kendall's usual tirade. It was one that she seemed to trot out regularly these days whether Makayla was working or not, a reflection of the same reactions and arguments she'd been having with her family for years. Admittedly, this particular opinion seemed to be rearing its ugly head more often now that their mother's wedding was quickly approaching.

Did Makayla work entirely too much? The answer to that was completely subjective. Okay, sure, she'd just been complaining that the staff meetings seemed to be never-ending these days. And yes, okay, her sister was correct in the fact that Makayla was not supposed to be in the office today. What no one seemed to understand, though, was that her job as a senior editor was never done. That was especially true considering she worked for Divine Mahogany Magazine, one of the leading Black publications in the country. A publication whose editor-in-chief was currently looking for a protégé and future replacement.

Makayla had never been one to apologize for going after what she wanted, and she certainly wasn't about to start now.

"Kendall!" Makayla said, her tone clipped as she cut her sister off. "Sis, I love you, but you have five minutes to get to the point before I very respectfully hang up this phone."

The best way to deal with any of the women in Makayla's family was to be direct. Otherwise, they'd be on the phone for another three hours despite the fact that Makayla knew Kendall probably had a laundry list of work to do herself.

"Fine! You have a date tonight. How's that for getting to the point?" Kendall responded, and Makayla could perfectly picture the smug look on her sister's face.

"A—excuse me?" she asked, confused. She was sure she'd heard her wrong.

"A date. You know, those things people go on so they don't end up old and alone. An outing made for romantic purposes?"

"Bitch, I know what a date is. What I don't know is why you're telling me that I have one."

"Because Lizzie set one up for you, of course."

Of course. Makayla should've known that Lizzie, the youngest sister in this equation, was involved in this somehow.

"No. No. Hell no. I told y'all after the last one that I was done. I am *DONE* with letting the three of y'all set me up. I don't need your help getting a date, and furthermore, I don't want it. Wasting my time dating right now is not on my agenda. How many times do I have to say that before y'all get the picture?" Any and all peace that she had before answering the phone immediately flew out of the window of her twenty-third-floor office and hit the pavement running.

For the last three months, her sisters and mother had been on a nonstop mission to find her a man. Ever since her mother announced that she was getting remarried, somehow, the focus had been placed on getting rid of Makayla's single status instead of directing their attention to getting ready for the wedding. Makayla resisted at first before finally deciding to humor them because, if nothing else, it afforded her the opportunity for some good food on someone else's dime. After nine dates, all of which could be described as subpar at best, homegirl was exhausted. Exhausted by the same old first date questions. Exhausted with the concept of finding yet another outfit for the night, which would ultimately be wasted on whoever she was meeting.

Exhausted with sitting across from men who not only couldn't and wouldn't keep her attention but quite frankly reminded her of why she was happily single in the first place.

Makayla had no desire to be someone's girlfriend, fiancée, wife, or anything in between. She certainly wasn't sleeping with any of the men that her family had set her up with. She could manage to find a sexual partner on her own, and when she couldn't, she knew exactly how to take care of herself in a way that left her both relaxed and satisfied. Unfortunately, it seemed that that sentiment was not exactly resonating with her family.

"We know what you said, M&M. We just don't agree. As the older and wiser sister who is happily married, trust me when I say that we know better than you do. So, I say again that you have a date tonight." Makayla had to fight back a gag at her sister's words. It was obvious that her childhood nickname was supposed to help ease her feelings about the situation. It wasn't working.

She closed her eyes in frustration. This was the issue. No one ever fucking listened to her. "Why are you even the one calling me if this is Lizzie's setup?"

"I volunteered," Kendall said, her voice filled with glee.

"Kendall—" Makayla started, but she was cut off by a second voice.

"Makayla, baby, it won't hurt you to go out with the man at least once. Your sister is just trying to help. We all are."

Makayla pulled the phone away from her ear. Of course, Kendall had ambushed her with her mother on the phone. The two of them were probably together wedding-planning while concocting this scheme.

The soft tone of her mother's voice washed over Makayla, and she immediately knew that she would say yes for no other reason than she didn't have the heart or the time to argue with her. Makayla looked at the clock and saw that her time had dwindled significantly since beginning this conversation, and if she wanted any hope of actually getting some work done before her meeting, she needed to end it now by giving both women what they ultimately wanted.

"Fine, Mommy. If it means that much to you, I'll go."

"Excellent!" her mother responded in a giddy tone.

"Don't get too excited. I'm agreeing to go, not agreeing to marry the man."

"Oh, don't be so negative, little sis. From what Lizzie told us, Reggie is tall, dark, and handsome. Three points right there. And I'm pretty sure she mentioned he's a travel writer. Isn't that right up your alley? Y'all can bond over work or whatever." Though what Kendall was saying made complete sense, she could sense her sister's shade in that last statement. Instead of responding, Makayla chose to ignore the comment.

"I said I'd go. No need to try and list his bullet points. Just send me the details. And make sure you include his picture this time. I have to go."

"Coming your way now," Kendall said, every word laced with smug satisfaction. Makayla was going to strangle her sister later. Both of them. It was inevitable.

"This is it, y'all. I'm serious. After this, I'm done, so you better hope he really is the keeper the three of you seem to think he is." After promising not to flake on the date and an added promise to call her mother later, Makayla ended the call and slumped back in her chair.

Why her family had such a hard time taking no for an answer, she would never understand. It was somewhat her own fault. Makayla had always given in to their desires and whims, especially lately, but this entire ordeal was beginning to grate on her nerves. Long-term romantic commitment was just not Makayla's cup of tea. It didn't fit her the way it did the rest of her family. She was perfectly happy focusing on her career and casually dating. It wasn't that she didn't believe in love. For better or worse, all the other women in her family had found it, though it hadn't always been easy. Still, the struggles she'd seen them go through just didn't seem to be worth the time and effort. Why put herself through that for something that she wasn't even sure she ultimately wanted anyway? She just wished everyone else could understand that too.

———

After finishing up her meeting that had run almost an hour over the scheduled time, Makayla was exhausted and ready to go home. She was definitely going to have to cancel this supposed date. She was drained and overwhelmed, so the last thing that she wanted to do was sit across from another one of her family's picks and act as if she wanted to be there. It wasn't like she'd actually agreed to this. Okay, so maybe she had *technically* agreed to be there, but obviously, that decision had been made under duress, so did it really count?

Truthfully, she'd just made up her mind to cancel and head home instead to soak in her oversized bathtub when her mother called. The woman had radar. Every time Makayla was poised to make a decision that would contradict what Delilah wanted, her name magically appeared on caller ID. Delilah Michaels, soon-to-be Harris, made it her mission to ensure that things went exactly the way she wanted them to.

"Hey, Mama," Makayla said with a sigh as she climbed into the car she'd ordered. Even though she had her own vehicle that she was perfectly capable of driving, she'd figured out a long time ago that getting from her brownstone in Oakwood to downtown was a lot easier to do when she wasn't the one fighting traffic.

"Hey, baby. Just checking in to see if you'd made it home yet to get ready for your date."

"I'm leaving work now, Mommy," she said, holding back her frustration. Her mother was predictable as hell.

"You're just now leaving? Girl, you're supposed to meet that man in like an hour! Now, you mean to tell me you can be on time for work but can't be on time to make a good first impression on your date?"

"Mama, my job pays me to be on time. I don't know this man from Jojo on the corner, and I certainly didn't ask to be set up with him. Quite honestly, I'm two seconds from canceling. All I want to do is go home, get in the bed, and——"

"Oh no, ma'am, you're going on this date. You agreed to it, so you're going."

"I only agreed because y'all strong-armed me into it this morning. I could've sworn all of y'all were there when I said no more dates or introductions. Hell, I'm pretty sure Percy heard me say it too."

At the mention of his name, Makayla heard her future stepfather's muffled voice in the background. Her mother covered the phone, more than likely to say something along the lines of, "Oh, hush, fool, no one was talking to you." Despite herself, Makayla couldn't help but laugh.

Makayla confirmed that Percy was, in fact, there when she said those exact words. The thought of him made Makayla smile. At fifty-eight years old, Delilah had finally found the love and happiness she had been looking for throughout most of her life. Love and life hadn't always been kind to her, so knowing that she was happy, no matter how much she fussed about Percy, made Makayla happy as well. Her mother lit up whenever Percy was in the room or when his name was mentioned, and it had been decades since anyone other than her daughters had put that sort of smile on Delilah's face. Even though her mother refused to listen, Makayla knew she had good intentions. She wanted this sort of love for her daughter. What she didn't seem to understand was that it just wasn't in the cards for Makayla.

"Anyway, like I was saying before I was rudely interrupted, you are not canceling your date. Based on what your sister told me, he seems like quite the catch. And it sounded like you two had a lot in common. Aren't you even the least bit curious how you'll get along?"

Makayla should've known that this was coming. From the moment that Kendall mentioned her date's job as a travel writer, she'd known that her family hoped that would be the thing that drew her in. She'd never admit it to any of them, but after she'd gotten off the phone earlier, she'd been curious and decided to look him up instead of waiting for her sister to send his picture. He was pretty cute, she had to give him that. At least Lizzie had good taste in that department. And she hadn't done too bad in the credentials department either. Imagine Makayla's pleasant surprise when she discovered that he'd actually written a few pieces for Mahogany. A few of her favorite pieces, actually. That, more than anything, showed that the date might not be a total waste. Still, she was tired, and this date was just one more thing keeping her from her bed. There was no way that her mom was going to let this go. There was only one way to handle this.

"Don't worry, Mommy, I'm not canceling the date."

Makayla made a mental note to send her date, Reggie Johnson, a message. Maybe he wouldn't mind pushing their meetup back by an hour. Part of her hoped that he would just cancel for her and save her the trouble. With her luck, she knew she probably shouldn't hold her breath.

"Good. Lizzie went through a lot of trouble to set this up, so the least that you could do is follow through, baby. Who knows, you may have fun!"

Makayla doubted that, but she didn't voice those thoughts. Instead, she sent off the text message and listened as her mother told her about her latest wedding decisions. It was time to make her way home to get ready for a date she hadn't wanted to attend in the first place.

CHAPTER 2

Makayla

Well, at least he has good taste in restaurants, Makayla thought to herself as the car pulled up in front of the Thai fusion restaurant.

She grounded herself with a deep breath before thanking the driver and climbing out of the car. Despite the seventy-five-degree weather earlier, the temperature had dropped with the sun, and a slight breeze kissed her thick mahogany legs. Makayla ran her hands over the black leather skirt that hugged her shapely figure in the best ways. This was one of her favorite skirts, hitting her just above the knee, form-fitting but not too tight that she couldn't walk comfortably. She'd left the first few buttons on her white button-up open, giving the perfect view of her cleavage, and rolled both sleeves just a little to expose her forearms. Half of her burgundy knotless braids were piled on top of her head in a high ponytail, leaving them cascading over her shoulders. Just because she didn't want to be on this date didn't mean she wasn't going to look good.

She walked into Taam Thai and greeted the hostess with a

smile. "Hi, I'm supposed to be meeting someone here. Reggie Johnson."

Her eyes scanned the area behind the hostess stand in an attempt to find the man whose picture she'd received earlier.

"Right this way," the hostess said with a smile as she led her to a table right between the bar and the window. Had he known this was her favorite part of the restaurant? Makayla preferred to be able to watch the bartenders work their magic while also being able to gaze out at the sidewalk traffic. This end of downtown Oakwood always provided visual entertainment no matter the time of day, but at night, that entertainment seemed to be especially…unique.

As Makayla approached the table, she couldn't help but take in the man in front of her, dark hair just longer than close-cut.

The perfect length to grab onto.

The thought skittered across her mind before she could stop it. Makayla couldn't even be sure where the thought had come from. Well, no, that was a lie. Considering how fine her dinner date was, it didn't exactly surprise her that she'd immediately gone to that place. As handsome as his face was, she could only imagine how good it would look between her legs.

She took in his smile, so bright that she wasn't sure how every person in the room wasn't staring his way. That smile was definitely a panty-dropper, and by the electricity she was feeling, her panties were ready to hit the floor all by themselves. As he stood to greet her, she couldn't help but think that the dark checkered jacket would've looked a mess on someone else and yet seemed to compliment his rich espresso-colored skin perfectly, not to mention his broad shoulders and thick thighs filled out his crisp white v-neck and dark jeans rather nicely. Her heels added a bit more height to her usual five-foot-eight frame, bringing her almost eye-level with her date. That had to place him somewhere around six feet. She couldn't help but pull her bottom lip between her teeth when she took notice of his strong build. His stubble only added to his sexiness, and she found herself wondering what it would feel like scraping against her inner thighs. He was fine as hell, and she was sure that he knew it. The pictures she'd seen of him hadn't done him justice.

"Reggie?" she asked.

"That would be me. Which must mean you're Makayla, right?"

"In the flesh," Makayla responded with a smile. She held out her hand, and instead of shaking it like she expected, he placed a soft kiss on her knuckles. Corny—but smooth, nonetheless.

"Well, damn, is the color coordination we have going on a sign of good things to come or an inkling to run like hell?" he asked in a deep timbre. He cast his smile in her direction as he moved around the table to pull out her chair.

"Give me five more minutes of conversation and I'll let you know," Makayla responded with a smile of her own as she took her seat. Their server quickly made her way to them, asking if she wanted anything to go with the water he'd ordered for the table. Makayla requested a Sake Tini, which she noticed earned her a smirk from her date.

"Fair enough. So, I guess you're familiar with the restaurant, huh?" he asked, referencing her drink order.

She raised an eyebrow. "Yeah, it's one of my favorites, but I'm sure my sister already told you that, right?"

He shook his head with a chuckle. "Actually, no. Lizzie mentioned you liked good food and that Thai was one of your favorites. I figured that meant you'd enjoy the food here. It's one of my favorites, and to be honest, it reminds me of some of the places I visited when I was traveling through Thailand a few years back."

"Oh, right. My sister did mention something about you being a travel writer." Reggie nodded. "So, would you say that makes you an expert on all things food?" she teased.

"Maybe not an expert, but I definitely know a thing or two

about a few things. Speaking of which, I heard you work for Divine Mahogany."

Makayla beamed. "A senior editor for Divine Mahogany, to be exact."

"Well, excuse me. I guess I stand corrected," Reggie said playfully. "Actually, I've submitted a few pieces to y'all over the years."

"I wasn't going to say anything, but I may have looked into you just a bit after I agreed to this date," she said. "We always conduct our own research, right?" She couldn't even bring herself to look sheepish.

"Right," Reggie said, smiling as he sat back in his seat. He was clearly impressed and surprised by her honesty. "So, what did you find out? I imagine I passed the test since you're sitting across from me."

"You measured up pretty well. Actually, that piece you wrote on Iceland's natural springs and glacial lakes? I have to admit, it's the reason Iceland is now at the top of my travel bucket list."

"I appreciate that. Honestly, when one of my old editors suggested I make the trip, I told him he was out of his damn mind." They both laughed. "My black ass in Iceland? Had to be a joke, right? But honestly, it was a once-in-a-lifetime experience. I figured most of us thought the same way I did when it came to Iceland, so when y'all reached out for a piece on unlikely Black travel havens, I knew I had to include my experience in my article."

Makayla found herself nodding along with his explanation. In truth, even though she enjoyed Reggie's writing, she hadn't expected to enjoy his company. Yet here they were, conversation flowing naturally. This was shaping up to be a pleasant surprise.

"Well, you certainly got a few points from me on that one," she teased.

Something flashed in Reggie's eyes as they scanned over her, and she felt a shiver run down her spine. "And what exactly do these points lead to?"

Makayla pulled her bottom lip between her teeth. "You don't need to worry about all that," she responded. "Just know they're a good thing."

Reggie only chuckled in response, the sound causing heat to run through her. He gave a nod. "Well, I look forward to finding out, Ms. Makayla Michaels."

"Oh, I'm sure you do, Mr. Reggie Johnson."

Makayla watched as his tongue glided over his plump lips. She could feel him watching her. Had someone turned the heat up in the restaurant, or was that just his gaze lighting her on fire? Whatever the case, Makayla brought her eyes up to meet his. There was a challenge being issued there, one she refused to run away from.

Doesn't mean you have to run toward it either, she chided herself as she watched him take a sip of his sake.

She took a sip of her drink to gather herself before she said something completely out of pocket. She was here for a good meal and to get her family off of her back. That was it and that was all. The last thing she needed to do was get caught up in some form of cute banter.

After what seemed like hours of silence, Makayla cleared her throat. "So, how do you know my sister? I didn't exactly get a whole lot of details on that front." Her eyes scanned his face and focused on the flex of his jaw. Damn, she was a sucker for a man with a sexy ass jawline.

Okay, so he's fine. And what, sis? You didn't even want to be here, remember? Stay focused!

"Actually, I've only met Lizzie a couple of times. Alonzo and I go way back, though."

"Really?" she asked, surprised. "And how old are you again?" She hadn't even meant to ask the question, but Makayla rarely exercised any type of filter. Her sister's husband, Alonzo, was amazing, but he was also almost forty-five years old. From the look of him, Reggie was closer to her own age of thirty-four than Alonzo's.

Reggie laughed, and the throaty sound caused her pussy to clench involuntarily.

Down, girl, she thought to herself as she subtly rubbed her thighs together to relieve a bit of the pressure.

"Thirty-five," he answered. "So yeah, to answer your next question, he's a bit older than me, but he's good people." Makayla nodded in agreement. "I met him a few years back through mutual friends. He was looking to get into partnering with a restaurateur in Barcelona, and I happened to be there at the same time. We got to talking, realized we both had roots here in Oakwood, and just sort of hit it off."

"Okay, then, Mr. Johnson. Well, I guess if you have the Lonzo stamp of approval, then you can't be too bad."

"Hmmm, sounds like I just earned a few more points in my favor then."

"It would seem that way, wouldn't it?" Makayla let a flirty smile play on her lips as the server came by to take their orders.

To Makayla's surprise, the date wasn't a disaster. Not even close. As much as she hated to admit it, her sister had been right on the nose with this pick. Reggie was funny, didn't seem to be intimidated by her, and had amazing taste in food. When she took the lead in ordering for the table, he made no move to stop her or correct her choices. Instead, he watched with rapt attention as she rattled off the different dishes she wanted: steamed dumplings, sushi bombs, drunken noodles with Pad Kra Pao and volcanic chicken, and finally, the Tongue Thai sushi roll, which was one of her personal favorites.

"I guess I should've asked if you had any dietary restrictions before I ordered all of this, huh?" Makayla asked as she placed some of the drunken noodles and volcanic chicken onto her plate. She looked over at him as he brought his cup of sake to his lips.

With a shrug, he responded, "If I did, I would've let you know or just ordered something else. Luckily for me, I don't have any real food allergies, and I'm down to try just about anything at least once."

"Anything?" she asked, kicking up her eyebrow. Her voice unintentionally took on a suggestive tone that she could tell he hadn't missed. Not with the way his eyes darted down to her lips. She definitely hadn't meant for the question to come out that way, but clearly, her subconscious had a mind of its own.

"Anything," he nodded, his tone mimicking hers.

Shit, was it hot in here, or was it this fucking chicken? Makayla cleared her throat and took a sip of her drink. It seemed that he was determined to meet her word for word. She could respect that. Hell, a part of her even appreciated it. Makayla didn't believe in bullshitting or holding back. If she saw some-thing—or someone—that she wanted, then she went for it without question. Of course, that attitude had led to plenty of men telling her she was "more aggressive" than they liked their women. That wasn't any skin off her back, just saved her the trouble of giving them the chance for a second date. Yet another point in his favor.

So he's not completely fragile. Does that really change anything about where this is headed?

"So, why a freelance travel writer?" she asked, steering the conversation toward cooler waters. No matter how much fun flirting with Reggie might be, she didn't exactly want to give him any ideas.

He nodded. "I honestly couldn't imagine doing anything different. What other career could I have that combines all of my favorite things into one? I get to do what I love: write, travel, encourage other Black people to travel, and eat some damn good food. I'm living the dream."

If anyone could understand that, it was certainly Makayla. "Is it safe to assume that doing what you love keeps you busy?" she asked.

"Oh, for sure. I'd say, depending on the year, I spend about six to eight months traveling from one place to the next."

With that sort of timeline, Makayla couldn't imagine that he had much time for a relationship.

Bitch, does it matter?

Yes! Gives me the perfect excuse to give my sisters when I tell them that another one bites the dust.

Now that she thought about it, Makayla wondered what exactly Lizzie had been thinking when she set this up. A man who was out of town that much was definitely more suited for Makayla's philosophy on dating, sex, and relationships, not her sisters'. Up until now, anyone that her sisters and mother had set her up with had definitely been more their speed. Men ready to settle down. Men who wanted families. Men who would ultimately become a pain in her ass.

"And so, you being in Oakwood now is…"

"Me finally coming home after being gone for way too long. Like I said, I love traveling, and I love what I do, but there's nothing like being home, you know. To be honest, I've been thinking about slowing it down a bit. I've been traveling damn near nonstop for almost ten years. It's just been feeling like now is a good time to reset. Readjust. Reevaluate. Living in constant motion can be…exhausting."

Makayla nodded in response to his words but didn't move to interrupt.

"And at the end of the day," he continued, "if I'm always on the go, maybe I'm actually running from something and don't even know it. One of my best friends pointed out to me that if I never lay down roots anywhere, what will I really have to show for this life that I've created for myself? No one to come home to.

Nothing permanent besides a few friends who are like family. Even then, I've missed so many big moments that when I do finally get back here, sometimes it feels like I'm starting from scratch." He paused for a moment and Makayla could tell something else was weighing on him.

"And if I'm being honest with myself, my writing has been a bit stale lately. Like all of my feelings of being exhausted with traveling are starting to come through in my articles. I know I'm better than that. Maybe finally coming back and giving myself time to actually settle will revitalize me, you know? Help me figure out what direction I want to take my writing in."

There it is. Now she understood why her sister had put this date together. The phrases *"settling down"* and *"no one to come home to"* definitely sounded like buzzwords that would've set Lizzie's ears on fire and her mind whirling. Then, of course, there was the fact that he looked like sex on a stick and happened to be a writer, two things that they both had in common. And while she may not completely understand why he felt the need to be settled, she could respect it. She just hoped he didn't expect to do that settling with her.

"Well, if nothing else, it seems like you're self-aware. I don't know about Maybe all you need is a new perspective. Hopefully being home helps to give you that."

The two of them smiled at each other and Makayla tried to ignore the feeling radiating through her. She'd never admit it, but being able to connect with someone on this level was…well it was nice.

After another hour, the two of them decided to call it a night. Reggie paid the bill without a second thought and even gave a snort when she offered to leave the tip. That was certainly fine with her. Makayla had paid for her share of dates over the years. It had never been a problem for her because fair was fair, right? Still, that didn't mean that she was about to argue over who got to foot the bill. If a man wanted to prove himself by shelling out money for her company, who was she to tell him no?

Makayla led the way out of the restaurant. She knew without a shadow of a doubt that his eyes were on her ass, so she added just a bit more sway to her walk for his benefit. Once they'd cleared the doors and stepped off to the side, she turned to look at him.

"So, my rideshare should be here in a few," she said, holding up her phone.

"Damn, trying to get rid of me already, huh? Guess this didn't go as well as I thought," Reggie joked, rubbing his hand along the back of his neck.

Makayla laughed and shook her head as she tilted slightly to look up at him. "I promise you, that's not it. I had a really great time," she explained, surprised that she actually meant it. "And trust me when I say I did not expect to be able to say that." The slight breeze in the air had Makayla pulling her thin black jacket tighter over her chest.

"Same," Reggie said with a smile of his own. "Though I wouldn't say it was a surprise. I had a good feeling about tonight, and my feelings are usually spot on." After a brief pause, he took a step closer to her.

"So, since we both had such a great time," he began again, reaching out and linking their hands, running his thumb over hers.

Shit. There her damn panties went. She was slick with need, and damn if she didn't wonder what his fingers could do to her if she gave him half a chance to show her.

"I know this great soul food spot. Another favorite of mine. I think you'd love it. Maybe we could check it out. The macaroni and cheese and fried fish would definitely be right up your alley," he said, but even before he finished, Makayla was shaking her head.

"Listen, I did have a great time, but I'm not really interested in doing this again." She winced inwardly when she saw his confused reaction. "I told my sister I'd go out with you mostly because I knew she wouldn't let the issue drop if I didn't. My whole family is sort of…actually, very overly invested in my relationship status right now. They've been trying for months to set me up. Honestly, you're the first guy who hasn't, well…" She paused, wondering how to say it, "Gotten on my damn nerves."

At that, a laugh burst from Reggie's chest. Well, at least he didn't seem to be offended. That was a win in Makayla's book. She would hate to have to cuss him out after such a good night.

"Okay, understandable. But tell me this, since we both agree that this date wasn't totally horrible, what's the harm in going out again?" he asked with a shrug.

"Well, for one, at the risk of sounding petty as hell, I don't really want to give Lizzie the satisfaction of thinking that she was right. And two, I just honestly don't have the time. I love my job, and while my family hates when I say this, my job is my life right now. And my goal right now is to move up in that job. If I have to give up some free time to do that? Well, I don't really mind. I'd rather spend the little free time I have curled up with a glass of wine and a good book, not making small talk over dinner just to keep someone else happy. So again, as much fun as this was… going out again just isn't going to be a thing. I don't wanna set you up when I know what it is from the beginning."

Reggie nodded in understanding. "That's fair. Setups aren't usually my thing either, but Lizzie and Alonzo have been talking you up for weeks. Months, actually. I figured I'd test my luck." He shrugged. "Can't say I regret it."

"Surprisingly enough, I don't either," she agreed. "Look at you beating the odds, Mr. Johnson."

He smirked at her, a bit of heat showing up behind his eyes. "It's what I do, Ms. Michaels." He took a step away from her as her ride pulled up to the curb. Walking over to the car, he held the door open for her. "Well, if your schedule ever frees up and you can't think of anything else to do, give me a call. We can try for a repeat."

Makayla smiled as she got into the car. "I'll keep you in mind."

CHAPTER 3

Makayla

The fact that Makayla managed to leave work early was a miracle that deserved celebration. Of course, her family probably wouldn't see it that way, but that was fine. She would applaud herself for sticking to the plan so that she would be on time to meet them. She shot a text to her best friend, Jasmine, letting her know. In true best friend fashion, Jasmine immediately responded with a Snoop Dogg dancing gif. See, this was why she kept her best friend around. If no one else was going to celebrate her, Jasmine certainly would.

Making her way through the bustle of downtown Oakwood toward the bridal shop was a feat, but she honestly didn't mind the walk. It was a beautiful day, and it gave her a bit of time to gather her thoughts before she walked straight into the lions' den. She knew the women were going to ask how her date with Reggie went. She'd managed to successfully avoid them this long, but her time to stall had come to an end. It'd been a few weeks since her date with Reggie, and other than the check-in text message where he'd given Makayla the name of the soul food restaurant he loved, the two of them hadn't talked.

She'd been busy up until now and hadn't had much time to dwell on the date itself. Or maybe what she was really trying to avoid thinking about was how when she last found herself using her favorite toy in the shower, it had been the vision of Reggie's lips gliding over hers that had floated across her mind. And the feel of his strong fingers on her hand. And of course, that was followed up by the moment she'd noticed the thick print in his pants as they stood to leave. The orgasm that hit her was one of the best she'd had in a long time. Having Reggie be part of that experience had honestly thrown her for a loop. Sure, he was attractive, and yes, he was a "catch," but he wasn't for her, so why should he be starring in her fantasies? The entire experience confused and frustrated her all at once.

Great, and now here she was, thinking about that thick print once again. Makayla was so lost in thought that she damn near walked right by the bridal shop where they were supposed to be meeting for the dress fitting. Luckily, the sight of Lizzie scrambling out of the car and onto the sidewalk snapped her out of her thoughts.

"Oh my gosh, so I'm not the last one here! Perfect," Lizzie said as a little body came barreling toward Makayla, nearly knocking her off her feet. "Christian! What have I told you about doing all that? You are getting too big. You almost knocked your Auntie right on her behind."

"Sorry, M&M," Makayla's nephew Christian said with a pout.

"Aww, it's okay, C-Money. It'll take more than your cute little self to knock me on my ass," she said, scooping him up and peppering him with kisses. His pout turned into laughter as Lizzie rolled her eyes and lifted her bag over her shoulder.

"Come on here, y'all, before Mama and Kendall have a whole fit."

"Now why would they do that? We're on time, just like they

asked us to be," Makayla said, hiking Christian up onto her hip and following her sister into the shop.

"Because you know damn well that they probably got here at least thirty minutes early, which means that no matter how on time we are, we're still thirty minutes late."

"And that's a fact," a voice that sounded suspiciously like her older sister said.

Sure enough, there was their mother smirking as she waited in an oversized chair with Kendall sitting beside her. While Delilah looked happy as can be to see the two women, Kendall clearly had an attitude. Her arms were folded across her chest, and she was looking at Makayla like she wanted to skin her alive. Makayla knew that it had nothing to do with what time the women had arrived at the shop. No, that attitude was most definitely due to the fact that Kendall had called Makayla no less than twice a day trying to get the details about her date. Makayla, of course, had pointedly ignored each and every call.

She didn't understand why Kendall was so pressed to know the details of that night. It wasn't like she'd been the one to actually set her up with Reggie. Maybe Kendall was feeling some type of way because Makayla had shut down all of the guys that she'd tried to set her up with. In fact, the last man Kendall had introduced her to had promptly gotten cussed out after making a comment about how Makayla should probably lose a few pounds if she wanted to get and keep a man. She'd made sure to hand Kendall her ass at the end of the night too.

"Well, hello to you too," Makayla said as she kissed her mother on the cheek and pulled Kendall into a reluctant hug.

Before the group could get into any small talk, the shop consultant informed them that everything was ready for them in the dressing area.

"Come on, y'all. Let's get these fittings started so we can go over the new details for the wedding." Kendall's tone made it very clear there was no room for discussion. God, Makayla hated it when she used that know-it-all tone. Kendall had taken the lead on helping their mother plan the wedding and made it a point to hang that over everyone's head from the beginning. Especially Makayla.

Taking a deep breath, Makayla promised herself she would not let Kendall get under her skin today. Their mom deserved to have a drama-free fitting, and that's exactly what she was going to get.

Forty minutes later and Makayla's pledge was being tested beyond measure. Any hope that Kendall would play nice today had quickly flown out the window the minute they'd gotten to the private area. It seemed as if every chance she got, her older sister found something negative to say about Makayla.

Stand up straight. You look so homely when you slouch.

God, you really aren't worried about how you look in that dress M&M? I really envy how you just don't care.

Do you really think you should show that much cleavage?

Maybe we should pick another dress color. I mean, this shade of peach looks great on me, Mom but it just isn't complimentary on everyone.

Makayla was absolutely ready to lay her older sister out, and she was sure steam was practically pouring out of her ears. The only thing that kept her from going off completely was the fact that she didn't want to embarrass her mother, nor did she want to show her ass in front of Christian. Her nephew did not deserve to witness one of his aunties get her ass beat by his other auntie. Her eyes flicked over and found his cute self-preoccupied with his Nintendo switch.

"So, Mommy wants to do some wedding party events leading up to the big day. Just some fun things to get everyone in the spirit, ya know? So far, we've come up with karaoke, of course, and a paint and sip night."

"Oooh, I love the sound of that! Like a way to unwind from all the wedding day stress and jitters," Lizzie said, gushing.

Delilah nodded. "Exactly! Who says that the reception is

supposed to be the only fun event throughout the whole wedding process?"

"I think that's a great idea, mommy. Just let me know when everything is once y'all have the dates firmed up. That way, I can make sure I don't schedule anything for those dates. I wouldn't miss this for the world." Makayla sent a smile and a wink in her mother's direction.

"I haven't even told you the best part yet," Kendall said, her tone just a tad bit too chipper. "Each activity is going to be couple-based."

"Wait, what?" she asked, turning around so fast she damn near fell off the pedestal. Makayla's entire body froze at her sister's words. She couldn't be serious.

"Everyone has to bring a date for each event. Sort of like a wedding date night scenario. Since weddings are all about celebrating love, we thought why not showcase all of the love we have right here in the wedding party?"

The feeling left Makayla's fingers as she clenched her hands into a fist. *Don't let her get to you. Don't let her get to you.*

"And who came up with that...amazingly clever idea?" Makayla asked through clenched teeth.

"Me," her mother said quickly, sensing the tension that was building. Makayla took one look at Kendall and knew that while Delilah might think this was her idea, Kendall was most certainly the real mastermind behind this scheme. She fought the urge to roll her eyes at the smug look on her sister's face.

"Is there a problem?" Kendall asked, kicking up an eyebrow.

Makayla took a deep breath. "No, not at all. I'm just saying I thought the wedding party activities were supposed to be for… you know…people in the actual wedding party. Not like friends or significant others."

"Well, technically, most of the people in the wedding party are couples," Lizzie said, clearly holding back her laughter.

Makayla truly could've kicked herself because Lizzie was

right. Delilah and Percy had opted to keep the wedding party small. Makayla and her sisters were the bridesmaids, while Percy's son Jack, his fiancé Joseph, and Kendall's husband, Greg, were his groomsmen. Alonzo, unfortunately, would not be at the wedding due to a work trip that fell on the same weekend.

"Besides, we really didn't want to leave anyone out. Just because Alonzo can't be at the wedding doesn't mean he shouldn't be able to participate. And Percy and I want everyone to join in on the fun."

Makayla couldn't argue with that. She knew how happy everyone was for the couple, and it was just like her mother to want to plan things so that no one would be left out.

"Well, no big deal. With Jasmine on my arm, I'll definitely give y'all a run for your money in the cute plus-one department."

Her mother made a face, biting her lip, while Kendall rolled her eyes.

"You have to bring an actual date, Makayla. Not your best friend who you do everything with."

"Says who? Y'all know she would love to do the type of stuff you have planned. And why should she miss out?"

Her mother's face turned thoughtful as if she made a good point, and Makayla damn near sighed in relief.

Score one for me.

Of course, Kendall refused to let her have the win and promptly burst her bubble. "That won't work because Jasmine's already going to be invited with her very own plus-one."

"Okay, so we'll be each other's date. I still don't see the problem."

Kendall tilted her head and rolled her eyes. "Let's be honest, M&M, the only reason that the whole double dating concept doesn't work for you is because you're really the only single one in the group."

Makayla took a deep breath and closed her eyes. She was two

seconds away from strangling her sister. Why was she so determined to make things difficult?

When she opened her eyes, Makayla saw the tell-tale look of
pity that seemed to appear on her mother's face more and more
these days. Delilah's look nearly gutted her. Makayla may not
always agree with her mother, but she didn't want to break the
woman's heart either.

Before she could think twice about what she was saying, the
words slipped out of Makayla's mouth. "Actually, Kendall,
Reggie and I have been dating for a couple weeks now so I don't
know if I exactly qualify as single."

Shit, now why the hell did you go and say that?

The looks on the women's faces said it all: they were confused
as hell. Well, Delilah was confused but clearly excited. Lizzie was
confused, too, since Makayla had made the mistake of telling her
flat out that the two wouldn't be going out again the day after
their date. She'd have to rectify that at some point. And
Kendall…

Kendall looked downright suspicious as if Makayla's pants
had caught fire right before her eyes.

"Is that right?" her older sister asked, eyes narrowed.

"Yep," Makayla said with a shrug. "I didn't exactly want to
say anything since you guys seemed so invested. You know, just in
case things didn't work out. It just seemed easier to keep it to
myself for now."

"Oh, baby!" her mother said, practically bouncing up and
down while pulling her into a hug. Lizzie also seemed to be
excited, though Makayla could tell she'd have to answer a few
questions later.

"I still don't get it. Why not just say something earlier? We
would've found out eventually when he showed up to the
wedding," Kendall said, folding her arms across her chest.

Makayla rolled her eyes. "Because honestly, it wasn't any of your business. I'm grown. I don't have to tell y'all everything. Besides, I wasn't even sure if I would be asking him to come to the wedding with me."

"Well, I guess you better get to asking, then."

"I mean, don't you think it's a little awkward to ask a man I've only known for a few weeks to be my date not only for my mother's wedding but also for all of the pre-wedding activities? What are y'all trying to do? Scare him off?" Makayla prayed her tone carried a joking note and didn't reveal that she was completely full of shit.

"If he's scared off by a few little group dates, then I'm pretty sure he's not gonna make it far in this relationship anyway," Lizzie said with a laugh. "Besides, based on what I know about Reggie, I'm pretty sure he can handle it."

"Mmmm, I hope so, because M&M is as sour as she is sweet," their mother added with a laugh.

Makayla couldn't help but laugh right along with them. "I swear, y'all are shady as hell."

"Yeah, yeah, yeah. The point is, if he's your new boyfriend, why not bring him along? This way, you can kill two birds with one stone. You get to show his very fine ass off, and we get the chance to get to know him." Damn, why did Lizzie have to be so sensible?

Makayla chewed on her bottom lip. She could feel each woman's eyes on her. Now that she'd put this out in the atmosphere, there was no way she could take it back. That would only lead to more setups and more men that she did not want to deal with. It also meant she would never hear the end of this from Kendall.

"OK," she said, finally giving in. What else could she say?

"Perfect," Kendall said. "I'll put you and Reggie down for paint and sip next Thursday night. And I'll send you the rest of the itinerary so y'all can both put it on your calendars."

"Can't wait," Makayla mumbled. She had one week to pull this whole thing together. What the hell had she gotten herself into? More importantly, how could she convince Reggie to help get her out of it?

CHAPTER 4

Reggie

A s Reggie sat across from Makayla, he couldn't help but shake his head. "I've gotta say, when I told you to give me a call if you wanted to go out again, I didn't think you'd actually do it."

Makayla stopped short and gave him a look.

Shit.

Reggie immediately backtracked. "Don't get me wrong. I sure as hell hoped you would call, but you seemed so…determined not to. I figured I just shouldn't get my hopes up." To say that he'd been shocked to hear from Makayla after a few weeks of radio silence was an understatement. He'd honestly thought she'd called him by mistake when he'd answered the phone after his Friday morning workout session.

But damn, he was glad she'd called. Reggie bit his lip as he watched her. With her knotless braids pulled up on top of her head, he could see her beautiful mahogany face with no problem. Her skin seemed to have its own glow, and it made it difficult to stay focused. He took in her deep brown eyes and the long lashes that framed them. Makayla's cheeks were the gift that kept on giving, forming their own adorable ass pockets every time she smiled. The gold hoop in her nose kept catching the light and drawing his attention to it. Then there was the fact that his eyes kept drifting to her plump lips.

Her body was its own temptation entirely. She was soft in all his favorite places. From the moment she'd walked through the door, he'd been blown away. Reggie couldn't deny that her thick body was a show-stopper. Her jeans practically looked painted on. And of course, there was the ass that had mesmerized him so much he hadn't been able to get it out of his mind since that first date. *Brick house* didn't even begin to describe how stacked she was. Looking at her now, he wanted nothing more than to get his hands on her. Between being gorgeous and witty, Reggie couldn't imagine anyone meeting Makayla and not wanting to spend more time with her.

Take a sip of water, bruh. You're looking real thirsty out here.

The tension in Makayla's shoulders seemed to ease once she realized he hadn't meant any harm by his comment. "Well... I have to be honest. I actually had an ulterior motive for calling you," she admitted.

"Damn. So, it wasn't my winning smile and charming personality that made you hit me up?" he asked, throwing that exact smile at her across the table.

She rolled her eyes. "No, Mr. Johnson, I'm sorry to report that is unfortunately not the case." The smirk she attempted to hide made him wonder if she was telling the whole truth.

"Was it the promise of good soul food?" he asked, eyes flicking toward the fried catfish on her plate.

Makayla let her smirk loose this time as she added a bit more hot sauce to her fish and just a dab to her greens. "Well, since I'm on an honesty streak here, the mention of good fried fish definitely piqued my interest. I'm a sucker for good food. But no... that wasn't the reason either." She paused. "Well, not the only reason."

Reggie noticed her hands beginning to fidget. She was nervous. But why?

"I have a proposition for you."

Reggie raised an eyebrow but didn't respond, taking in the way she pulled her bottom lip between her teeth. He couldn't help but wonder when else she made that motion. How hard did she chew her lip when she was frustrated? Concentrating? Focused? How deep would those teeth dig if she was warm, wet, and slippery around his—

"Reggie, are you listening? Is there something on my face?" she asked, interrupting his thoughts just as they were headed down a path that would certainly make the way he was sitting uncomfortable. The last thing he needed to be doing was sitting at this damn table with a fucking hard-on.

Maybe stop acting like a perv and get yourself together, then.

"Sorry. Zoned out. That tends to happen when I get a bite of Sylvia's sweet potatoes," he joked before putting down his fork. "You have my full attention."

Makayla took a deep breath and put her own fork down. "Okay. So, I don't know if Lonzo or Lizzie told you, but my mom's getting remarried. That's sort of what started this whole 'find Makayla a man' adventure. Everyone is sort of hoping that setting me up will somehow lead to my own wedding."

Reggie's eyes went wide, making Makayla laugh. "Haven't you heard? Apparently, being the last single member of my immediate family is the biggest crime I can commit at this point."

"That...that sounds like a whole lot of pressure," Reggie said. He had no idea what that sort of pressure felt like, but he could tell it weighed on her, even if she tried to act as though it didn't.

"Just par for the course these days."

He nodded but furrowed his brow in confusion. "So, what exactly...umm..." He wondered how to phrase his question.

"You're trying to figure out what exactly this has to do with you, right?"

Reggie shrugged. "Just a little bit."

"I may or may not have told my sisters and my mom that we were dating now." The words flew from her in such a rush that Reggie wondered for a moment if he'd heard her correctly. Based on the sheepish look on her face, he had. "Which may or may not have led to a conversation about how you were going to be escorting me to the pre-wedding activities and the actual wedding."

He nearly choked on his drink.

Reggie's eyes went wide, and he was glad he'd put his cup down before he took another swallow.

Makayla groaned. "I know, but I panicked. We were just there at the dress fitting, and they dropped this bomb on me. Next thing I know, I'm trying to come up with every reason in the book why I don't need a date, and my mom looks at me with that pitiful look. My older sister is staring at me with this smug look on her face. And shit, it just came out. By the time I realized what I was saying, it was too late. Even if I wanted to go back and admit that I actually don't have anyone to go with me, that would just give them a reason to keep trying to set me up. Trust me when I say that I just can't deal with that again."

Makayla sagged in her chair, looking utterly defeated. Reggie had to admit that he didn't exactly like to see that look on her face. It left him unsettled.

"I'm pretty sure that I like this even less than you do, but I swear to God, if I have to sit through one more setup orchestrated by my sisters or my mother, I'm going to pull every one of these braids out of my head."

Reggie sat in silence for a few moments before he cleared his throat. "Okay, so let me get this straight. You lied to your family and said that we've been dating for the last couple of weeks. You said this, even though in reality, you curved my ass to the left without a second thought and went about your merry way? And now, to keep them off your ass, you need me to pretend to be your boyfriend so that they leave you alone."

Makayla nodded.

"And how long do you think this little scam you came up with will last? Like what happens once the wedding is over?"

Does that even matter? This whole thing sounds like a trainwreck waiting to happen.

"I figure a week or two after the wedding, I'll just tell them that things didn't work out and that this is why I didn't want to tell them in the first place."

Well, shit. Was homegirl for real? By the look on her face, absolutely she was. Reggie still couldn't fathom how the hell she thought this was a good idea. She clearly hadn't thought about the fact that this could lead to even more problems. It wasn't like a fake boyfriend was a permanent solution.

Maybe Reggie should've been put off by the entire thing, but honestly, he was curious. Could he really go along with this little plan of hers? Hell, was she actually ready to commit to her own plan? He may not know much about Makayla, but she seemed like the type of woman who never let anyone see her sweat. He wondered if she really came up with this on the fly or if she'd seen it in a movie somewhere. These schemes may work in movies, but this was real life. They couldn't possibly get away with this sort of thing, could they?

Are you actually considering this shit, bruh?

Honestly? Yeah, he was. Reggie may not know a lot about Makayla, but from what he'd gathered, she didn't ask for help lightly. She sure as hell didn't seem like the type of woman who put herself in uncomfortable positions just for the hell of it. And he had wanted the opportunity to get to know her, right? Wasn't this the perfect way to do that?

He must have taken a bit too long to process what she'd said because next thing he knew, Makayla was putting her napkin down on the table and pushing back her chair. "Listen, forget I even brought this up. I don't know what I was thinking. It was a wild ass idea, and now you're probably regretting even getting mixed up with my ass." She gave a light, slightly uncomfortable laugh. "Listen, dinner's on me. I'll cover the check and then get out of your way. It's the least that I can do."

Just as she reached for her wallet, he threw out his hand to stop her. "Wait a minute." Makayla wrinkled her nose in confusion. "I'll do it," he was saying before he could think twice about it. "Under one condition."

She narrowed her eyes. "I'm not going to fuck you," she said, and Reggie burst out laughing. The way she'd said it had so much force that it managed to knock some of the tension from the space.

"Okay, good to know, but that's not what I was going to say." Out of all the things that had crossed his mind when she brought up this idea, having sex with her was not one of them. Sure, he'd been thinking about it beforehand, but he'd be willing to bet the same thought had popped into her mind as well. That was clear based on the looks she'd sent his way on their first date. That wasn't what this was about though.

"I was going to suggest we do a tradeoff. For every fake date we go on, you have to let me take you on a real date."

"I don't *have* to do anything," she snapped.

He let out a chuckle. "You're right, ma. My bad. I didn't mean to offend you. Let me rephrase. In exchange for being your fake date, I would like to take you on a few real dates. Even out the playing field a bit."

Makayla gave him a contemplative look. "So, you're telling me that while we're fake dating, you want to actually date me?"

Reggie gave her a simple nod. "That's exactly what I'm saying."

"No," she said quickly as if she wouldn't even give it a second thought.

"Why not?" he countered.

"Because that defeats the whole purpose of this plan. I already told you that I have no interest in dating for real."

"Fair enough, but look at it this way. If we're going to go through with this, it has to be believable, right? That means meeting up and getting to know one another outside of the time we spend with your family. So why not have a little fun while we do that?"

Makayla didn't look too convinced, so he continued. "Look, I'm not in the habit of forcing anyone to date me. I am, however, in the business of making connections, getting to know good people, and going after what I want."

"And what you want is me?" she asked skeptically.

"No, what I want is to get to know you. That's what dating technically is, right?" he said nonchalantly. "We don't have to put any pressure on it, but I don't see any drawbacks here. Besides, I put one hundred percent into everything that I do. If we're not going to actually commit to this, then your family isn't going to buy it. That means you'll be right back at square one when this thing is over."

If it's over.

As much as she might want to disagree, he knew that she had to see the logic in what he was saying. She relaxed back in her seat and shook her head. "Ok, fine. You're right. A date for a date. I can agree to that as long as you can agree to two things."

"Shoot."

"One, respect my time. I understand you're doing me a favor here, but that does *not* mean that I'm just at your mercy. If I have to cancel because of work, can't talk, or just don't feel like being bothered, you need to be okay with that. Otherwise, this isn't going to work."

"Understood, and I can absolutely respect that. And I hope you'll offer me the same courtesy," Reggie said. The last thing he wanted was for Makayla to feel as though she didn't have any choices in this arrangement. He was trying to get to know her, not control her.

"Without a doubt. As long as we can agree to respect one another and be considerate, we shouldn't have any problems."

"You have my word."

"Good."

After a few moments of silence, he cleared his throat. "So, what was number two?"

"Number two?" she asked as she scrunched her nose in confusion. Why was she so fucking cute when she did that?

"You said I had to agree to two things. We went through the first thing. What's the second?"

She eyed him warily as if debating whether or not she wanted to answer him. He knew which side won out when a smirk appeared on her face. "Two, I have no intention of sleeping with you, so that's off the table."

Reggie gave her a smirk of his own as he leaned in. "Baby girl, I promise to keep my hands to myself if you can promise to do the same."

CHAPTER 5

Reggie

"Y ou agreed to do what?!" Reggie's best friends, Lucas and Avery, exclaimed at the same time. They both stared at him as if he had three heads sprouting from his neck. Suddenly, he remembered why he'd put off telling the two of them about this little arrangement.

Reggie scooped another handful of popcorn and settled back onto the couch. "I agreed to be her boyfriend until her mom's wedding." He said it as if it was the simplest thing in the world. Truth be told, he knew it sounded a little...out there. The more he thought about it, though, the more invested in the idea he became.

"Let me get this straight. You're going to pretend to be her boyfriend at these lovey-dovey ass events while also trying to be her actual boyfriend behind the scenes?" Lucas asked as he leaned forward in his seat. Reggie nodded.

Lucas muted the movie and scoffed. "Do you realize how ridiculous this sounds?"

Before Reggie could respond, Avery cackled. "I feel like I've seen this in a movie somewhere. Or maybe I read it in a book. Either way, this has to be the wildest shit that you've ever agreed to."

Reggie shook his head, not even the least bit surprised that his friends were using this opportunity to clown him. The fact of the matter was he was intrigued by Makayla. Intrigued enough that yes, when she'd turned him down for another date, his pride was a little hurt. Reggie was sure she had been feeling him during dinner. The chemistry between them was off the charts. There had been no misjudging the heat in her eyes during their suggestive conversations or the way the other parts of their discussion flowed seamlessly.

Reggie understood that for her, work came first. He could respect her work hustle because he had his own, but he was also a romantic at heart. One that went after what he wanted. Relationships had never been in short supply for him, whether long-term or otherwise. Even when it came to issues such as long-distance, he'd never seen it as a problem. Of course, oftentimes his partners didn't exactly have the same attitude. While he may not feel the compulsion to get into a relationship right away now that he was home, he could readily acknowledge that being back and creating stability for himself did make a relationship even more enticing to him.

He'd been in no mood to rush that until Makayla had walked through the door of the restaurant. Between her slight attitude, voluptuous body, and husky voice, it was hard to deny the woman was the sexiest person he'd ever laid eyes on. Combine that with her drive, sense of humor, ability to carry a conversation, and taste in good food, and all bets were off. As far as Reggie was concerned, he'd found the woman of his dreams. If pretending to be her boyfriend gave him a way in to see if those dreams could come true, he damn sure wasn't going to miss out on the opportunity.

"No, but seriously, Reg, all jokes aside, you sure this is a good idea?" Lucas asked. Reggie could see the genuine concern in his friend's eyes.

"If I'm being one hundred percent honest, the answer to that is fifty-fifty in either direction. On the one hand, Makayla is cool peoples. Like on the surface, she seems like the whole package. She's about her business, bad as hell, and we just vibe. Plus, she has no problem calling someone out on their shit. I'm hard-pressed to think we wouldn't be good together just based on what I know now."

"But…" Avery said, already knowing he had more to say.

"But," he started, "she's very upfront about the fact that dating isn't her thing. And while I totally respect that, I can't lie and say I'm not a little worried about where this could end up. Either I'll end up in way over my head and she'll be over me before we can even get started, or I'll realize I made the worst mistake ever and want to dip out within the week. Shit, what if I really fall for her and she plays me to the left again?"

Now that he was giving voice to his reservations, he was second-guessing his decision.

"I don't mean no harm, but you left yourself open to that. I mean, you've always been a risk-taker, but this is wild, even for you." Avery was shaking her head.

"I know, I know." He ran his hand over his face. "But some-times you have to take the risk to get what you want, right? So maybe this will all be worth it. If nothing else, by the end of this, I'll have an interesting ass story to tell." He shook his head. "But I have to say, it feels like I met her for a reason."

Reggie had been raised to believe in fate. Some things and people were put in your path for a reason. As wild as it sounded, he had a feeling that if he saw this through, what he found at the end would be completely worth it. He took a sip of his beer and looked up at his friends.

Avery and Lucas both looked at each other like they had more to say but seemed to decide against it. Instead, they just shrugged and sat back.

"If you say so," Lucas said, kicking his feet up onto the coffee table. "We won't question you too much about it."

Avery didn't seem to share his sentiment, but Reggie held up his hand to stop her before she could say anything. "Just trust me, Avery. I know what I'm doing."

She looked at him skeptically but gave him a nod. "I'm pretty sure you don't, but I'll leave it alone for now. All I'm asking is for you to be careful. The last thing I want to see is you get hurt."

"Without a doubt."

As the trio settled in to watch the kick-off of the Oakwood Stallions pre-season game, Reggie's phone vibrated. Pulling it out of his pocket, he saw Makayla's name flash across the screen. The smile that appeared on his face certainly wasn't fake as he answered with a quickness.

"Well, Ms. Michaels, to what do I owe this pleasure?" he asked, a playful note in his voice.

"Mr. Johnson," she said just as playfully. "I just wanted to see if you were good on the details for Thursday night. It's only two days away."

"Yeah, I think I'm straight. It's at Lizzie and Lonzo's house, right?"

"Yep. Right outside of Oakwood in Birch Harbor. Do you already have the address, or should I send it to you?"

"No, I've actually been once or twice before, so I should be able to find my way there."

"Oh, okay. Well, great."

The silence settled. Just as it began to get awkward, Reggie cleared his throat. "Should I swing by your place and pick you up or..." he said, letting the end of his sentence taper off. If they were dating, should they arrive together? He didn't want to make any assumptions, but figured that it wouldn't hurt to ask.

"No, not this time," Makayla said without hesitation.

"Oh, you don't want your new man to know where you live, huh? Afraid I'm a stalker or something?" Reggie said in mock offense. He couldn't stop the warmth that filled him when he was rewarded with her full-bodied laugh.

"Mmmm, something like that. You can never be too careful these days."

"Well, damn. I was just joking, but I guess you're right," Reggie said with a laugh of his own.

"Don't worry, I'm just fucking with you. Truth is, I have to be there early to help set everything up. My best friend offered to cater, so of course, I've been roped into being her assistant."

"So, I get to meet the family and the best friend tomorrow night, huh? That's a lot of pressure on a brother."

"Something tells me you have no problem when it comes to handling pressure," Makayla responded, her voice dipping just a bit. The sound went straight to his dick. Damn, was he already this far gone off of practically nothing?

"You're right about that," he said, hoping he was keeping his voice somewhat under control. He ran his tongue over his bottom lip and almost said something else but heard Lucas clear his throat as Avery stifled a laugh. So maybe he didn't have as much control over himself as he thought.

"Well, it sounds like you're busy, so I'll let you go. See you Thursday."

"Looking forward to it," he said, and after a few moments of silence between them, he heard the line go dead.

Reggie turned to see both of his friends watching him. "What?" he asked.

They both watched him before turning to each other. "Fifty bucks says he's head over heels for her ass by date number two," Avery said to Lucas.

"Shiiiit, a hundred says by date number three, she's ready to cut his sprung ass loose," Lucas responded.

"Fuck both of y'all," Reggie said, kissing his teeth, which only sent the two of them into fits of laughter. He settled back into his seat and put his phone away. He had no problem admitting that he was feeling Makayla. The issue was he had no way of knowing if those feelings would be reciprocated.

CHAPTER 6

Makayla

"Girl, what the fuck are you doing all that fidgeting for?" Jasmine asked. She popped Makayla's hand for what had to be the third time in the last thirty minutes.

"Ouch, bitch!" Makayla said, snatching her hand back from the dessert table.

Jasmine leaned over to fix the tiered tray that Makayla nearly sent tumbling to the ground. "Listen, you're about to mess up my whole mini tart vibe, and I worked too long and too hard on this. What is your problem?"

"He's going to be here any minute," Makayla hissed.

Jasmine raised an eyebrow. "Girl, what are you so flustered over this man for? It's not like this is your first time seeing him. You've been out with him twice at this point."

"Yeah, but I certainly wasn't introducing him as my fake boyfriend either of those times."

Jasmine rolled her eyes. "This was your idea, bitch! You can call it off at any time."

Hiding her plan from Jasmine hadn't even crossed her mind.

The two of them had been best friends since the ninth grade; they told each other everything. When Jasmine snuck out of her house to meet a senior during their sophomore year to have sex for the first time, it was Makayla that covered for her when she was freaking out the next day because she was too sore and anxious to go to school. When Makayla lost her grandmother's priceless locket, it was Jasmine who helped her look for it for weeks before her mother realized it was gone. The two were truly two peas in a pod.

"Call it off and give Kendall the satisfaction of thinking I made the whole thing up? Have you lost your mind? That heffa would just love for me to turn and run with my tail between my legs," Makayla said, shaking her head.

"You know, this weird rivalry you and your sister have has led to some out-of-this-world shit, but I'm pretty sure this takes the cake," Jasmine said, laughing.

Makayla sent her best friend a side-eye. "So glad you find this entertaining."

"All I'm saying is you made your bed with this man, so now you have to fuck him in it."

"Bitch, that is *NOT* the saying, and you know it." Both of them burst out laughing at their silliness.

"Ok, fine. The point is this man has agreed to help you with an idea that is straight out of a movie. Those movies you claim you can't stand, by the way." Makayla tried to ignore the accusatory tone the other woman was giving her and instead focused her attention on rearranging the fruit tray and charcuterie board. "So, put on your big girl thong and get it together."

Makayla took a deep breath, trying to center herself. Jasmine was right. She'd gotten this train rolling, and while she was sure that Reggie would let her call it off with no problem, she knew she would regret it if she did. Turning Reggie away now would only put her right back at square one. She would try and get through tonight with no problems, and if things got too dicey, she would come up with an excuse to get the two of them out of there.

Honestly, the paint and sip night was probably the best way to break the ice with her family and this dating situation. Not only was it low-key, but it should be easy to set up the vibe she wanted when everyone was more concerned with not fucking up their pictures instead of clocking her and her new "boyfriend."

"Fine," she said grudgingly. Jasmine's own date, a five foot ten, dark brown skinned, model-esque beauty with locs that flowed beyond her ass, walked up just then carrying a platter filled with decorative cookies. Considering Jasmine only reached about five foot three, the woman towered over her, not that Jasmine seemed to have any complaints. Makayla watched as her bestie smirked at whatever the other woman whispered in her ear before handing her the treats and walking away.

"Well y'all are cute," she said with a raised eyebrow. "Will I get to see more of this one or are you changing up your date depending on the event?"

"Have you seen the legs on that woman? Matter of fact, have you seen the legs on her while they're wrapped across my shoulders? The plan is definitely to keep her around."

"You are so nasty," Makayla giggled.

"Maybe so, but unlike you, I intend to have as much fun with my date as possible."

As if right on cue, the doorbell rang. Before she could make a move, her mother's voice floated to her from the front room.

"Well, hello! Aren't you a tall, dark drink of water?" Delilah said. Makayla had to fight not to gag. There was no way her mother was flirting with her damn man. Okay, maybe he wasn't exactly her man, but Delilah didn't know that!

"Woman, I know you're not over there flirting with that young ass boy like I'm not standing right over here," Percy's voice called.

"Oh, hush! I'm just welcoming our guest. You know you're the only drink that I want to get my mouth on," she purred.

No fucking way.

Makayla knew she had to grab Reggie and get him the hell out of that foyer before her mother made a show of actually following through on her declaration to Percy.

"Mommy, please! You're going to scare the man away," she said, coming around the corner and into the foyer. The older couple was practically wrapped around one another. Thankfully, Reggie wasn't running out the door, though he did look a bit sheepish with his hands tucked into his jeans. Makayla might have thought it was cute if she wasn't so busy being embarrassed by her mother's behavior. God, it felt like she was a teenager all over again.

"Oh, girl, please. I'm sure he doesn't mind. Isn't that right, baby?" Delilah asked, smiling up at Reggie.

"Not at all, ma'am," Reggie answered with a smile. Makayla could actually see her mother melting right in front of her eyes.

Well, at least he has the charming part down pat.

"Uh-uh, there are no ma'ams in here! Please call me Delilah." Delilah offered up her hand, and Reggie kissed it lightly. Was she imagining things, or had hearts suddenly appeared where her mother's eyes should be?

"Very nice to meet you, Delilah. It's easy to see where Makayla gets her beauty from." He turned to look at Percy, who looked two seconds off from stepping between Reggie and her mother. "And you must be Percy. It's nice to meet you, sir. Congratulations on the upcoming nuptials," he said, holding out his hand, which Percy shook, albeit hesitantly.

"Nice to meet you too, son. Glad you could make it," Percy said with a nod.

Reggie pulled a bag from behind his back and handed it to Delilah. "I know Makayla said I didn't need to bring anything, but my grandmama raised me better than to come into someone's home without a host's gift." Shit, he was charming and had manners? If he didn't dial that shit back a little, her mother might actually cancel her wedding just to get a piece of him.

Hell, she may have to wait her turn, she thought to herself.

"Daaaamn, girl," Jasmine said, walking up next to her, clearly on the same page.

"I know," Makayla said, shaking her head. She walked over to Reggie, who pulled her into a hug pretty effortlessly and placed a kiss on her cheek. She lifted an eyebrow because what the hell was that about?

Well, he is pretending to be your man, girl. Isn't that what significant others do?

"Hey, baby," she said, smiling up at him. Makayla hoped that her smile didn't look as strained as it felt, especially considering that she could feel all eyes on the two of them.

"Hey, beautiful." The ease with which the words left him gave the illusion that they'd done this a hundred times over. He gave her a smile of his own, that same smile that almost had her melting the first time they met.

How does he do that?

Makayla mentally shook herself. She didn't have anything to be nervous about. She could do this, right? It was time to match Reggie's energy.

"You know you had no business coming in here getting my mama's panties all in a bunch, right? She's damn near ready to steal my man," she teased. She placed her hand lightly on his chest and gave him a small push. Reggie's hand wrapped around her wrist, and she felt a bolt of electricity run through her.

Reggie licked his lips, and she wondered if he felt it too. Damn, he made that look entirely too good. And why the hell did she have the urge to pull that tongue between her own lips and see exactly what it tasted like?

Reggie leaned down, one of his arms wrapping around her waist to pull her close. "Quiet as it's kept, there's only one woman whose panties I'm worried about right now." His voice was low enough that no one else heard his suggestive words. His lips grazed her ear, and this time, she had to fight to swallow her moan. A shiver went through her body. Well, shit, there he went again, ruining another pair of panties. It was becoming a habit of his every time they were together. She was either going to have to find a way to get him to chill, or she would just need to stop wearing them altogether.

The second option would definitely be good for easy access.

That's not supposed to be on the table, remember?

Well, shit, maybe it should be.

"Mmmm...is that a fact?" Makayla asked in a breathless tone.

"One hundred percent," Reggie responded, giving her hip a squeeze before giving his attention back to the group.

Makayla leaned away from him just a bit. She was feeling a little bit dizzy and just slightly out of control. She was losing control of this shit and fast. Looking up at him, she couldn't tell if any of this was having the same effect on him. At the very least, Reggie wasn't making any moves to let her go. In fact, he was doing just the opposite by tucking her into his side.

"Well, isn't this cozy?"

Makayla fought hard not to roll her eyes as Kendall walked into the foyer.

Deep breaths, girl. Deep breaths.

"Reggie, this is my big sister, Kendall. Kendall, this is Reggie." She sent a raised eyebrow in her sister's direction.

"Nice to meet you, Reggie," Kendall said, her tone suggesting it was anything but.

"The pleasure is all mine."

"Though I have to admit, I'm a bit surprised you came. Almost as surprised as when Makayla told us you two were dating."

Kendall's voice was a bit too smug for Makayla's liking.

"That's Kendall-speak for she thought I'd made the whole thing up." It was difficult as hell to keep the irritation out of her own voice.

Reggie chuckled, and Makayla joined in. This was their own private joke, and no one even realized it. "Nah, it's very real. Glad I could shut down any doubts."

"Me too," Kendall said, though her tone of voice still didn't match her words.

Makayla couldn't stop the smug feeling that went through her. "Come on, Mr. Very Real. Let's introduce you to everyone else and get you a drink." She took his hand and led him past her sister into the family room.

CHAPTER 7

Makayla

How the fuck was it possible for this man to be so charming? Everyone who crossed his path seemed to fall under his spell. Her mom's friends, Percy's family —hell, even Jasmine seemed to be in awe of him, and she knew the entire thing was a scam. They were all practically eating out of Reggie's hand. It was honestly a bit amazing, if not infuriating, to watch. He was so relaxed with his arm draped over her chair. Meanwhile, Makayla couldn't get her body to relax no matter how many sips of wine she took.

As everyone laughed at something her mother said to Percy, Reggie leaned over, his lips once again brushing against her ear. "Relax, baby girl. You look ready to bolt out of the door any second now."

She fought not to shoot him a glare. "I am relaxed."

Liar.

"Want a little help with that?" he asked.

"Nope," she said, a strained smile appearing on her lips. Makayla could feel him staring at the side of her face. She just needed to get out of her own head. She took one deep breath and then another. Yeah, no. This wasn't working.

She sighed. "If I said yes, what sort of help are you planning on giving?"

The smirk on his face almost had her ready to pull her question back. "Would you excuse us for a second?" Reggie said to the group as he took hold of her hand.

All eyes were on them as they stood and made their way out of the room. After a quick look around to determine where they were, Reggie pulled her into the hall bathroom.

"What are we doing in here?" Makayla huffed.

"Do you want to call this whole thing off?"

His bluntness caught her off guard, causing her to stumble over her words for a moment.

"I— What?"

"Do you want to call this whole thing off? I'm only asking because you're clearly uncomfortable. It's fine if you are. We can go out, finish the night, and then once it's all said and done, you don't have to see or hear from me again."

Makayla contemplated his question. On the one hand, it was an easy out. She could probably pull herself together enough to get through paint night. It might be a pain in the ass, but if she made this their first and last event, she could figure out the rest later. It was tempting, but backing down wasn't in her DNA.

"I appreciate the offer, but I always finish what I start."

A smile spread across Reggie's lips. "So do I." He laced his fingers with hers and took a step toward her until she was backed against the seat.

"Ummm…ever hear of personal space?" Makayla asked with her face turned up.

He chuckled, clearly unoffended by her tone or the look on her face. "Close your eyes."

Oh, hell no.

Makayla cocked her head to the side, looking at him as if he'd lost his mind.

"Relax. I promised to keep my hands to myself, and I'm a man of my word. I just need a little space to work here. Close your eyes. Please."

The urge to tell him no was strong, but she swallowed it. He'd said he would help her, and as much as she wanted to grumble about it, Makayla couldn't deny that she needed to calm her nerves, especially if she intended to go through with this whole scheme.

"Fine," she grumbled.

He gave her time to follow the direction before giving his next one. "Now, take a few deep breaths and let them out slowly."

Makayla did as requested until she'd done it three times. The muffled voices from the other room filtered into the space, mixing with the soft pattern of her breathing. The sound reminded her of white noise, but soon even that began to fade.

After her last deep breath, she felt his lips graze her ear, and she nearly jumped out of her skin.

"You control everything that happens here, Makayla. Every handhold, every hug, every interaction and impression." His soft words swirled around her, helping her to focus.

"Nothing here happens tonight that you don't want to happen. We're here to relax, paint some horrible ass pictures, and have a few drinks. You could run circles around anyone in that room. So, take another deep breath, collect your thoughts, and then head out there and be the boss we both know you are."

That last sentence made her smile. Reggie was right. She'd never let anyone run her out of any room, especially not her family. She damn sure wasn't going to start now.

When Makayla opened her eyes, Reggie was staring down at her, one eyebrow raised.

"Thanks," she said, voice soft.

"Anytime."

"Ahem…" The sound came from the other side of the door and was followed by a heavy knock. "Are y'all going to stay in there all night, or will you be joining us anytime soon?"

Kendall.

Reggie stepped out of her space. He gestured toward the door, allowing her to take the lead. Squaring her shoulders and grabbing his hand, Makayla opened the door to find her older sister standing there with an irritated look on her face.

"Our bad," she said, placing a smile on her face. "Guess we got a little distracted."

They slid by her and headed back into the room with the other guests. As they entered, it was hard to miss the rest of the room's expressions. Makayla knew she should probably be at least a little embarrassed, considering what everyone probably thought they were up to, but she couldn't bring herself to feel that way. Not even when she realized that just about everyone in the room was staring at them.

Lizzie looked like she was practically bursting at the seams. Both her mother and Jasmine had mischievous looks in their eyes, though Makayla was willing to bet it was for two very different reasons. Everyone else at least made an attempt to feign indifference. Everyone except for Kendall, who had walked in behind them.

"I mean, if y'all need a room, I'm sure Lizzie could point you toward one," Kendall said with her arms crossed over her chest. She was clearly aggravated, for whatever reason.

"My bad. I should take the blame on this. Just wanted a little alone time with baby girl here. I guess I just lost track of time. I'm not sure if anyone can really blame me, though," he said, shooting Makayla a conspiratorial glance.

"Well, maybe you could keep it under wraps. Or at least warn us next time. I may have to have something a little stronger than wine if you're going to be sneaking off every five seconds for the rest of the night."

"Oh, girl, stop being such a hater. Don't act like you and Greg haven't gotten down and dirty in public before. Remember my twenty-first birthday?" Lizzie shot at her with a pointed look.

Kendall immediately went red. "That was years ago, and that's completely different!" she said, exasperated. She looked over at her husband for support, but he was currently looking extremely interested in anything but looking at her.

"Yeah, okay, if you say so," Jasmine snorted. Everyone remembered that night fairly well since Kendall had practically climbed Greg like a tree right in the middle of the dance floor. There was also the added note of her trying—and failing—to whisper to him that she wanted to "ride him into the sunset."

Kendall quickly scooped up her glass of wine, downed it, and mumbled something about needing a refill. Her hasty exit sent everyone into a fit of laughter and thankfully took the attention off of Makayla's antics. Reggie gave her hand a squeeze as they took their seats.

Once things calmed down and they were settled again, Delilah cleared her throat. "So, Reggie, tell me a little about yourself. Are you from Oakwood?" she asked.

He nodded, picking up his glass and bringing it to his lips. Makayla suddenly had a strong craving for the cognac he was sipping on. On instinct, she took it from his hand and took a sip herself. He looked at her with a raised eyebrow.

"Figured I'd have a taste," was her only response.

Reggie chuckled. "Have at it, baby girl." Turning back to her mom, he said, "Yeah. I was actually born and raised in Oakwood."

"And your parents?" she asked.

"Mommy…" Makayla groaned.

"No, it's okay," he said with a small smile. "Actually, my parents didn't raise me. My mom died when I was about two years old, and my dad dipped out not too long after that. I guess he couldn't handle raising a kid on his own."

"I'm so sorry to hear that," Delilah said, slight distress showing on her face.

"Everyone has a story, right? That's just part of mine. When I was three, he dropped me off with his mom, Lovey. That's who raised me, and honestly, it was probably for the best. My grand-mother was definitely a force of nature. She was…a mess," he said with a laugh, "but in the best possible way. She was a damn good cook, too. She's actually the reason I have such a love for food and traveling. We were always going places and trying new things together. Lovey always said that she knew I had a restless soul, and it was important to feed and nurture it."

Makayla watched him as he spoke. Even though he lit up when talking about his grandmother, she saw sadness settle over him as well. She clearly wasn't the only person who noticed because her mother reached across the table and squeezed his hand.

"When did she pass?" she asked softly.

Reggie swallowed, and Makayla found herself tucking into his side, hoping it offered him a bit of comfort. "About ten years ago. Colon cancer," he said, his voice thick with emotion. "It's been tough without her, but I'm making it."

Damn. It had never crossed Makayla's mind that tonight would lead to such a heavy conversation. This may have been stressful for her, but the last thing she wanted was for Reggie to be uncomfortable. She could feel him tense up. Without a second thought, she leaned over and placed a light kiss on his cheek.

He gave her a small smile and returned her kiss with one of his own on her forehead before turning back to Delilah. "I know she would've loved baby girl here. And I like to think she would've been proud of me for not only living my dream but managing to scoop up your daughter. She always said I'd find a woman that would knock me clear off my feet and right on my ass. Apparently, she was right."

Wait, what? That was…unexpected. Was he just playing to

the crowd, or did he really mean that? There was no way that statement could be real. Not when this was all for show. Not when they were still just getting to know each other. Makayla wondered if she looked as shocked as she felt. If she did, no one seemed to notice, given the chorus of awwws that flowed through the room.

Fuck. If she wasn't careful, Reggie was really going to have her caught up. He was playing this a little too well, and honestly, she didn't know if her game was up to par.

The rest of the night went by without a hitch. Kendall eventually let go of her attitude, probably thanks to all the wine, and even she succumbed to Reggie's charms. Other than suggestive looks from Lizzie that she tried to ignore, everyone was on their best behavior.

By the time everything was all said and done, Makayla was ready to deem the night a success. After insisting on helping with cleaning up the aftermath of the paint and sip, Reggie offered to give her a ride home. She'd been ready to turn him down and catch a ride with Jasmine and her date until her best friend nixed that idea. If they were an actual couple, then it made sense for her to ride home with him. At least, that was the logic that Jasmine had given her as they whispered to one another while packing up the catering equipment.

"Let that man give you a ride home, M&M! And while you're at it, I suggest *you* give *him* a ride when you get home," Jasmine said, breaking down the cupcake stands.

"Jasmine!" Makayla hissed, which only widened the devious smile on her best friend's face.

"All I'm saying is, if you're going to commit to this whole thing, you might as well take it all the way. And considering how much time y'all spent in the bathroom earlier, I don't think he'd turn you down."

Makayla rolled her eyes. "I told you we didn't do anything! He just helped me get out of my own head. *That's it.*"

"Mmhmm, well, maybe you should be returning the favor," Jasmine snickered.

"You know what? At this point, I'm going to let him take me home just so I don't have to deal with your bullshit."

"Whatever you need to tell yourself, friend," Jasmine said with a knowing smirk before she turned to finish cleaning up.

With a sigh, Makayla made quick work of the rest of the table before heading to the front hall to meet Reggie.

"Ready to head out?" he asked, reaching out for her hand.

She could literally feel Jasmine's gaze burning a hole in the back of her head. "Yep." She turned around. "Mommy, we're leaving!" she called down the hall.

Delilah came rushing down the hallway and practically yanked Makayla off her feet as she pulled her into a hug. "I think he's a keeper," she whispered into her daughter's ear.

"Moooom," she groaned before pulling away.

"It was very nice to meet you, Reggie," Delilah carried on as if her daughter hadn't said a word. "You'll be at karaoke night at the end of the month, right?"

"Of course," he said with a smile.

Delilah looked downright giddy at his answer. Makayla thought for sure that she would have to pry her mother off of him with a crowbar, but thankfully, they managed to make it out of the house unscathed and without tools.

"You sure you want to set yourself up for more of this?" Makayla asked as she climbed into his truck.

"You kidding me? I can't think of anything better," he said with a chuckle before pulling off.

CHAPTER 8

Reggie

Sunday had always been Reggie's favorite day of the week since they were something like a guilty pleasure. No schedule, no timeline, just Reggie doing whatever he wanted. It was a tradition carried over from growing up with his grandmother, Lovey. She always said that what happened Sunday set the tone for the rest of your week. If Sunday was a stress-free day, then it ensured the rest of your week was the same.

Saturday was the designated cleaning day when Reggie was little. Of course, if you asked him, there was never much to clean. Lovey could never be accused of keeping a dirty house. Still, he could always count on the fact that while Saturdays were filled with Diana Ross, Gladys Knight, and imaginary dust bunnies, Sundays were strictly for pleasure.

Even now, all these years later, Reggie kept the tradition going. He was nothing if not reliable. It didn't matter where in the world he was, Sundays were for him. That was probably why Lucas had no problem finding him at Diane's. It was a staple in the Oakwood community, one he and Lovey had visited every Sunday, and something he still did whenever he was in town.

Diane and Lovey had grown up together, so this place always felt a little bit like home.

"I don't remember inviting you to my spot," Reggie said with a smirk as Lucas sat down across from him.

"When has that ever stopped me before? Besides, you and Lovey brought me here all the time back in the day. So technically, it's *our* spot."

Reggie let out a snort. "Yeah, whatever, man. Just know that you're paying."

"Why me? You're the big-time writer, remember? I know you're pulling in the big money."

"Yeah, well, I may be the big-time writer, but I happen to have a best friend who's a big-time realtor. From what I heard, he's pulling in some great money too. In fact, I could've sworn he was supposed to be doing an open house this morning, not here bothering me."

"That's not for a few more hours, so lucky you, I have plenty of time to chill."

"Yeah, lucky me."

It didn't take long for someone to come and take their orders and soon the two were digging into their food. The taste of Diane's biscuits and sausage gravy took Reggie right back to his childhood. He chuckled when he remembered how Lovey used to say that Diane almost made her biscuits as light and flaky as she did. *Almost.* The thought caused Reggie to laugh out loud.

"What's so funny?"

"Remember when Lovey and Ms. Diane got into that argument over these damn biscuits?"

Lucas let out a snort of his own. "Yo, I thought those two were going to come to blows. Especially after Lovey told Diane that her biscuits were drier than the ones at Popeyes."

That had both of them chuckling. Reggie's grandmother had been a trip. "You know after that, she didn't let me order these damn biscuits for like three months? We never stopped coming here, but she told me that if she saw those biscuits on my plate again, she was gonna snatch me up. Had my little ass terrified."

"Yeah, well, lucky for you, Ms. Diane has plenty of other good shit on the menu to get down on."

"You're right about that."

After another minute or two, Lucas cleared his throat. "It's good to have you home, bruh."

"It's good to be home."

"Is it?"

To anyone else, it may have seemed like an odd question, but Reggie understood what his friend meant. There was a reason he'd stayed away from Oakwood for such a long time. Ever since his grandmother died, being here—being back home—had been difficult, to say the least.

"I won't say it's been easy. I mean, shit, I see Lovey every- where. I always have. It's like she's imprinted on Oakwood. That's the thing I hate and love about being here. Everything reminds me of her."

Lucas nodded. "I know. And I get it. I mean, it can't be easy to see the person you love the most everywhere you go."

"It's definitely not."

"I gotta say, when you said you were home for good this time, it surprised the hell out of me."

Reggie chuckled. "Yeah, I gotta be honest, it caught me by surprise too."

Reggie's relationship with Oakwood had been nothing less than complicated since Lovey had passed away. After losing her when he was twenty-five, staying in Oakwood had been too painful. Her last will and testament had left specific instructions that said he was to sell the home he'd grown up in and use the money to start over. Instead, he'd packed his bags and taken his first travel writing job. It took almost three years for him to set foot back in Oakwood.

By then, Lucas had his real estate license, which helped him finally follow through with his grandmother's wishes. By the time it was all said and done, he'd had more than enough money to buy his condo and set himself up. He'd also had enough of Oakwood and was soon back on the road.

That pattern continued over the next several years. Oakwood always called to him, be it his friends or the memory of his grandmother. Reggie always answered the call, but eventually, the very thing that had drawn him back to his hometown drove him away time and time again.

"I'm tired of running, Luke. I've been running from Lovey's memory for a long time, and…I'm tired."

Lucas set his fork down and leaned forward. "We've missed having you around. I know you visit and all that, but it's not the same as having you here on a regular basis. I've just never said anything because I knew how hard being here without her was."

Reggie nodded. "And I appreciate that. But it's time for me to admit that when Lovey told me to explore the world and do what I love, she didn't mean do it at the cost of cutting out my roots. I'm not saying I'm going to give up traveling, but I'm not going to use that as my excuse anymore. I miss being home. This is where I belong."

It had taken Reggie a long time to figure that out, probably longer than it should have. He was thirty-five now, and it was beyond time for him to stop chasing something he couldn't find out in the world. Not when it was right here in his hometown.

"You won't get any protest from me. Believe that." The two men dapped each other up before returning to their food.

"I'm sure the women of the world would disagree, though," Lucas said with a smirk.

"I'm sure they'll find a way to survive."

"Speaking of, how was that paint shit the other night? Did y'all pull it off or what?"

"It was actually a pretty good time. I mean, her moms is wild as hell, and her sister Kendall is a trip. For a minute, I was sure that Makayla was going to call the whole thing off. She looked ready to bolt right out the door."

"I'm assuming she didn't, though?"

"Naw. I pulled her to the side, asked her if she wanted out. When she said no, I did my best to help her relax, and it must have worked because we were good to go for the rest of the night. Didn't take much. I mean, ole girl can do bad all by herself. I just did what I could to keep up."

Lucas nodded, but Reggie could tell there was more that he wanted to say.

"Thoughts?"

"Just one."

Reggie waited for his friend to elaborate. "Care to share with the class?" he asked when it became clear that Lucas wasn't going to say anything on his own.

"I'm pretty sure she's going to knock you right on your ass, and you don't even realize it."

"I'm pretty sure you're right."

CHAPTER 9

Makayla

When Reggie called Makayla a little over a week later on a Wednesday during work to ask, "Rocky road or cookies and cream?" her first reaction was to ask him if he was high. To his credit, he'd laughed off her question and proceeded to explain that he wanted to know which flavor she preferred.

————

"Cookies and cream, but I would choose chocolate chip cookie dough before both."

"Questionable, but answer accepted."

"Is there a point to this line of questioning? I'm sure you already know this, but I'm at work."

"I do, my bad. Is today a late day, or do you think you'll get out of there within the next few hours?"

"Ideally within the next two hours, if someone would stop distracting me." She knew her tone gave off how agitated she was, but he didn't seem to mind.

"Well, I definitely don't want to get my ass beat," he said with a chuckle. "So listen, there's this food truck, Justice for Desserts, that's supposed to be over in Washington Square tonight. I'm checking it out, partly for work and partly because, well, who doesn't love dessert?"

"Tick-tock, Reggie."

"Right, okay. Look, I know that's not too far from your office, so if you want to check it out with me, meet me, say around...six? Dessert for dinner type of situation. Just think about it, and let me know. We can even count it as our first date-for-a-date trade-off."

———

Makayla had fully intended on passing up Reggie's offer, but by the time 5:30 rolled around, she was starving, in need of some stress relief, and curious. That's how she found herself in the middle of Washington Square, wondering where the hell Reggie was.

"So, which was more appealing? The ice cream or the date?" a voice said from behind her.

She couldn't help the smirk that crossed her lips. "The ice cream. Without question." Makayla turned to face Reggie, and somehow, he looked even better than he did the last time she'd seen him.

"Ouch." He clutched his chest as if she'd really hurt him. "Well, I gotta respect your honesty, I guess. A hug for my wound?"

Makayla rolled her eyes but allowed him to pull her into a hug anyway. "Don't be such a baby," she teased.

"And the shots just keep on coming." Reggie shook his head, but she could tell he didn't mind. "I'm glad you came out, no matter what the reason is."

"If we're being honest, today feels like it really should be a dessert-for-dinner day, so as irritated as I was about you calling me earlier, I needed this."

Reggie nodded in understanding as they began to walk toward the busy truck. "Want to talk about it?"

"Two of my editors have been working my last nerve lately. Everything I say or do, they want to give pushback on. And they're at each other's throats over every little thing. I swear, sometimes I think adults are worse than children."

"You're probably right about that. Especially since adults think they know every damn thing."

Makayla let out a snort. "Sad, but true." She looked around. "So, what's the deal with the truck? Do they only have ice cream, or am I in for several dessert-type treats?"

"Oh, they definitely serve up more than ice cream. One of the reasons I'm writing about them is because of their rolling menu. They aren't open every day. You have to watch their socials to see when they pop up, but every time they do, there's a whole new menu. Supposedly, it's whatever the owner comes up with that day. But word on the street is there's never been anything that wasn't a hit."

From the look of the crowd, whatever the owner was doing was working. Makayla was already anticipating adding this to her regular food truck rotation. Once they checked out the menu, she finally decided on a maple bourbon donut topped with chocolate chip cookie dough ice cream, while Reggie went with strawberry shortcake funnel cake topped with strawberry ice cream.

"Exactly how much whipped cream does one person need?"

"There is no limit to the amount of whipped cream acceptable on dessert, okay? Take your judgment elsewhere." Makayla took her whipped cream-to-dessert ratio very seriously.

"Okay, okay. Don't fight me. Death by whipped cream is not on the agenda today," Reggie laughed.

She couldn't help but laugh along with him. "Cute, real cute."

The two of them found a stone bench that wasn't occupied

and took a seat. After a few spoonfuls, Reggie reached his spoon over, going for her food.

"Uh-uh!" she said, snatching her tray away quickly. "What do you think you're doing?"

"Sharing is caring, right? I know they taught you that in school."

"Mmmm, I must've missed that lesson. What I do remember, though, is supply and demand. I have the supply, so I get to make the demand."

"I don't think that's how that works," Reggie said skeptically.

Makayla shrugged. "Suit yourself." She made a show of her next bite of the sugary treat, exaggerated groans and all, and Reggie nearly choked on his own mouthful.

"All that, though?"

"All that," she confirmed.

"Fine," he said with a sigh. "What's the demand?"

She thought for a moment. This had come on a whim, but considering the amount of time they were going to be spending together over the next several weeks, why not take the opportunity to get to know him?

"That first night we went out, at the Thai fusion restaurant, you mentioned something about settling down. Isn't this whole thing with me sort of…counterproductive to all that? I mean, you can't have time to find 'the one' if you're sorta kinda dating me."

By the look on Reggie's face, that clearly wasn't what he'd expected her to say. "One, you say that like you're going to hold me hostage forever. Two, who said I was looking for 'the one?'"

"I mean, you didn't say those words exactly, but it was implied. I guess I'm just curious."

After tossing her question around in his head for a while, Reggie cleared his throat. "To answer your question, I don't think this is counterproductive. I know you're adamant about not wanting to really date, but the truth is I think you're the type of person I'd like to spend time with. So far, I have a good time every time we're together. I have a bit of a knack for picking up on these sorts of things. So, in my mind, why waste someone else's time when my focus could be here?"

"Right, but my point is it doesn't have to be here at all. Because eventually, this thing between us is going to end, and once it does, what are you going to be left with?"

"I think I'll make out ok in the end," he said, smirking at her as if he knew something that she didn't. "Don't worry about it too much. Just relax and enjoy the ride."

She scoffed but didn't say anything. Just as she was about to hand over her tray, she snatched it back. "Exes never made the cut?"

Reggie groaned. "Not this question."

"What? It's a fair question." He looked at her skeptically, and she cocked an eyebrow at him. "Please?" Makayla asked, giving him a fake pout.

With a sigh, he shook his head. "Okay, fine. Umm...let's see. I guess it just never worked out because the reality of love is a lot different than the idea of love."

The look on her face must have told him he'd have to give her more than that.

"I tend to go all or nothing when I'm in a relationship. I've never done anything halfway. Now, that's great for a while, but considering the job I have and my aversion to staying in one place for too long, it doesn't exactly make for great relationship terms."

"What do you mean?" Makayla said, face scrunched in confusion. She handed over her tray and offered him a taste. This conversation required a sugar rush, and a deal was a deal.

"I mean, not everyone wants to pick up their life and move every few months. Beyond that, sometimes it's easier to bask in the moment when everything is great and happy. When there's nothing but beaches, amazing food, discovering new places, and great sex, of course, a relationship looks amazing. But take those things away and start facing the realities and demands of everyday life…things start to go downhill real quickly."

She thought for a moment. "Downhill on whose end?"

"Both. I wasn't always my best self. I made more than a few mistakes, I'll own that. Even beyond that, though, it's hard to give someone what they need when you don't know what it is either of you is looking for."

"Is that what happened in your last relationship?"

Reggie nodded as he cleared his throat. "I met Kari in Costa Rica. I was gone from the beginning. She had this voice that just…it hypnotized you." He gave a light chuckle.

"To be honest, Costa Rica is probably the longest I've ever stayed in one place. I was there for almost a year. I would go off on assignment still, but I always came back to Kari. She had that effect on me."

Reggie paused and put both trays down. He rubbed his hands against his jeans and gave a weak laugh. "It never mattered what she did, I always made excuses. When she disappeared for days on end, I acted like it didn't bother me. When she complained about me not paying enough attention to her even though she was just about the only thing I was focused on, I cut back on my writing. I didn't even realize how much I was giving her until she couldn't give me the one thing I asked for."

"What was that?"

"To come back and visit Lovey." He sighed. "I hadn't been back in about two years at that point. Her birthday was coming up. Just because she's not here anymore doesn't mean I can't come visit and celebrate her, right? I wanted Kari to come back with me this time. Wanted to introduce her to my friends.

"It took all of thirty seconds after the words left my mouth to register the look of horror on her face. Took another two minutes for her to explain how she never wanted things to get that serious between us. Coming back here just wasn't something she was ready for. I don't know if she meant ever or just at that moment.

I don't think she knew either. It was clear, though, that we wanted different things."

Reggie looked directly at Makayla, the raw look in his eyes hitting her square in the chest. "Hurt like hell when she left. I ended up hightailing it out of Costa Rica, coming back here for a few months, then heading to Phuket. That was a little over a year ago. Haven't dated anybody since." He knocked shoulders with her. "Until now, I guess. I decided to just focus on myself and work, two things I'm sure you know a lot about."

Makayla offered him a genuine smile. When she'd asked her question, she hadn't known it would lead to this conversation. As heavy as it was, she felt like she had a better sense of who Reggie was. He didn't have all the answers like she thought he might. Maybe they were more alike than she thought.

"Just one day at a time, right?"

"Right."

They watched each other for a while, a silent understanding growing between them.

"Sooo…are you ever gonna give me my shit back? I know my ice cream has to be melted by now," Makayla finally said, giving him as much attitude as she could muster.

"If it is, it's not my fault."

"Of course, it's your fault!" she screeched, shoving his chest. He caught her hand before she could do it again, and Makayla felt her heart give a stutter.

They stayed like that for a moment. "So is it my turn to ask a deep dark question?" he asked, not making any move to let her go.

Before she could answer, she heard the last voice she expected.

"Aren't y'all just the cutest!"

CHAPTER 10

Makayla

"Please tell me that's not Lizzie," Makayla said, her eyes shut tight. She had to be imagining this. No way in hell was her luck that bad. She peeked through one eye to look at Reggie.

"Hate to break it to you, but that's definitely her," Reggie said with a grimace. Clearly, he grasped the gravity of the situation and thankfully, he let her go.

"I should've known anywhere there was a dessert truck, M&M would be nearby," Lizzie teased as she and her husband, Alonzo, appeared in front of them.

"M&M?" Reggie's tone was all too amused.

"It's what we called her growing up. She could sniff out candy like a bloodhound. Mommy has a real sweet tooth, but to keep us kids out of her stash, she used to hide them in random places around the house. Somehow, Makayla always found them. I still don't know how she did it." Lizzie's laugh was infectious because pretty soon, Makayla was laughing right along with her.

"I have a weakness for chocolate. It's her own fault. Besides, she really just recycled her hiding places over and over again."

"Interesting," Reggie said. "No wonder it was so hard to get you to share tonight."

Makayla scoffed and shook her head as she turned to her sister. "So great to see you as always, little sister. What exactly are you doing here?"

"It's date night," Lizzie said, gesturing to Alonzo. "Besides, this truck is amazing. We were thinking of trying to get them to do Christian's birthday party in a few months. Lonzo and I thought this would be a great test run."

Makayla gave her brother-in-law a hug after he dapped up Reggie. She wasn't usually this rude by ignoring him. She loved Alonzo. He was so sweet to Lizzie, and he loved Christian as if he were his own.

"What are you two doing here?" Lizzie asked, wiggling her eyebrows suggestively.

"Baby, don't be so nosey," Alonzo chuckled as he pulled his wife in close.

"I'm just curious, that's all!"

Of course, she was. Lizzie had been trying to corner Makayla ever since she'd said she was dating Reggie that day in the dress shop. Up until now, she'd managed to avoid this conversation, but it looked like her luck had run out.

"Date night," Reggie answered. "Guess great minds really do think alike."

"I guess so." Makayla did not like the twinkle that she was seeing in the other woman's eye.

"You know, I was just telling Alonzo how cute you two looked together the other night at Paint Night. Looks like my instincts were right." She leaned back into Alonzo and looked at the two of them. "Speaking of which, I'm glad to see we didn't scare you off completely. Between Kendall and our mom, I know things got a bit intense."

"Don't worry about it," Reggie said, shrugging the whole

thing off. "Makayla already apologized. I've never been afraid of a little pressure, so I didn't mind."

"Oh, she apologized, huh? I bet that was fun." Lizzie shot her sister a wink.

"Lizzie!" Makayla hissed.

Lizzie shrugged and went on eating what looked like pineapple upside-down cake as if she was the most innocent person in the world.

Before Makayla could say anything else, Reggie wrapped his arm around her shoulder and pulled her in close. "Relax, remember," he whispered in her ear. The feel of his breath on her skin sent shivers down her spine. He placed an unexpected kiss just below her ear, and she pulled her bottom lip between her teeth.

She almost forgot her sister was even there until she heard Lizzie clear her throat. "Should we give y'all a minute?"

"Maybe give us more than that," Makayla said as she leaned into Reggie. "I mean, it is date night, after all."

"Ooop! You don't have to tell me twice. I can absolutely take a hint," Lizzie said eagerly. Makayla laughed at her sister. "Come on, baby. I want to grab something for Chris before we head home."

The couple said goodbye and headed back toward the food truck. Makayla couldn't even pretend she didn't see Lizzie's gesture to call her. Bless her heart, but Lizzie had never learned the art of being inconspicuous. She went to tell Reggie as much, but when she turned, she noticed the heated gaze in his eyes.

"More than a minute, huh?" he asked in a low, gruff voice.

"Had to find some way to get rid of her." Makayla's own voice was just above a whisper.

"Well, I hate to break it to you, but just because she walked away doesn't mean we don't still have an audience. Doesn't look like Alonzo or that truck is holding her attention."

"Yeah, well, Lizzie has always been the nosiest out of all of us."

They both laughed at that and shook their heads. When the laughter settled down, there was something else left in the moment, something that seemed to burn her inside and out. She didn't have to wonder if Reggie felt it too. Not as he brought his hand up to cup her chin. She felt her breathing stall just for a moment. Reggie's lips hovered over hers, giving her plenty of time to stop what was coming. Instead, she leaned in just a bit more, his scent intoxicating her. He pressed a soft kiss just to the right of her lips and then to the left. Shit, that definitely wasn't going to improve her breathing, but she couldn't find room to complain. Not when he finally gave her what she'd been anticipating.

What probably should have been a light, easy kiss soon turned into anything but. His tongue tangled with hers before he sucked on it lightly, eliciting a low moan from her. He tasted like strawberries and bourbon. Nothing had ever tasted so damn good. Makayla brought her hand to the back of his head, pulling him in, ready for more, and he seemed to happily oblige. The two of them lost themselves in the kiss, which gradually became more insistent until they were finally interrupted by a few distracting giggles.

They pulled away from one another and saw that the sounds had come from a group of kids not too far away from them. The two were just lucky enough to catch the disapproving look from their parents.

Makayla made a poor attempt to hold back her laughter. "Maybe we should get out of here," she said to Reggie as she grabbed their trash.

"Good idea."

CHAPTER 11

Makayla

"Thank you for tonight. I needed this little break," Makayla said as she and Reggie came to a stop in front of her brownstone.

"No problem. After all, what are boyfriends for?" he teased her.

Makayla let out a laugh. "I suppose you have a point."

The two of them made their way to the sidewalk in front of her house, and she tried to use the time to pull herself together, to no avail. As she turned to look at him, it hit her that resisting her attraction to him may just be a lost cause. The way the street lights backlit Reggie had his skin glowing, and his eyes drifting over her body damn near set her on fire. Just like their kiss earlier, his heated gaze was strictly for her.

Makayla was never one to shy away from awkward moments. No, she would much rather say whatever was on her mind. That was why the next words out of her mouth were, "So, about that kiss…"

Reggie chuckled. "What about it?" he asked with a cocked eyebrow.

"Do you kiss all of your fake girlfriends like you want to blow their backs out or was that just for my benefit?"

Whatever he had been expecting her to say, it wasn't that. The deep, full-bellied laugh he let out sent Makayla into her own fit of laughter. He took a step closer to her, the twinkle in his eyes promising mischief. "I like to offer the full boyfriend experience. I figure if I give 110%, my Yelp reviews will skyrocket."

"Oh, is that so?" she asked, tilting her head to the side.

Reggie nodded. "Mmhmm. Though I have to admit, I may have pulled out my A-game for you." His eyes darted down to her mouth.

His tongue slid over his lips, and Makayla could barely fight back the shudder that went through her entire body. Damn, she wanted nothing more than to wrap her legs around his shoulders and put that tongue to the ultimate test. Could he feel the heat radiating off of her? Could he sense the tingle that had just hit her between her thighs? It didn't matter because both feelings drove her closer to him.

"Well, do you have any of that A-game left?" she asked boldly.

His fingers traced along her jawline before situating them under her chin to tilt her head back just a bit. "I do. I seem to remember someone telling me to keep my hands to myself, though."

She hummed and moved forward, pressing her body against his. "I've never been all that great at following rules, even when they're my own."

Before she could second-guess herself, Makayla surged forward, gripping his forearms as his hands moved to her hips. The moment her lips touched his, the hunger that had been pulsing through her went into overdrive. She wasted no time parting his lips with her tongue, hoping to get another taste of the dessert he'd had earlier. Makayla felt it all the way in her toes when he suckled on it lightly. His hands moved from her waist down to her ass, palming it as he pulled her as close as possible. Makayla let out a gasp as she felt his erection at the apex of her thighs. Her own hands moved to either side of his face, keeping him right where she wanted him. She nibbled at his bottom lip, hoping to make him feel just a fraction of what she did.

Fuck. Why does he taste so fucking good?

She let out a whimper that he devoured as he spun and lowered her onto the small stoop that bordered her steps. The new position gave him just the leverage he needed to tilt her head back further. He wasted no time getting his fill of her. Makayla brought her thighs up to bracket either side of him as his hips hit a slow stroke that had her pulling away to let out a throaty moan. Fuck all if she wasn't ready to reach right into his jeans and pull out his length so that she could feel the real thing. Hell, she just might with the way his lips trailed down her neck to suck on her pulse point. She was practically squirming underneath him right here out in the open. Her breath came in pants and whimpers as she soaked through her panties, and at this point, she couldn't bring herself to think about anything else.

His fingers trailed across her covered slit, causing Makayla to let out a raspy "Shit!" as she arched into his scraping touch. At the very same time, several yipping barks that she was 95% sure weren't coming from her rang out behind him. Her eyes snapped open, and she was met with the very disapproving stare of one of her neighbors, out walking her trio of Yorkies.

"Umm… Evening, Mrs. Wharton," she said, attempting to catch her breath as her legs dropped and Reggie leaned into the crook of her neck.

"Makayla," the older woman said before giving a small tug on the leashes in her hand. She shot the couple one more withering glance before making her way down the street to her own home. Once she was out of earshot, Makayla felt more than heard Reggie trying to hold in his laughter.

"Shut uuup," Makayla said, her laugh mixing with a groan as

she pushed his tall frame away. "I cannot believe you have me out here getting down and dirty with you in the middle of the damn sidewalk."

"I'm pretty sure you started it, Little Miss I Don't Follow My Own Rules." Reggie helped her stand and made sure to readjust himself in the process.

Makayla rolled her eyes. Yeah, ok, he was right. She had been the one to make the first move. And it wasn't like she made any real attempt not to get carried away. Still, despite the fact that she knew Mrs. Wharton was probably on the phone right now spreading her business to the other old biddies in the neighborhood, she couldn't bring herself to regret their little adventure into exhibitionism. Quite honestly, with the thick ass third leg she'd felt through his jeans, she was ready to ask him if he wanted to come inside to finish what they'd started.

Any chance of that went out the window when Reggie placed a quick kiss on her lips and began backing up.

"Go inside, Makayla," he said.

She raised an eyebrow. "By myself?"

He nodded with a smug look on his face. "You're not quite ready for what would happen if I went inside with you, baby girl. Besides…you owe me a date. If I give you everything you want now, it will only ruin the fun later."

He winked as he leaned against the car. He looked every bit like a sculpted god and she thought about protesting. Her eyes darted down to his pants, the bulge that greeted her causing her to swallow. Still, she took a shaky breath and tried to give him the most casual shrug that she could.

"If you insist. I guess I'll just have to…take care of myself." And considering the mess he'd made of her panties and the filthy images currently floating through her mind, she knew she'd have no problem giving herself a much-needed orgasm. From the intense look she could feel him giving her as she walked up her steps, she was sure that Reggie knew it too.

CHAPTER 12

Reggie

Reggie couldn't believe how nervous he was. This certainly wasn't an emotion that he experienced often. Sure, pursuing women wasn't new to him, but he rarely went into a situation unsure of himself. Either he and his date hit it off, or they didn't. More often than not, things tended to go his way, and when they didn't, he chalked it up to the game and kept it pushing. That was just life. No harm, no foul, no real loss. This date with Makayla felt different, though. He needed this date to go well. He wanted to believe that this thing with Makayla, despite her reservations, had the potential to develop into something more.

This entire situation was new to him and not just because of the fake dating aspect. Makayla's entire energy was electric. There was no other way to describe it. Each time he was around her, he felt a jolt slide down his spine, through his veins, and all the way down to his fingers and toes. Her presence commanded attention, even when there were plenty of other things to focus on.

Take the paint and sip night with her family. Though he'd

encouraged Makayla to relax and go with the flow, his own calm had been completely fraudulent. Reggie felt like he was on the edge of a cliff for most of the night. It had taken everything in him to focus on his conversation with her mother instead of being enraptured by her scent. He'd had to remind himself over and over again not to stare at Makayla across the room while Lizzie teased him about what a horrible painter he was.

"I'm a master with words, Liz, not a paintbrush," he'd chuckled as his eyes traced Makayla's every move. When she tossed her head back laughing at something her best friend had whispered to her, his heart stuttered at the sound.

Her presence set Reggie at ease in a way that he wasn't used to. He certainly hadn't planned on opening up about his family or his history right up front. Neither were topics that he discussed often because the pain of losing his grandmother was still so fresh all these years later. Still, with Makayla sitting next to him, her mother's questions didn't strike the usual chord. And when sadness seeped into his voice and he felt himself begin to choke up, it was Makayla tucking herself into him that helped ground him in the moment. It made no sense that she could ease his spirit that quickly, and yet…she had.

Then there was their ice cream date. Her sister showing up had been unexpected, but they'd taken the bump in stride. It wasn't like it would hurt for her family to see them together outside of wedding events. Of course, running into Lizzie and Alonzo was a lot better than running into Kendall. He'd known Alonzo for a few years now, and he'd always enjoyed the little time he spent with Lizzie. The night hadn't been a complete bust, and for that, he was grateful, especially when he thought about how their night ended.

The taste of her was a problem in and of itself. He could've chalked their kiss up as a one-off, just something to sate both of their curiosity as they came down from a sugar high and the encounter with her sister. At least, he could have before the two of them had gotten lost in one another. There was certainly no denying the primal attraction between them.

Once you coupled that with what happened between them in front of her brownstone, Reggie was undeniably on edge, his teeth sinking into his bottom lip. Every part of him had wanted to take her up on what she'd been offering. He could still feel the way her body molded to fit his. Still tasted traces of the bourbon and chocolate chips that had been dancing on her tongue. It damn near kept him up these last few nights.

He'd wanted nothing more than to take her upstairs and show her exactly what she did to him. He was positive that his dick could do plenty of talking for him, but he was playing the long game, and he didn't have much time to do it. So instead of giving into the good time they both clearly wanted, he'd said goodnight and made sure Makayla got into the house safely. The cold shower he'd tried to take to calm down lasted all of sixty seconds before he was turning up the heat and stroking himself as he remembered the sounds she made as he pressed into her on the stoop and the feel of her legs hiked up over his hips. By the time he finished, he was too tired to do anything except fall into bed and pass out with images of Makayla dancing around in his head.

You are in waaay over your head here. That was all he could think as he scanned the parking lot for anyone who looked like her.

There was no other way to put it. To be honest, when he'd countered Makayla's proposal with his real date for every fake date idea, he hadn't actually expected her to agree. At most, he'd thought she would laugh her ass off, and the two of them would share a few jokes at his expense. Despite how…unorthodox her whole idea had been, he'd decided to help her out the moment she'd explained her situation. There was no way he could bring himself to leave her out to dry. It just wasn't in his character.

But instead, she'd thrown him a curveball and agreed to his offer. Their ice cream outing had managed to be a two-for-one, but tonight was different. They'd planned ahead for this, and he'd put a lot of effort into tonight. He was excited, despite his nerves, and he was pretty confident that she'd sounded the same when he called her earlier to confirm their date for tonight. Was it wishful thinking, or was she actually looking forward to spending time with him? Reggie didn't want to get his hopes up, but he'd certainly take his wins where he could.

The fact that she hadn't completely ghosted him so far was a win in his book. The two weren't in constant communication, but he'd found one reason or another to contact her every day this week since their ice cream outing, happy to see that she didn't seem to mind as long as he wasn't interrupting her at work. Their conversations flowed easily, ranging from childhood stories to funny work anecdotes to her venting about the latest bullshit in her office while he explained the deadlines he was working on. Whether it was actually talking over the phone or text messages, the conversations had yet to taper off or get awkward. He was hoping that same energy would transfer over into tonight's date.

After what felt like forever, a car pulled up in front of the skating rink, and Makayla stepped out of the back seat.

"Fuck," he let out, his throat going dry as his eyes dragged over every inch of her body. Reggie couldn't be more thankful for the warm August night than he was once he took in her long, thick legs in her chocolate-colored linen shorts romper. It felt like a double knockout when he noticed the buttons she'd left undone at the top, giving him the perfect view of her cleavage. Reggie wanted nothing more than to dip his tongue between the valley of her breasts while giving her braids the strong pull they deserved. How the hell was he supposed to focus tonight?

"If I've got you drooling like that, I can only assume that I look just as good as I thought."

Her teasing tone pulled him out of his trance. Caught, and he couldn't even play it off. Fuck it. It wasn't like he had anything to lose. "Looking good doesn't even begin to cover it," he said, pulling her into a hug. He took the opportunity to check to make sure she was only joking about the drool comment. With the impact she seemed to have on him, Reggie wouldn't have been surprised if it were true. Thankfully, though, it seemed he'd managed to keep some of his dignity intact.

The feel of her warm body against his was almost enough to pull a groan from his throat, but he held it together. Once they stepped apart, she took a good look at where they were.

"I can't believe you brought me skating."

Shit, had he made a mistake? He looked down at her face and breathed a sigh of relief. She actually looked excited.

"Yeah," he said with a nod. "If you think you can keep up. After all that shit you were talking the other night when I mentioned it, I figured I should check out your skills for myself."

"Oh, you ain't said nothing but a word," she returned with a smile of her own.

"We'll see." He didn't hesitate to take her hand in his and lead her through the entrance of the skating rink.

Roller skating had always been one of his favorite pastimes growing up. He could always be found here at the Down & Around skating rink just outside of downtown Oakwood with Avery, Lucas, and whoever else they were hanging out with in their crew. He'd had all of his firsts here—first time busting his ass, first job, first date, first real kiss. This old spot had a special place in his heart. After they'd talked about their favorite childhood memories late one night and he learned that Makayla had done all of her skating at a rink across town, he knew this was the perfect place for their first real date.

Walking into the rink was the perfect blend of going back in time and meeting a new friend. This was Reggie's first time back at his old stomping grounds in the past two years, and he had to admit, it was amazing. The owners had managed to keep the same vibe the place had growing up while also taking care to make modern upgrades. For the first time since he'd been back in Oakwood, Reggie actually felt like he was at home.

"Daaaamn, ok, ok, so maybe this place does have a little style," Makayla teased as she looked around. He smirked as he took in her face. Despite the teasing tone, he could see her appreciation for the rink in her expression. It eased some of the nervousness that had been plaguing him. Maybe he shouldn't admit this, but Makayla's opinion mattered to him, even though they hadn't known one another very long. In bringing her to the rink, Reggie was opening up a piece of himself to her. It felt good to know it wasn't all in vain.

"Well, of course, it does. You didn't think I'd vouch for somewhere that wasn't up to standards, did you?"

"I don't know. It still remains to be seen whether or not you have good taste."

"Considering my present company, I'm sure we can both agree that my taste is pretty damn top-tier," he said as his hand moved to her lower back. "Unless you're trying to argue a different point."

A smirk played at the edge of Makayla's lips. "I guess I'll give you that one, Mr. Johnson. One point to you. And an extra half-point for smoothness."

Reggie couldn't help but be pleased with himself.

"Well, I see some things never change," a familiar voice said behind the couple.

Reggie and Makayla pulled apart and turned toward the voice. Just as he suspected, Reggie found Vesta Jergens standing at her usual station behind the rental counter. A deep, wide smile spread across his face at the sight of his old friend, and he chuckled. "Been here all of five seconds, and you're already about to clown the fuck out of me, huh?" Reggie shook his head in mock exasperation as he stepped up to the counter with Makayla following his movement.

"I mean, we haven't seen you around here in what, almost

three years? Maybe longer. And the first time I do see you, what are you doing? Pulling out your corny ass lines for a gorgeous girl," she said, throwing a wink in Makayla's direction. "You are nothing if not predictable. What type of person would I be if I didn't point that out and clown you for it? Consider it payback for staying away for so long."

Reggie groaned. "Damn Vee, you know it's not even like that."

"I do? Are you sure?"

"Oh, so this is just a regular stop for the Reggie Johnson tour bus, huh?" Makayla said, joining in on the teasing.

"Not you too," he said, sliding his hand over his face.

"The *infamous* Reggie Johnson tour bus, okay," Vesta said with a giggle. "It's always been like this. I swear, any day he was on the schedule to work, there was a line of girls wrapped around the damn parking lot."

"Stop exaggerating, Vee, before you give me a bad rep," Reggie said as he leaned against the counter. He might have been concerned about Makayla taking everything that was being said seriously if it weren't for her over-the-top facial expressions. Still, if things took a turn, he'd have to shut Vee's storytime down before his date got the wrong idea about him.

"Exaggerate? Me? Never," Vesta said, feigning shock.

"Yeah, okay. And anyway, I don't remember anyone complaining about all the money that was being made on those busy ass nights. You're welcome," he said with a laugh.

"What can I say? Young Vee loved the money dollars, okay!"

Reggie and Vesta both laughed. He took a look at Makayla just as her eyes went wide, realization dawning on her face.

"Oh my gosh, wait! This is big, bad Vee? The older girl who broke your heart and left you devastated?" Makayla gasped. Suddenly, Reggie was regretting sharing that little tidbit about his first during one of their recent conversations.

"Big, bad, and devastated, huh?" Vesta teased, leaning over the counter.

"What was it you said the other night? You wanted to cry like a baby when she turned you down after you finally got up the nerve to ask her out?"

Reggie shook his head. "Hold up, I know I ain't say all that." He rubbed the back of his neck sheepishly because, truthfully, what he said hadn't been too far off.

"Mmmm... I'm pretty sure that's exactly what you said," Makayla said, winking at Vee.

"Oh, please! He really broke out the big sympathy guns for that one. If I recall correctly, it took all of twenty-four hours before that broken heart was repaired by Delia Glenn," Vesta responded.

"Give me a break! I was fourteen," Reggie said, propping himself up on the counter.

"Mhmm, fourteen and sniffing around something way out of your league," Vesta teased, sending both Makayla and Vesta into laughter.

Even though the jab was at Reggie's expense, he didn't mind. This may not have been what he had in mind for the start of the night, but it was all in good fun. Besides, seeing the smile on Makayla's face was most definitely on the agenda tonight so he wouldn't complain too much. Besides, although Vesta had turned him down—and rightfully so, considering she was four years older than him—she'd become one of his closest friends and the older sister he'd never had. He wouldn't trade that bond with her for anything.

"Are you finished or nah?" he said, folding his arms over his chest.

"Yeah, yeah, I'm done. For now, anyway." Vesta walked around the counter and pulled Reggie into a hug. "It's good to see you, Reg. We missed you around here." Once she pulled out of the embrace, she punched him in his shoulder, making him wince. "You were gone too damn long this time! You better be sticking around for a while."

"Damn, woman! Watch that right hook of yours," he said, rubbing the spot where she'd hit him. "And don't worry, I don't plan on making any hasty ass exits any time soon." He looked over at Makayla. "I'm starting to think I might have an extra reason or two to stay."

Vesta's eyes twinkled as she looked between the two of them. "Interesting. Very interesting." She gave Reggie a conspiratorial glance. "Well, come on then, don't be rude. Officially introduce me to your extra reason." She winked at Makayla, who blushed in response.

"Vee, this is Makayla. Makayla, as you've already figured out, this is Vesta. Vesta here is basically my big sister and, as you can see, an even bigger pain in my ass."

"Aww, don't be like that. You know I have to pick on you like only a big sister could."

"Really? Because here I thought you'd help me out by making me look good," he responded, a mini scowl on his face.

"Yeah, yeah, yeah, don't be such a baby. Anyway, it's very nice to meet you, Makayla. I hope you're keeping his big-headed ass on his toes."

"Oh, without question and it's very nice to meet you too," Makayla said confidently.

"My type of woman," Vesta said, giving her a high five.

"Are y'all finished, or are y'all done?" Reggie groaned. The two of them giggled, and he rolled his eyes.

"Sure, hotshot. I guess we'll give you a break," Vesta said, pinching his cheek.

He swatted her hand away playfully. "Thank you. Can we get two sets?"

"Sure." Vesta asked for Makayla's shoe size as she made her way back around the counter. After grabbing what they both needed, Reggie made a move to pull out his wallet.

"Now, you oughta know better than that, boy," Vesta scolded before shooting them a wink. "You two have fun. It's on the house."

"Thanks, sis." Reggie scooped up the skates and leaned over the counter to place a kiss on Vesta's cheek. She beamed at him before moving along to help another set of customers.

Reggie led Makayla over to an empty bench near the lockers where they could change into their skates. "You just loved that, huh? Have a good time watching her roast the fuck out of me?" he asked Makayla.

"I mean, watching you get all flustered and aggravated was sort of cute. Who am I to stop a good time? Besides, she seems cool. I can see why you were drawn to her in the first place," she responded, nudging his shoulder.

"I don't know. Now I'm wondering if I should just cut both of y'all off. I think you got a bit too much joy out of that." Reggie chuckled.

"I'd like to see you try," Makayla shot back. Her confidence was one of his favorite qualities.

"Keep thinking so highly of yourself, baby girl. You'll fuck around and find some shit out."

"Like what?" she challenged.

His eyes dipped down to her lips. When he managed to meet her eyes again, she was smirking. He swallowed the small lump that had formed in his throat and shook his head.

Behave, he thought to himself.

"Like how much it's gonna hurt when I give you this work on the rink floor."

"Hmmm…" she said, slipping her feet into the skates and bending over to lace them up. "Trust me when I say you'll be the one getting this work."

———

Reggie had to admit that Makayla was every bit of the beast on the floor that she'd said she was. Watching her circle the rink, hips moving in perfect sync to whatever song the DJ was spinning, was even better than anything he could have conjured up in his imagination. He made a point of keeping up, cracking jokes right next to her.

"Looking like you're moving a little slow there, Mr. Johnson," she teased as she pulled up next to him along the wall. He'd fallen back to watch her bob and weave through the crowd. He didn't quite want to admit it, but he needed a moment to catch his breath after the trick she'd just tried to have him pull. The two of them had taken to playing their own skating version of HORSE. They both had the chance to perform a trick that the other had to copy flawlessly. While he'd managed to land the jump-and-spin move she'd challenged him with, the sit-and-spin ending had been a complete fail that ended with him flat on his ass in the middle of the rink. It was a good thing that the rink was not only chill but not too crowded either. Even though they were having a damn good time, the last thing he wanted was to mess up anyone else's flow.

"Nah, I'm just giving you a break. I would hate to embarrass you out here."

Makayla froze for a moment before letting out a peal of laughter. She was laughing so hard that she nearly toppled over on her skates. "Embarrass me? I'm pretty sure I'm whooping your ass on your home turf. You're literally one letter away from losing."

"See, you're falling into my trap. I was just trying to lull you into a false sense of security." Reggie pulled her into him, one arm looping around her waist as their chests pressed together. He placed a soft kiss to the right of her lips, then to the left. His mouth moved to her ear as he whispered, "And I'm pretty sure it's working."

When he pulled away and gazed down at her, he could see

that her bottom lip was tucked between her teeth. He could practically feel the heat behind her gaze, and it took everything in him to pull away completely before taking off on his skates.

"You should've warned me that you like to play dirty," she called after him, her voice sounding like it was slightly caught in her throat.

"Where's the fun in that?" he said, shooting her a wink before he took off to do his next trick. The feel of her body against his and her eyes on him was just the energy boost he needed.

Reggie took off speeding down the lane as "You Dropped a Bomb on Me" by The Gap Band played through the rink's speakers. He looped around once, then twice, picking up as much speed as he could. Once he was ready, he completed a jump turn that sent him skating backward. He could see Makayla on the sidelines watching him with a twinkle in her eye as she moved her head to the beat. Reggie shot her a wink as he did his own little footwork that looked like something straight out of *Roll Bounce*, making her laugh. Just as he was ready to attempt the high kick and clap combo, he noticed a little boy darting out into his path.

"Oh, shit!" he said, moving to avoid him. The sharp change in momentum saved the little boy but sent Reggie crashing right into a wall. The impact sent him flying to the floor with a groan.

"Oh my God!" Makayla cried, skating over toward him with worry lacing her voice. "Shit, Reggie, are you okay? How many fingers am I holding up?" She held one hand in front of his face as she used the other one to brace his head a little.

He squinted a bit. "Four. Unless I'm seeing double, which means two."

She breathed a sigh of relief. "You were right the first time." She looked down at him in concern. "Are you sure you're feeling okay?"

His ass hurt, and his pride was more than a little sore, but luckily he hadn't hit the kid or his head. "Yeah, I'm good. I'm gonna need a hell of an ibuprofen, though. Otherwise, I'm going to be feeling this shit in the morning." He looked up at her with a slick smile. "I'd feel even better if you didn't count that as my last letter."

Makayla let out a throaty laugh, a sound he couldn't bring himself to get tired of. "That's a negative, Mr. Johnson. You have officially lost to the Queen of Rink." He gave her a fake pout, and she rolled her eyes. "Come on, you big baby. How about I buy you a drink and some cheese fries? Would that help?" she asked, holding out her hand to help pull him up.

Once he was back on his feet, he pulled her in close. "Only if you promise to kiss it better," he said in a low voice that only she could hear.

She looked up at him and winked. "Mmmm, let's go with no. But if you play your cards right, maybe I'll let *you* kiss something to make *me* feel better."

Reggie watched as she skated off the floor and onto the carpet toward the bar area at the back of the rink. This woman was truly going to be the death of him, and he couldn't find one reason to complain about it.

CHAPTER 13

Makayla

It had been a long time since Makayla had had this much fun on a date. Hell, it had been a long ass time since she'd been on a date, period. There was no shortage of guys asking to take her out, but she either always turned them down or canceled at the last minute. The few dates she had been on recently had been cut short either because of her schedule or her lack of interest. They certainly hadn't held her attention like Reggie was at the moment. Between their shit-talking, their little game, and Reggie busting his ass, Makayla had laughed more tonight than she had in a good while.

"Damn, I can't believe it took me this long to get back on some skates," she said. She shook her head as she pulled a cheese fry out of the basket in front of her. The two of them had wasted no time ordering food and drinks once they'd gotten their skates off and grabbed a table.

"Well, I'm glad to be the reason you were able to dust off your old skills," Reggie said.

"Even though those skills ate your ass up?" she teased.

"Oh, especially since those skills ate my ass up," he laughed.

"You are such a mess," she said with a giggle. She couldn't believe she was the sort of girl to giggle now. What was this man doing to her?

"I've been called worse, so I'll take that as a compliment."

The two of them sat in silence for a while before Reggie leaned over.

"So, I've been wondering something," he started as he took a sip of his beer. "What made you agree to this whole date-for-a-date idea?"

She raised an eyebrow at him as she sipped her own drink. "Regretting it already?" she asked.

"Never that, baby girl. Just curious," he said, raising his own eyebrow in the same fashion.

Makayla found herself looking down at the food on the table as she contemplated the answer to his question. She appreciated that he waited patiently while she tried to gather her thoughts.

"Honestly, at first, it was pure desperation. I don't think I expected you to agree to the whole fake dating thing in the first place. I mean, it's not like you knew me all that well. And this sort of shit probably isn't what you had in mind when my sister set us up. I was sure when I asked, you would think I'd lost my mind."

"I might have had that thought for a moment," he said with a laugh.

She rolled her eyes at him. "Rude ass." He chuckled, and she couldn't help the smile that played on her lips. "Seriously, though. You could've said no, but you took a chance and agreed to help me out. So, I figured anyone willing to do that for me... Well, that's probably the type of person who's worth a date or two."

She watched a wide smile spread across his face. "Well, no bullshit? I appreciate you taking a chance on me. I know you keep saying dating in general is a bit out of your box, so I hope I can make all of this worth your while."

Makayla gave him a smirk. "Off the record? You're doing pretty well so far."

She really hadn't expected things to go this well. She also hadn't expected to feel so relaxed with someone that she'd been thrown together with by chance. Makayla thought back to his openness at the paint and sip and found herself watching him as he stood to grab another beer. The way he seemed so at ease was almost unsettling. This should not be so easy. When it came to Makayla's dating life, nothing had ever felt this simple. Was this all a result of their natural chemistry or was it just the situation itself? After all, a fake relationship didn't have the same pressures of a real one. Then again, here they were on a real date, and she didn't feel any of the usual urgency to get this over with as soon as possible. She was utterly confused, another feeling she wasn't very familiar with.

Either way, her being so comfortable was the only way she could explain the words that came out of her mouth when he returned to the table. "Would it offend you if I said that the bar was low?" she asked.

One of his eyebrows shot in the air. "I feel like I just walked into the middle of a conversation," he said jokingly.

She laughed, heat creeping up her neck as she grabbed a napkin to clean her hands. "That's fair. Technically, you sort of did." She took a sip of her drink before she continued. "I said that you were doing pretty well so far—which you are, don't get me wrong. If I'm being honest, though, the bar…it's set pretty low at the moment."

He nodded as if he was clued into what she was saying. "Does that offend me? No, not really. Did it just pique my curiosity? Absolutely." There was a slight pause after his statement, the silence hanging thickly in the air. After a moment or two, he added, "We don't have to talk about it if you don't want to."

She shrugged as she pushed her drink to the side and leaned

forward just a bit. "I appreciate that, but no. I hate when people say something cryptic like that and then don't elaborate. What's the point of bringing it up if we're not going to fucking talk about it, right?"

He nodded in agreement but stayed silent. He was letting her set the pace of the conversation. Was the bar really low, or was he just killing the game without even trying?

"My last relationship wasn't exactly horrible. It just—" Makayla paused. "It wasn't a great fit. He was sweet, funny, and there was plenty of evidence to support the fact that he wasn't some freeloader who secretly lived in his mama's basement playing video games twenty-four hours a day at thirty-something years old," she said jokingly. "No off-the-wall custody battles or ex-girlfriends ready to jump out of the bushes on your girl. He was probably one of the least disrespectful and drama-free men I'd ever met in my life."

"But?" Reggie said, and she smiled because, yes, obviously, there had to be a 'but' somewhere in this conversation.

"But...I think hearing that work is my first priority and actu-ally understanding or experiencing that are two very different things. Everyone always assumes that women in their thirties who say they're career-driven are really just biding their time until they can find the right partner, whatever that means."

Reggie nodded in understanding.

"But what happens when there is no right partner? What happens when your job isn't actually just a placeholder for your significant other? That's where it fell apart."

"How long ago was this, if you don't mind me asking?"

"Three years ago." She gave a laugh that she hoped didn't sound anywhere near as bitter to him as it did to her own ears. "I honestly should've known better than to try and date someone I work with. My mom always said that you don't get your meat where you get your bread."

The next laugh she let out was genuine since it was a reaction to Reggie almost choking on his beer at her words. She felt a little lighter as some of the tension left her shoulders.

Makayla had a hard rule against dating people in her office. Other people in the publication world were fair game, but the people that worked at her magazine were strictly off-limits. She'd always figured it was a recipe for disaster. That was exactly what she'd told Nick when he'd asked her out one night while they were working late. A couple days later, he asked her out again. Her answer was still no. He was never forceful or pushy. He just always made it clear what his intentions were. Still, Makayla resisted because going against her rule could fuck up everything she was working toward. Eventually, though, after another late night, a few glasses of the whiskey she kept hidden in her desk, and two orgasms on the couch in her office, she decided to give it a try. If anyone was going to be able to understand the demands of her job and her ambition, it would be someone she worked with closely, right?

She said as much to Reggie before adding, "Imagine my shock when I was, in fact, wrong."

"What happened?" Reggie asked. She could see the curious look in his eyes, but there was something else there as well. Something she didn't exactly want to unpack at the moment.

"It started off small. We both tended to stay late in the office, but he started putting together some sort of semblance of a work/life balance because he was happy with where he was in the company. For a few months, he understood why I didn't make the same changes. He didn't complain when I needed to cancel dinner dates or when I said I needed space so that I could buckle down and focus on a deadline. Then, the longer it went on without changing, the more he got tired of begging me to pay attention to him."

"Is that what he said?"

"Yep. Those were his exact words, actually. He also made sure to add the fact that he didn't understand why I needed to stay late at work when he didn't. Oh, and of course, my personal favorite—if I really cared about him, then I should be able to devote just as much time to him as I did my job because that was how relationships worked."

"Seriously?" Reggie asked.

Makayla nodded. "Seriously. If I'm being honest, on some level, he was right. My job isn't a placeholder for my love life, but don't people say you make time for the things you want? So, by that logic, if what I really wanted was that relationship, then I had to take the time out for it. So, I did. I tried. I scaled back at work and started putting real effort into the relationship. There's no way for you to know this yet, but being intentional about stuff outside of work is huge for me. Dates? Scheduled. Family time? Marked down on my calendar. I like to be spontaneous when it's just me, but when it involves other people, I know setting a schedule is the best way to get me. It gives me time to plan and adjust, but it also means that I'm making a conscious effort to spend time with people. Hell, sometimes I have to literally schedule time for myself."

Reggie's hand slid across the table and engulfed Makayla's. She gave him a weak smile. "And I'm guessing that still wasn't good enough?"

"Apparently, being penciled in or taking the time to plan in advance wasn't actually what he was looking for."

"He told you that?"

"In the end, he didn't have to. When he started talking about moving in together and how that would be the perfect segue into my career taking a back seat, I knew he had me all the way fucked up." She let out another genuine laugh.

"And I'm pretty sure you told him exactly like that," Reggie said with a chuckle.

"I sure did. Told him exactly where he could take his bullshit because I wasn't interested in any of it."

She shook her head, thinking about the fight Nick had

attempted to have with her that night. She didn't have the energy or the desire to participate in any way, so instead, she'd left him there in the restaurant sputtering and confused while she made her way home to have a glass of wine and finish up some work ahead of her deadline.

"Good girl," Reggie said with a smirk. His words sent a jolt right to her clit.

What the hell was that?

His words stirred something unfamiliar inside of her. She was so lost in trying to dissect that unnamed feeling that she missed what he said next.

"Huh?" she asked, snapping back into the moment.

Reggie gave her a strange look but thankfully didn't call her out on anything. "I asked how things went at work after that. I can't imagine it was a walk in the park." His pointer finger traced over each of the lines on her palm slowly as if it would give him some insight into the rest of her story.

The feel of their skin-on-skin contact sent another shot of electricity straight between Makayla's thighs. She silently hoped that she wouldn't have a wet spot when she stood.

She took a big swallow. "Not as horrible as you'd think. Of course, he told a few of his work friends that I was a bitch who'd wasted his time. It's wild because up until then, I hadn't seen anything like that from him before. I was just sort of like what-ever, though. I'm good at what I do, so very few people brought his bullshit to my doorstep."

Her breath caught in her throat as his finger moved from the palm of her hand and began tracing along the edge of the inside of her wrist. "And anyway, everyone pretty much knows what type of person I am. It was less 'what's wrong with her?' and more 'did you expect her to do anything except die old and alone?'" Makayla said, attempting to make light of the whole situation.

Reggie looked her in the eye and held her gaze. "There's something I need you to know."

"Okay," she said hesitantly.

"Yes, compromise is important to any relationship, romantic or otherwise. I can't argue against that. But, just as equally important is making an effort." He leaned across the table, so close she was convinced he was going to kiss her. Instead, his face hovered just inches away from hers, not quite closing the distance as she expected. "But any man who can't see that you're not only worth the effort of pushing through but also that you're willing to make the effort to make your relationship work probably isn't really the man you need anyway. It's not about forcing you into a box that works for them. It's about finding someone willing to build something new that works for both of you."

Reggie's last sentence was said so softly she could barely hear him over the commotion around them, but she heard him all the same. It was surprising, really, especially since she could've sworn the only thing that she could really hear at the moment was static. As soon as he'd finished talking, he closed the distance between them, placing a soft kiss on her lips. He pulled away, leaving her a bit dazed. Once the confusion cleared and both his words and actions finally set in, she pulled him back in, this time for a kiss that literally snatched the breath from both of them.

The firm pressure of his mouth against hers was enough to set Makayla's entire body on fire. Reggie brought one of his hands behind her head to tilt her back just enough for him to deepen the kiss and part the seam of her lips with his tongue. He lapped into her mouth, his tongue gliding ever so slightly over hers, making her gasp.

Every part of her wanted to let him devour her right there in that moment, no matter who was watching, but it seemed Reggie had a different idea.

"I think it's time for us to go," he said, voice thick with need. Knowing that she was part of the reason for his change in tone excited her. It confirmed what she'd already gathered—she wasn't alone in the attraction she was feeling between them. "I need to taste you, and I'm pretty sure there may be some objections if I do it right here at this table."

She let out a full-bodied laugh before nodding. "Well, let's see if you can put your money where your mouth is. Because your skating skills turned out to be shit."

CHAPTER 14

Makayla

The ride back to Makayla's place felt like torture, and not just because they seemed to get caught at every light possible on the way there. No, it had more to do with the fact that Reggie's fingers had begun tracing circles against her inner thigh.

She felt something akin to wanton, the way she parted her legs and tucked her lip between her teeth, hoping...praying that his fingers would travel just a bit higher and make their way into her shorts. This had not been in her plans for tonight, and yet here she was.

Reggie seemed to know just what she wanted but refused to indulge her. He continued to torture her with his light touches, skirting just the edge of the bottom of her shorts before making his way back down again. By the time they were a few lights away from her house, she was practically whining at every touch, trying to adjust herself ever so slightly to get what she wanted. She knew her panties were soaked with her need; she could feel them sticking to her. If he kept this up, the evidence would be right there on her romper for him to see.

"Are you going to torture me the whole time or actually give me what your fingers are hinting at?" Makayla should've been embarrassed by her words, but she couldn't find the willpower to focus. Her skin felt itchy and hot to the point that it was driving her up the wall. Even though she wanted nothing more than for him to give her a taste of what he'd promised her, there was a part of her that was completely turned on by the thought of him denying her.

Reggie just chuckled as he pulled up to a stoplight a block from their destination. "I gotta be honest, baby, I'm having a damn good time teasing you."

She shot him a death glare that didn't last more than a few moments when his fingers made their way to the front of her romper and pressed the fabric directly against her wet pussy. The pressure parted her lips just enough that she felt the friction against her clit, causing her hips to jerk forward as her moan broke the silence. He scraped his nail against the thin fabric, drawing another roll from her hips, and then did it again. One of her hands shot behind her, attempting to grab hold of the head-rest. She rolled her hips forward, wanting more of that delicious contact.

"Fuck," she moaned. Desperate wasn't even the word. Suddenly she was right back in that moment with him on her front stoop. He really was turning her into some horny ass college kid.

Before she could form another thought, he moved his fingers, making her eyes fly open. "Why…" she started but followed his eye-line. They were at her house.

"Unless you want a repeat of last week, I'm thinking we should take this inside," he said.

She huffed in frustration, though she knew he was right. "I guess I'll lead the way." She undid her seatbelt, and as she moved to open her door, Reggie stopped her.

"What's wrong?" she asked, a confused expression on her

face. He shook his head and pulled her in for a kiss, practically devouring her in the best possible way. She matched his intensity, wanting nothing more than to taste every part of him.

He pulled away just enough to ask, "Are you sure you want to do this? I know what I said at the rink, but we don't have to do anything. Any taste of you I can get is worth it, even if it's just one amazing ass kiss." He paused to laugh. "Well…maybe two."

Instead of answering, she moved her mouth down and snaked her tongue out, flicking it along his pulse point. He groaned, and she couldn't help but smile against his skin.

"I appreciate the check-in, but I promise you, I more than want this. The question is, do you?" He wasted no time nodding in response. Not feeling as though any other words were necessary, she opened her door and made her way toward her steps.

It didn't take anything but a few moments for Makayla to make her way up the steps, grab her keys, and open the front door. With the force that Reggie used to push her against her entryway wall, though, you would've thought she'd taken a few hours to complete the simple task.

"Mmmm, someone's eager," she said with a giggle as his teeth found her neck. He grabbed her wrists, placing them over her head in a grip that was damn near punishing. The feel of him restraining her just enough to show her he was the one in charge had her head spinning. Or maybe that was the drinks.

"Would you prefer I slow down?" he asked with a raised eyebrow, his grip loosening to give her a clear choice.

She knew exactly what she wanted, so there was no need for hesitation. "Either taste me like you promised or let me go," she challenged.

The heat in his eyes sent a thrill through her as he moved a hand to grip her neck. "Don't move."

His tone left no room for debate, and as much as she wanted to see his control snap, this version of Reggie had her too intrigued to press her luck—for the moment, at least. Both of his hands skimmed her arms, fingers tracing invisible lines as they ghosted over her skin. Her breathing came in pants as he watched her with an intensity that she hadn't experienced in a very long time. Any chance of her panties being in decent shape after that car ride was already slim to none, but the anticipation of what was coming next only had her dripping even more.

Makayla tucked her bottom lip between her teeth, fighting to keep her wrists pinned to the wall exactly where he'd left them. Reggie's hands unbuttoned her romper before he roughly pulled down one bra cup and then the other, exposing their intended targets. His thumbs skimmed over her nipples, teasing them as he tasted her neck, licking and sucking in a way that drew whimpers from her. Whimpers that she tried to hold back, if only in an attempt not to let him know how affected she was in the moment. She should try to keep some part of her dignity, right? It didn't matter, though. The moment his fingers trailed below her waistband, he'd know exactly how much she wanted him right now. Hell, she was sure he could already scent it on her.

Makayla was so lost in thought that the rough pull of her nipple perfectly timed with a bite just above her collarbone made her yelp. She felt him smirk against her skin as he gave another tug of her nipple, this time pulling a low moan from her.

"All that talking you did earlier, no need to get quiet now." The roughness of his voice was the only indication that he was as affected by this as she was. That was the very thing she needed to steel her resolve.

"You want me to make some noise, baby? You'll have to earn that," she said in a breathy pant, issuing a challenge they both knew he wouldn't back down from.

"Oh, trust me, baby girl, I intend to."

He brought his lips to hers as one hand continued to massage her breast, and the other traveled lower. His movements felt like slow torture as he moved below her clenched stomach, unbuttoning the few buttons left. She didn't even have time to be impressed that he was doing it one-handed, not when he'd switched to her other nipple, pulling and coaxing it to life. Soon she was standing in front of him, romper open and skin exposed to the lingering cool air they'd brought into the house with them.

The moment his fingers dipped below her panties and made contact with her dripping slit, Makayla let out an involuntary gasp and arched into his touch. Any thoughts that he might take it easy on her were lost when he gave her a punishing kiss at the exact same moment that his finger pushed through her lower lips and traced over her clit. The unexpected contact sent her reeling, and she moaned into his mouth as his tongue tangled with hers. She'd expected the same teasing strokes Reggie had given her earlier, but instead, he wasted no time circling her clit with his finger just rough enough to elicit loud moans from her.

"This is what you want, right?" he asked as he pulled away just enough to look at her. A whimper escaped her as he pulled his hand out from below her waistband. She closed her eyes, her whole body feeling as though it were on fire. She felt a sharp sting against her pussy that sent her eyes flying open, revealing Reggie's face just inches away from her own. Had he just spanked her pussy? She got her answer when he gave her another smack that left her squirming. Fuck, she loved that. How did she not know before tonight that she loved that? Even with her underwear still on, she felt the force behind his movements, maybe even more so since they were soaked through.

"I'm talking to you, Makayla." Shit, had he said something? She couldn't remember. Her world was going fuzzy around the edges, and all she could think was how much she needed his fingers back on her clit because she had been so close to coming and...

There was only a moment to process that the soft material covering her pussy had been moved to the side. This time, the smack landed against her swollen, exposed clit. She let out a moan because goddamn, that felt so fucking good. "Yes. Fuck yes. I want it," she responded, his question coming back to her.

"Tell me what you want," Reggie said, pulling her earlobe between his teeth. The slight tug made her whimper again. Her nipples were aching from the attention he'd given them, and she felt just the tip of his finger trace over her clit.

"I want...I want to come," she said in a gasp. "Please make me come."

"That's a good girl," he said with a chuckle.

He pulled away, leaving her confused for only a minute before she realized what he was doing. He brought her arms down before helping her out of her romper. Makayla's eyes never left his as she unhooked her bra and let it drop beside her. She went to do the same with her matching panties, but he stopped her.

"Nah, leave those on," Reggie said, looking at her as if she were a full meal. She couldn't wait for him to treat her like one.

Reggie followed the path her one-piece had taken, sliding down her body until he was on his knees in front of her. He took care to slip her legs out of her romper and place them on the floor. Makayla watched with hazy eyes as he draped both legs over his shoulders, one after the other, resting his head between her thighs. With her ankles locked behind his neck, it was easy to imagine that he was trapped right where she wanted him. The look on his face as his tongue darted across his lips made her wonder exactly which one of them was actually trapped. He looked like this was just where he wanted to be. Who was she to deny him what he wanted?

He moved the wet black material to the side, giving him the perfect view of her glistening lips. "You're fucking dripping for me, did you know that?" he asked, though he seemed to be speaking those words directly to her pussy. Makayla didn't mind, and by the fresh wave of slickness that flowed from her at his words, she knew her pussy didn't, either. His tongue slowly licked along her seam, and she couldn't resist the urge to move one hand to the back of his head, his soft waves giving her just enough to hold onto.

"And she's just as sweet as I thought," he said, his voice thick with desire.

He gave her lips another long lick, and this time, she groaned right along with him. "Reggie, I swear to—" Her demand was cut off before she could finish the thought. His fingers parted her lips, and his tongue flicked over her swollen clit in a way that tore a moan from the bottom of her throat. He alternated between licking and sucking her, one hand gripping her quivering thighs and the other making sure she stayed wide open and exposed as he gave her clit the attention she craved. When his tongue lashings quickened, she couldn't help but respond with needy whimpers. She found herself applying pressure to the back of his head, her fingers tightening in his hair as she pushed him deeper between her thighs.

"Fingers," she managed to gasp between moans. "I need… mmmm, shit… fingers…please." She couldn't bring herself to care that she was begging. Not when she was so close to that sweet release, the familiar feeling pooling in her stomach.

He didn't hesitate to oblige her. Keeping her lips parted but loosening his grip on her thigh, so that he could push one, then two fingers into her hot, wet heat. By the third stroke of his fingers, she was coming apart around them, moaning and whimpering and whispering just how good it all fucking felt. She hoped like hell that they were just getting started.

CHAPTER 15

Reggie

R eggie was diving straight into the deep end. He was drowning in Makayla's honey, and fuck, if this was how he died, he'd surely die a happy man. The taste of her on his tongue, the feel of her warm and wet around his fingers, and the sound of her moaning, whimpering, and coming apart for him had him ready to worship at her altar for as long as she'd let him. Even with the way his dick was so hard it was ready to bust a fucking hole in his jeans, he didn't want to get off his knees. He didn't want to move from this spot for anything.

"So. Fucking. Good." Each word came with a soft kiss against her sensitive clit. After the last word, he took extra care to draw the kiss out. He hoped that it conveyed every filthy, dirty thought he was having about her at that moment. He lapped at her, loving every twitch that his movements elicited.

"Are you gonna stay down there all night, or are you going to let me return the favor?" she asked breathlessly.

Reggie couldn't help the chuckle he let out. Even now, legs hiked up, face flushed, and chest heaving, she was still mouthy as hell. Still ready to let him know exactly what she wanted without shame or hesitation. He'd never met a woman like her, and he was sure that he never would again. He knew that there were men out there who didn't like it when their partners gave directions in the bedroom. He was the opposite. He wanted to know what she liked, how she liked it, and how often she wanted whatever it was. The moment when she'd told him she needed his fingers to send her over the edge had turned him on beyond belief. He wanted more.

"You clearly never learned that patience is a virtue, huh?" Reggie said, unhooking her legs from around his head, setting her down on her feet, and putting her underwear back in place. He waited on his knees, watching her carefully. He could see that her legs still had a slight tremble to them, and the last thing he wanted was for her to lose her balance. He shouldn't have been surprised when she decided to take matters into her own hands and pulled him up by his shirt.

"What can I say? Some lessons just didn't stick. You, however, were clearly a star student." She pulled him in for a kiss, and the feeling of her sucking lightly on his tongue, tasting herself on it, drew a groan from deep within his chest.

Makayla pulled away from him, and it was almost pitiful the way his lips attempted to follow. She smirked and said, "Now, let's see how your leg strength holds up."

He immediately caught her drift, gripping her underneath her thighs and lifting her until they were wrapped around his waist. Her covered pussy pressed flush against the front of his jeans, and the friction made her bite her lip.

"Did you know it drives me out of my mind when you bite your lip like that?"

"Maybe," she said in a singsong voice. She peered down at his hard length pressed between them. "I showed you mine. Are you gonna show me yours?"

His laugh must've been enough of a yes for her because she quickly directed him upstairs to her bedroom. The simple kisses they shared along the way only stoked the sexual tension between them. Makayla wasted no time going in for a deeper kiss, one that was all tongue and teeth. It was like she couldn't get enough of his taste. She bit down lightly on his lip just as he entered her bedroom, and Reggie let out a growl as he tossed her onto the bed.

"Keep playing, baby girl. Go 'head," he said in warning as he stripped off his shirt.

Makayla rose to her knees slowly, allowing him to take in the sight of her supple, heavy breasts. How the fuck was she this damn intoxicating? She beckoned him closer with a single finger, and he happily obliged. He wondered if she could feel just how intense his gaze was as he watched her undo his belt and jeans.

The moment her hands dipped below his waistband and wrapped around his throbbing length, another groan left his lips. He had no problem being vocal when something felt amazing, and goddamn, there was nothing better in that moment than the feel of her hands on him. He was already slick with precum, and she gazed at his dick hungrily, ready to devour it whole. As her thumb grazed the tip of his head, he made no attempt to stop the "Fuck..." that escaped his lips.

Her grip was the perfect amount of pressure, and he wasn't even sure if she realized it. Hell, maybe she did. It didn't matter. All that mattered was that he'd do just about anything to hold this moment in his mind. She looked like the picture of perfection as she gave him a rough stroke, perfectly timed with his pants and briefs pooling on the floor around his ankles. Each stroke pulled more and more precum from his hard length, the feeling hitting him in his knees. Was it his imagination, or did the timing of her strokes match the rhythm of his heartbeat? Reggie closed his eyes, so focused on what her hands were doing that he didn't expect it when she wrapped her lips around the tip. His hips bucked as curses flew from his mouth, and his eyes shot open.

What he saw almost had him releasing straight down her

throat. She gripped him at the base with one hand as her tongue glided over his tip before she sucked his length completely into her mouth. Reggie could just make out Makayla's other hand moving not so subtly beneath her panties. It wasn't hard to figure out what she was doing, not with the way she began moaning around his dick as she bobbed her head and tried to keep eye contact with him. Every time he hit the back of her throat, he felt her gag and watched her eyes flutter shut. She was clearly enjoying this just as much as he was.

"So damn gorgeous," he grunted as her eyes began to water while she gagged around him. Nothing should sound that fucking good. How could anything sound that fucking amazing?

"Just like that," Reggie said, bringing his hand to the back of her head, tangling his fingers in her braids as he helped guide her motion. She was doing just fine on her own, but that didn't stop him from thrusting into her mouth. Each push was a test of her reflexes and reactions. Watching those beautiful eyes flutter shut as she moaned wantonly and tears began to slide down her cheeks let loose the primal side of him. His thrusts became faster, but any fear that it was too much for Makayla disappeared the moment she took her hand away and gave him the control he needed to fuck her face however he wanted. As she started to ride the hand buried between her thighs, she brought the other hand up to his sac, lightly dragging her nails over one side and then the other. His knees almost instantaneously buckled, and he pulled back to give them both a moment to catch their breaths.

"Fuck, baby, you keep doing that, and I'm going to finish right down that pretty throat of yours."

"Threaten me with a good time, why don't you," she said, pulling her hand from its hiding place. Two of her fingers were fucking drenched, and he was just about to pull her up for a taste when she spread her juices across his tip before taking it back into her mouth. She picked up her rhythm, gagging and choking, stroking his balls at the same time, trying to bring him to the release he promised her.

Heat pooled in the bottom of Reggie's gut, and he closed his eyes as the tell-tale tingling started in his thighs. He felt his balls begin to tighten, and he couldn't stop his fingers from doing the same in her hair. As much as he wanted to finish right where he was, he began to pull her off. "Shit, I'm about to come, baby," he groaned.

Instead of moving, Makayla sucked him to the back of her throat, relaxing it and moaning around him. He thrust his hips, fucking her throat with such force he wondered if he was pushing her too much. She gave him her answer when she tightened her grip on his thighs, digging her nails in and drawing a hiss from him. Reggie clenched his teeth, a guttural groan forming behind them as he released his cum right where she seemed to want it. He wished he would've kept his eyes open so that he could watch her swallow every drop, but he just couldn't.

"Goddamn," he said with a gasp once he finally caught his breath and gazed down at her.

Makayla pulled off of him, smirking as she wiped the corners of her mouth, and laughed. The sound had his dick hardening all over again as if he hadn't come just a few moments ago.

He didn't hesitate to bend down and kiss her hungrily. They both moaned as they tasted one another on each other's tongues.

"Condoms are in the nightstand," she whispered against his lips once they managed to separate from one another.

Reggie nodded and stepped completely out of his pants before making his way to the nightstand as she instructed. When he turned around, condom in hand, the sight of her stole his breath. There Makayla was, leaned against the headboard, legs spread, underwear discarded, a finger stroking and parting her lower lips. For a moment, he was just stuck staring because holy hell. How the fuck did they end up here? How did he get so lucky?

"How do you know I didn't want to be the one to take those off?" he asked, gesturing to the panties on the floor.

"Maybe if you're lucky, you'll get another chance."

He chuckled. "Oh, I'm damn sure going to make sure of that."

Reggie climbed onto the bed and placed one, two, three kisses against her lips, each one longer than the last. Her hands bracketed his face, holding him still. He couldn't get enough of her, and he was glad to see she felt the same.

His lips moved along her jawline, wanting to taste every part of her skin if she'd let him. His teeth nipped at different spots, and he made note of which ones made her moan and which made her squirm. When he reached the crook of her neck, he gave her a hard bite, drawing a pained moan from her. His tongue snaked out to soothe the ache, and he basked in her appreciative sigh. Her pebbled nipples drew his attention next as he licked and sucked them like a man starved. Makayla whined underneath him, arching her back to push him further into her breasts. He'd never look at Hershey's Kisses the same because his favorite candies could never compare after an experience like this one.

"Reggie, please," Makayla moaned, her hands traveling down his chest.

"Please what, baby girl?" he asked before he blew on a nipple. She arched into him, and he smirked, pleased with her reaction. "Use your words." His tongue dragged slowly across the hardened bud.

"I want it," she said, out of breath.

"I can't hear you." His tongue trailed along the path between her breasts, tasting her overheated flesh.

"I want you," her teeth clenched as her hand reached between them and gripped his dick, "to fuck me."

As if he really needed any more incentive. Reggie only wanted to hear the words come out of her mouth. Still, she gave him no other choice but to oblige as she fit the length of him between her lips and rolled her hips, coating him in her wetness. A series of gasps fell from her lips every time his head knocked against her swollen clit.

"Fuuuuck, baby," he groaned, sitting back. He opened up the condom wrapper and rolled it onto his dick. "Don't worry, baby girl. I'm going to take real good care of this pussy, I promise."

He notched himself at her entrance and gazed down at her. Makayla looked like a fucking goddess. Her deep brown skin was glistening, and the lust was clear in her eyes. He wished he had a camera, but his memory would have to suffice for now.

The minute he slid into her, Reggie knew he was fucking gone. If he thought the feel of her around his fingers was maddening, the way her walls gripped his dick damn near drove him beyond the point of no return. Reggie pulled out until just the tip of him was left in, and just when he was starting to miss her warmth, he thrust into her again. His rhythm never faltered as he positioned himself over her, resting on his forearms as his hips rolled into her over and over again. Makayla's moans were like his favorite song on a soundtrack that he wanted to put on repeat. He had absolutely no control over his own groans or the way her name rolled off his own tongue.

Every snap of his hips seemed to hit a new depth, and soon, he was bottoming out with each stroke. More. All he wanted was more. Reggie leaned to one side, moving his hand down to grip her thigh as he pushed into her harder. Her heat pulled him in willingly, and her knees settled on either side of him as she rolled her hips to meet each thrust.

"This what you need, baby?" he asked, pressing his forehead to hers.

Her moans were the only answer she gave, but that wasn't good enough. Nowhere near it. "Answer me, Makayla," he growled. He forced more power into his thrusts as he sat up on his knees and gripped her hips with both hands. Makayla's own hands struggled to find purchase over her head as she looked for something, anything to grip as he fucked her within an inch of her life.

"Yes. FUCK! Yes," she gasped as he tilted her hips up, allowing him to hit the spot inside of her that bowed her back completely off the bed. "Fuck, Reggie. Shit, that feels so damn good." Her eyes rolled to the back of her head as evidence of the truth in her words.

Makayla's walls began to clench, forming a vice around his dick. There was no way he could keep this going. She felt too fucking good. He refused to give in to the feeling, though, and resolved to ensure she reached her peak first.

"Look at me, baby girl." Reggie thought she'd resist, but instead, her eyes met his. A stutter? A skip? He couldn't be sure which one his heart had done, but damn if the look in her eyes didn't practically end him right there. Whatever he'd been about to say escaped him. The only thing he could focus on was the fire lighting her beautiful brown eyes. If he wasn't careful, he'd get lost in them.

"Like what you see?" Makayla managed to ask as her hips met his thrust for thrust.

"Absolutely." His eyes never left hers as he trailed one hand between them. His thumb began stroking her clit to a rhythm that matched his hips. Each snap came harder, each swipe of his thumb faster, and before long, she was letting loose a keening cry as she found her release. Her legs shook as she played with her own nipples. He could only assume that she was trying to make the feeling last as long as humanly possible.

She let out a small shriek when he pulled out quickly and flipped her over, pulling her ass high in the air. She was out of breath and slightly disoriented but did her best to match his energy as she arched her back, pressed her head into the pillow, and held onto the sheets as tightly as she could.

Reggie slid back into her at this new angle, and a growl was immediately forced from his throat. Her pussy dripped with the evidence of her orgasm. His hand came crashing down on her ass cheek, and she moaned in response.

"You gonna take this dick, baby girl?" She nodded. "Good. Show me how you take this dick."

She looked over her shoulder at him and gave him a breathless laugh. "Gladly."

The moment she thrust back against him, Reggie decided that nothing was going to keep him out of this pussy. Not work, food, family, or responsibilities. He was willing to live right here and dedicate the rest of his life to her. Why wouldn't he when her center was gripping him tight without a second's hesitation? He let her control the pace, her thrusts backward coming faster and faster. The motion of her ass and the feel of her had him entranced. The only sounds in the room were her wetness, their skin slapping together, and both of their moans.

As soon as he felt her purposely tighten her walls around him, all bets were off. Reggie met her thrusts with forceful ones of his own, and suddenly the rhythm she set became lost. She reached back, her hands working to put some distance between them as she whimpered.

"Uh-uh, baby girl," he said, pushing her hands away. "You wanted all this dick and that's exactly what you're going to get," he grunted, not slowing up. He leaned down and took her hand, guiding it to her pussy. "Play with that pretty pussy. Make her come for me again."

Watching her do exactly what he said was a sight in itself as Makayla reached under them and stroked her clit furtively. She continued to whine and whimper as he fucked into her over and over again. Before long, he felt his balls tighten again. His hand wrapped itself in her braids, and he gave a tug.

"Shiiiiit!" she sobbed. He used his other hand to pull her up off the mattress until her back was pressed against his chest. He thrust into her, one hand moving to grip her neck while the other met with her fingers between her thighs. She used her free hand to pull his face closer until it was nestled in the crook of her neck.

"Reggie," she gasped as he took over for her fingers, strumming her clit like it was his favorite instrument.

"Go ahead, baby, I've got you. Let go."

His words triggered exactly what he hoped for, and soon, she was exhaling his name on each throaty breath between a string of curses. He refused to let up, chasing his own release as his hips snapped frantically. Reggie pinched her clit with just enough force to have her sobbing through her orgasm, her body shaking uncontrollably. Her walls clenched around him once more, and that was all it took to send him off the edge of his own cliff. His groans were muffled in her neck as she milked him for all he was worth.

By the time the two of them came down from their sexual high and collapsed on the bed, Reggie was spent. He wasn't even sure if he had the strength to pull himself from on top of her. He dug into his reserves to do just that, climbing off of her and making his way to her en suite bathroom to dispose of the condom. He grabbed a fresh washcloth, wet it with warm water, and stepped back into the bedroom. Makayla lay peacefully on the bed, drifting off to sleep, and a feeling of warmth spread over him. This wasn't where he expected things to end up tonight, but he damn sure wasn't going to complain.

He made quick work of cleaning her up, being careful not to wake her, and tossed the washcloth back into the bathroom before climbing under the covers with her. Nothing felt more right than having her pressed against him as he wrapped his arm around her waist. Makayla snuggled in close, and soon, the sounds of her light snoring filled the room. The last thing he thought before drifting off to sleep was that whether Makayla realized it or not, Reggie was a fucking goner.

CHAPTER 16

Makayla

The first thing that Makayla noticed was the thickness pressed up against her ass.

Well, that's not my usual wake-up call.

The second thing she noticed was the thick arm wrapped around her waist that kept her pressed against the unexpected stiffness. She shifted slightly, turning so that she was face-to-face with the owner of both. Reggie. A smile spread across her face as she watched him sleep, his brow furrowed and his breathing light. The events of the night before came flooding back to her. That brought her to the third thing she noticed: the delicious soreness between her legs.

Makayla was no stranger to sex. In fact, despite her single status, before last night, she would've gone on record saying that she wasn't a stranger to good sex. Hell, great sex, even. But last night? Last night, she was pretty sure that could be classified as out-of-this-world sex. With a dick and mouth that bomb, she couldn't believe that some woman hadn't already scooped Reggie up for themselves. Oh, well. She was damn sure glad that he was available and hers.

Wait, what?

Okay, the sex was amazing, but claiming this man as hers? That was going a little far, wasn't it? The dick had her wildin', and she needed to lock that thinking down immediately.

Yeah, well, letting a nigga spend the night isn't exactly the best way to lock this shit down now, is it? Her inner voice really needed to stop dragging her like this.

Makayla couldn't even remember the last time she thought about letting a man stay the night at her place. That wasn't to say that her sexual partners never came over. On the contrary, her regular rotation of late-night booty calls weren't strangers to her home, just like she wasn't a stranger to theirs. Spending the night, though? That was a big no-no. She'd decided a long time ago that boundaries were important, and that was one of the biggest. Typically, once everything was said and done, she freshened up and left or walked them right on out of the house. Makayla rarely got any questions or pushback about it at this point. So this —Reggie sleeping peacefully in her bed after a night of fucking her with his mouth, fingers, and that beautiful ass dick of his— was uncharted territory.

"You know, watching someone sleep could be considered very creepy, right?" Reggie said. His voice was groggy with sleep, and his eyes were still closed.

She couldn't help but smile. "So I've heard. Good thing you're not really asleep, then. It means I get a pass."

He chuckled before wrapping his arm around her thick waist and pulling her into his body. "Good morning," he said, placing a light kiss on her lips.

She accepted it without protest and didn't even recognize herself when she whined once he eased away. "Good morning."

"By the look on your face a second ago, you were either mesmerized by my handsome face, or you were overthinking this whole thing."

She kissed her teeth. How dare he act like he knew what was

going on in her head? Was she that easy to read? She began to squirm in his hold, attempting to pull away in irritation, and huffed when Reggie refused to loosen his grip.

"Uh-uh. Don't try and run away now just because I'm right," he teased. He placed another kiss on her forehead as she mushed his chest.

"Nobody in here is worried about what you *think* you know. I'm just trying to get away from your morning breath. You should've warned me about all that before I let you all up in my face first thing in the morning."

"Mmhmm, sure," he said. He clearly didn't believe her. "Let me put you out of your misery then."

He gave her another peck before pulling away and throwing the comforter off of them. Makayla sat up and watched as Reggie climbed out of bed. She was pleasantly surprised to see that he was still naked from the night before. She couldn't help the little groan that escaped her as she watched his very tight ass walk to her bathroom. She was such a sucker for a man with a nice ass.

He shut the door, presumably to handle his business before she heard the sink running. A few moments later, he opened the door and poked his head out. "Do you have an extra toothbrush?"

"Second drawer to your left," Makayla called back to him as she pulled herself out of bed. She cursed as she realized that she'd been so tired that she hadn't tied her hair up the night before. Rookie mistake. She quickly grabbed her edge scarf from her nightstand and tied it around her head. Good dick was not an excuse for raggedy edges, especially when her braids were pretty fresh. After piling her braids up on top of her head and grabbing a night shirt and throwing it on, she looked around for her cell phone. She came up empty, which meant it unfortunately had not made the trip upstairs with them. At least she knew she hadn't slept in too late. According to her clock, it was just after ten a.m. Okay, so a little behind schedule, but Makayla still had plenty of time to shower and get herself together before she had to meet Jasmine for their standing mani-pedi appointment in a couple of hours. Now, she just needed to get the fine ass specimen in her bathroom out the front door.

Speaking of, she couldn't hear anything coming from the bathroom anymore. Makayla turned and found the man in question standing naked in the doorway, dick thick and inviting against his thigh. Her mouth watered as she remembered just how amazing that dick tasted. Once she had the added pleasure of remembering what it had done to her pussy as well, she had a slightly messier reaction. Clearly, her pussy remembered, too, because it was damn near purring right now. She rubbed her thighs together in an attempt to relieve the ache.

She walked toward him slowly, a woman on a mission. "Do you have somewhere to be in, say…the next hour or so?" Her eyes couldn't seem to find his. They were too focused on the beautiful appendage between his legs.

"Nah. Don't you have plans to meet Jasmine today, though? Mani-pedis, right?"

Makayla finally pulled her eyes up to meet his. "I did. I mean, I do. I have a little time, though. And it wouldn't kill her if I was just a little late, right?" Her legs brought her closer to him. She wanted to wipe the smirk from his face, but she wanted something else even more. Maybe she could get a two-for-one special.

"Oh, really?" he asked.

"Mmhmm," she said, her hand reaching out to grip him. His dick twitched, reacting as if she were an old friend. If Reggie played his cards right, her pussy might just be his new bestie. He groaned as he began to harden in her hand. She gave him two pumps before pulling her hand away and pulling the t-shirt over her head.

Sliding by him into the bathroom, Makayla made her way to the shower. After checking the water's temperature, she stepped inside. Just before shutting the frosted glass door, she looked at him. "Coming?" she asked.

"Not yet, but I will be. And so will you." Reggie followed her into the shower without hesitation.

A snort escaped Makayla's lips as she shook her head. "We'll see about that," she said with a grin before pulling him in for a kiss.

———

Makayla was absolutely late getting to the nail salon, but the three orgasms that Reggie pulled from her were worth it. She could swear that she could still feel his strokes as she walked through the front door of the salon. Maybe that was why she felt a little unsteady on her feet. It didn't take long for her to spot Jasmine sitting in one of their usual pedicure chairs, tapping away on her phone as her feet soaked in the blue water.

"I'm here, I'm here," Makayla said, giving her friend a quick kiss on the cheek before claiming the seat next to her.

"Yeah, late as hell! I was just getting ready to call up the National Guard to look for your ass," Jasmine said.

"Oh, please. If you were calling the National Guard, it would not be for me. We both know you'd be calling ole girl with the fat ass and the blunt bob to see if she was in town. What was her name? Tierra?" Makayla responded. She rolled her eyes, waving her friend off.

"Now see, why did you—" Jasmine's sentence cut off abruptly.

Makayla looked over and saw the other woman looking at her with narrowed eyes.

"Oooooh shit," Jasmine said.

"What?" Makayla said, looking at her in confusion.

"You got some dick, didn't you?!" Jasmine said excitedly.

"Huh?" Makayla looked away instantly and hoped that her neck didn't look as hot as it felt.

"Nope, you know better than that. If you can huh, you can hear. Your ass absolutely got some dick last night. Look at you, all glowing and shit!"

"I did not get dick last night," Makayla insisted. When she looked up at her best friend, the girl looked at her skeptically. A sly grin spread across Makayla's face. "I got some bomb ass dick last night *and* this morning."

"I KNEW IT!" Jasmine shrieked, drawing the attention of just about every customer in the shop.

"Girl, calm down before you get us put out!"

"Oh, please. As much money as we spend in this place, they are not going to put us out. Don't change the subject. Spill the tea. Who was it?"

"Reggie," Makayla said simply.

"Oooh, your fake ass man who wants to be your real ass man? I told you that you should climb him like a tree. I could just tell that man was carrying a whole third leg in his jeans, with his bowlegged ass. The ultimate hint that he had the right equipment to dick you up and down."

Makayla fell into a fit of laughter. Jasmine was a damn fool, but she couldn't deny that her bestie was telling the absolute truth.

"Siiiiis, I'm telling you, that man is…whew. The things he did with that mouth and dick of his." She rubbed her thighs together just thinking about it.

"It was that good?"

"The shit was practically talking to me," she said with a sigh, her mind drifting off to the events of that morning.

"I swear to goodness if you start quoting Nina from *Love Jones*, I will leave right now, wet feet and all," said Jasmine.

Makayla rolled her eyes as her technician started her pedicure. "All I'm saying is, Nina was onto something, okay?"

"Mmhmm, okay, sis. You just make sure you don't get caught up like Nina did," she said, giving her a pointed look.

Makayla rolled her eyes, brushing her friend off. Despite the connection she felt with Reggie, she knew there was no danger of her falling in too deep. Amazing sex or not, Makayla fully intended to keep herself and her situation under control. Still, a little voice in the back of her mind told her that would be easier said than done.

CHAPTER 17

Makayla

Two weeks had passed since Makayla and Reggie's roller-skating date. Somehow, in that short amount of time, the two of them had fallen into a rather comfortable routine. Regular, easy conversations. Very hot phone sex, which she had to admit she hadn't done in years. Oh, and of course, there was the very surprising dinner date when Reggie dropped by her office with sushi. She'd casually mentioned that she'd managed to work through lunch that day, and so he'd taken it upon himself to make sure that didn't happen with dinner. That one may or may not have ended in a quickie right there in her office.

What they were doing went above and beyond Makayla's usual boundaries, yet she couldn't bring herself to complain. Those boundaries had originally been put in place because other men always tried to demand too much of her time. That wasn't an issue with Reggie. He never asked for more than she was willing to give. Maybe that was why his doing an unexpected office pop-up hadn't irritated her. Why his messages or phone calls never felt like a distraction or a chore. Should Makayla be analyzing why she was okay with everything that was happening between them? Probably. Was she going to do that? Absolutely not. Ignorance was bliss, right?

"So, why karaoke?" Reggie asked, pulling her out of her thoughts as the two of them made their way down the sidewalk.

The breeze in the air almost made Makayla regret the high split in her flowy forest green skirt and the sliver of skin her white scoop-necked top revealed. The heated look in Reggie's eyes every time they scanned over her made it worth it, though. He was looking at her like he wanted to turn around, take her right back home, and fuck her senseless. If her entire family wasn't waiting for them, she might just let him. Instead, she had to satisfy herself with the way his arm wrapped around her waist as his thumb made slow circles against one of her soft spots. Makayla had to admit that Reggie's reaction to her body certainly made her feel smug as hell.

"Karaoke's a big thing for our family. Singing has always been one of my mother's favorite things to do. Literally any and every talent show her school or church had, she participated in it no matter what. I think half of the people that knew her growing up expected her to try her hand at singing professionally. She thought about it, but life sort of…happened. Anyway, she passed her love of singing onto us, though, for the record, Lizzie can't carry a tune to save her life." Makayla couldn't help but laugh. They teased Lizzie about it mercilessly, and the youngest sister always took it in stride.

"Anyway, once a month, we get together to do karaoke. It doesn't matter what we have going on in our lives, karaoke night is sacred. That's actually how mom met Percy." A smile crossed her face at the memory of the night her mother was belting out Whitney Houston's "I Wanna Dance with Somebody" and Percy wandering in trying to figure out who was giving Queen Whitney a run for her money. "He took one look at her little ass on that stage and fell in love. At least that's how he tells the story."

"Well, how does your mom tell it?" Reggie asked curiously, pulling her in just a bit closer to shield her against the slight breeze.

"Mommy says that he barged in and fucked up her set. Cussed him out from top to bottom. According to her, he felt so bad about it that he almost had a breakdown right then and there and the only way to stop it was to agree to go out with him. If you can't tell, she has a flair for the dramatic," laughed Makayla.

Reggie laughed along with her. "Yeah, your moms is wild as hell, baby girl."

"Where do you think I get it from?" she teased with a wink. "Karaoke is usually a family affair, but tonight it'll just be the adults. Kendall's mother-in-law offered to watch all of the kids for the night so that everyone could sort of cut loose."

Reggie nodded. Makayla looked up at him, and his profile nearly stole her breath away. How the fuck did he keep doing that to her? As she watched him, she couldn't help but think about the way that jaw flexed when he was inside of her, delivering long, slow strokes that made her toes curl and her sex clench. Just the thought left her hot and ready, slick with need. Damn, she needed to get it together before she ruined the panties she was wearing.

"You good?" Reggie asked, gazing down at her. She wondered just how much heat showed behind her eyes because the look that crossed his own face told her he could guess what she was thinking about.

She cleared her throat and looked away. "Yep." She could've sworn she heard him chuckle but chose to ignore it. "Anyway, whenever it's your turn to sing, you'll pick a slip of paper out of the fishbowl. You can't show it to anyone else unless it's a group song. Scoring is completely subjective, and the loser has to settle the tab at the end of the night."

"Oh, so y'all get down for real, huh? I bet everybody breaks out in dance routines and everything," he said, teasing her. She couldn't even deny it. She and her sisters were known to bust out a choreographed routine or two.

Makayla shrugged. "We're competitive as hell, but it's all in good fun, I promise. And try not to cry too hard when you get your ass kicked tonight." She shot him a wink before opening the door to Sing It Low.

Even though they were right on time, the party seemed to be in full swing. Makayla couldn't help but smile. The main room was packed to the brim, but she wouldn't have expected anything less on a Saturday night. She made sure to throw a smile at the owners who were behind the bar. Her family had been coming here for so long that the owners practically considered them family as well, which was why they never had a problem getting their favorite private room whenever they came in.

Makayla grabbed Reggie's hand without a second thought and guided him toward their usual room in the back. Sure enough, when the two of them walked in, her family was already there, all smiles and laughter. Her sisters all practically squealed as the couple walked in, pulling her into a hug and immediately jumping into who they thought would kill their performances tonight.

This was what she loved about karaoke night. No matter what bullshit was going on in the family, everything seemed to be put aside when they walked through these doors. This was her happy place. This was the one place where she could relax around her family, no judgments, no arguments.

As she watched her mother come over and speak to Reggie, she felt a tug on her heartstrings. Part of her wondered if she was crossing a line by inviting him into their space. Despite the great conversation and amazing sex—fucking amazing sex—Reggie wasn't really her boyfriend. He wasn't actually family. Hell, did he even qualify as a friend? Lying to her family this way, in this space—it felt wrong.

It doesn't have to be a lie.

The thought flitted across her mind so quickly that she wasn't sure if she'd heard herself correctly. She must be really losing it. Yes, the dick was bomb. Thick, dark, long. The type of dick you dreamed about once you had it. The type of dick that ruined lives and started wars. Yes, the man attached to the dick was a force in and of himself, one that seemed to be pushing her limits in the best possible ways. The fact remained, though, that she did not do relationships. Reggie's penchant for giving her great orgasms and even better conversation was not poised to change that. She was certain of it.

CHAPTER 18

Makayla

Almost two hours had passed since they arrived, and Makayla was officially lost in the moment. As the night wore on, an invisible weight had lifted from her shoulders, one she hadn't even noticed, to be honest. Drinks were flowing, food kept coming, and every few moments, someone—usually Makayla—falling over in a fit of laughter. She'd really needed this. The fact that she and Kendall had even managed to put their attitudes aside proved just how magical their karaoke nights really were. The fun she'd had when the two of them had climbed on stage after drawing "Rollin' with Kid 'n Play" from the song bowl was unmatched. They'd even fallen into their old dance routine that they'd crafted growing up. It was as if no time had passed. Their performance had received high scores, and even Jasmine had admitted to being just a little jealous of the duo.

"I cannot believe we still remember every bit of that routine," Makayla said, laughing as she and Kendall made their way to the bathroom.

"You! I'm shocked we managed to pull it off. I thought for sure it was going to be over when we did that dip and high kick combo," Kendall said with her own laughter.

"We're definitely going to feel that in the morning," Makayla said, shaking her head. "But it was absolutely worth it after seeing the look on Mama's face." The move had practically sent their mom to the floor. In the back of her mind, Makayla couldn't help but wonder if her mother had intentionally made sure that song was in the rotation. She was always attempting to find ways to get the two of them to stop going for one another's jugulars. Hmmm... Well, mission accomplished, at least for today.

"Oh, without a doubt. We might need to move up that spa day because we're going to need it," Kendall answered.

"Or you could just get Greg to put those big hands to good use," Makayla teased as they walked through the bathroom door. She'd thought her sister would agree with her, but instead, she seemed to tense up. "Ken, what's wrong?" she asked.

The blank, tense look that appeared on the other woman's face disappeared so quickly that Makayla wondered if she'd imagined it. "Oh, girl, nothing. I might just have to put that idea to use," she said, her laughter sounding a lot more forced than it had a few moments ago.

Makayla wanted to worry but decided against pushing any further. They were having such a good time. The last thing she wanted to do was ruin it by sticking her nose in her sister's business. The two finished up in the bathroom and headed back to the private room just as another round of drinks arrived. Makayla took a seat next to Reggie, who leaned in without hesitation to snag a kiss from her.

"I swear y'all are like cuteness overload. Give it a break already!" Lizzie groaned as she threw a fry at the two of them.

"Haters never prosper, sis. Remember that," Makayla said with a laugh.

Lizzie stuck her tongue out before turning to the stage as Percy's son and his fiancé got ready for their turn. Makayla turned to Reggie, tugging on his beard just a bit. It had grown out some since they'd first met, and she had to admit that it only increased his sex appeal.

"Uh-uh. Don't play like that. You tug on this beard, you better be ready to do something about the reaction you get."

He smirked at her as his hand gave her thigh a firm squeeze that had Makayla swallowing a whimper. Between the whiskey she'd been drinking since they arrived and that powerful grip of his, she was absolutely willing to follow through on what he was suggesting.

"Who says I'm playing?" she asked, testing the waters. She lifted her leg and draped it over his thigh.

He cocked an eyebrow up at her as his hand took advantage of the new position and inched up toward her center just a bit more. "Oh, word?" Reggie asked, issuing a challenge of his own.

She was just getting ready to respond when she felt a tug on her arm that caused her to yelp. The momentum of the pull tipped her backward toward the culprit.

"Little girl, I know that man of yours is fine as hell, but save all that freaky shit y'all got going on for when you leave, okay?" her mother stage-whispered in her ear. She found herself blushing at the reprimand. She could tell her mother was only teasing, but that didn't stop her skin from heating. They had been about to get a bit carried away. This was a room full of people, and if her mother had noticed, then she knew the others probably had too.

"My bad, Mommy."

"Don't worry, baby. Where do you think you get it from?" Delilah said with a wink. She leaned back into Percy's embrace. "Now go ahead and get your little butt back up there and put on a show for Mama."

Makayla hadn't even realized that the two men performing

had finished up already. She groaned playfully and stood, knowing this was her mother's way of getting her to cool off. Reggie gave her an encouraging squeeze that had her swatting his hand away.

"This is your fault, you know."

He chuckled as she rolled her eyes. Makayla fished around in the song bowl before pulling out a small slip of paper. When she saw the title she'd chosen, she couldn't help but shoot Reggie a mischievous smirk. She quickly walked over to select the song in the system, grabbed the microphone, and cleared her throat.

"This special little number goes out to my plus-one tonight," she teased.

Everyone oooooooh'd in unison, and she watched as an embarrassed Reggie rubbed the back of his neck. Makayla couldn't help the little shimmy she gave as the beat began to flow through her. She added a cute little bop to her movements as the '80s tune played through the speakers. She strutted across the stage as she sang along to Deniece Williams's hit record, "Let's Hear It for the Boy." Makayla couldn't hold back her grin as Reggie groaned while the others in the room began to clap along. Despite the catchy upbeat tempo of the song, they all knew it was about a man who wasn't really worth a damn. Still, it had always been one of Makayla's favorites, sending her straight into pop star mode. Every time she heard it, she couldn't stop herself from pretending she was starring in her very own music video.

By the second chorus, everyone in the room had joined in on the song. Makayla fought hard to keep her composure as her sisters and Jasmine stood up and acted as her backup dancers, breaking out some of their best moves. She glanced at Reggie, who was laughing along with everyone else as he bobbed his head to the beat. Once the song finally came to an end, she gave a dramatic bow to a very enthusiastic standing ovation.

"Let's hear it for the boy, huh?" Reggie said with a smirk after Makayla jumped offstage and made her way back to him.

"Eat your heart out, Reginald," she laughed.

"Oh, I plan on eating something. Trust me on that," he leaned in and whispered. Makayla couldn't help the whimper she let out as he nibbled on her ear. The moment was over far too quickly for her liking. It was his turn to pick a song.

"Fix your face, baby," he said as he chuckled.

Reggie grabbed a slip of paper from the bowl. Whatever was written there practically had his eyes glowing. The look he shot her only made her more nervous about whatever he was about to do. He wasted no time making his way to the stage and submitting the song of choice. As soon as the music began playing through the speakers, Makayla knew she was in trouble.

As Bobby Brown's "Roni" came through the speakers, Makayla let out a groan and sank down in her seat. She wanted nothing more than to disappear into the floor. This damn song did something to her, and Reggie was looking at her like he already knew it. Jasmine didn't make it any better when she slid next to her, elbowing Makayla as Reggie started singing along with Bobby.

"Ummm…friend?"

"Yes?" Makayla responded, her throat suddenly going dry as Reggie crooned into the microphone about a very specific tenderoni. She wasn't sure if she was mesmerized by the sound of his baritone voice, which he managed to fit into the song perfectly, or the way his eyes seemed to undress her as he sang. Both were equally tantalizing.

"I'm not sure if you are aware, but you're in deep shit here."

Makayla couldn't even deny it. "I think you're right."

She wished she could explain the magnetism that she was feeling. The heat behind Reggie's eyes was pulling her in even more than his actual voice. She rubbed her thighs together, attempting to relieve the pressure in her core, but it just wasn't working. He may not be giving her any Bobby Brown-era dance moves, but damn if the way he licked his lips as he sang didn't have her dripping. Even her breathing pattern had changed. She was vaguely aware of her family and friends hooting and encouraging him. The smile on Reggie's face let her know that he knew just how trapped in his web she was. Makayla hadn't even realized she was practically panting and leaning forward until Lizzie gripped her shoulder and pulled her back onto the couch. When had her sister come and sat next to her?

"Ma'am, stop looking like you're about to jump on stage and ride that man from here to glory right in front of us," Lizzie snickered.

"Hell, if she doesn't, someone else in this room just might," Jasmine said matter-of-factly.

"Both of y'all can kiss my ass," Makayla said, shooting them what she hoped was a scathing look.

"No, thanks, but he just might," Lizzie said, inclining her head toward Reggie, who'd just gotten off stage to an even greater round of applause than she'd been given.

"Somebody throw some panties at the man!" Delilah shouted with a cackle.

Makayla couldn't even feign embarrassment because truth be told, if he had been on stage any longer, she may have done just that. Hell…the night was young. She still might.

"On that note, who's next?" Percy asked, clearly ready to change the subject. Who could blame him? His fiancée was practically ready to buss it down for Makayla's date.

While the group debated who was next, apparently leaning towards a duet between Alonzo and Greg, Reggie walked over to Makayla and raised an eyebrow. "You good?"

She shook her head. "Not at all."

He frowned. "Damn, was I that bad?"

She wrapped one hand around the back of his neck and pulled him toward her, lips grazing his ear. "Terrible. Awful. In fact, you were so bad that we have to get out of here right now."

Before he could say a word, she pulled away so she could look him in the eye. "Cause right now, all I can think about is fucking you."

CHAPTER 19

Reggie

It took all of two seconds after Makayla's confession for Reggie to decide that he didn't need to stay for the rest of karaoke night. She hadn't even waited for his response before she went to tell everyone that they were going to head out for the night. Reggie couldn't even bring himself to feel any shame as the entire room gave him a knowing look. Her mother was the only one who protested, pouting and saying something about the night not even being close to over. Once Reggie offered to cover the tab the group had already accrued in the few hours they'd been there, her protests came to a screeching halt, and the two of them were able to escape the karaoke bar unscathed.

He couldn't be sure if it was the alcohol or his performance on stage, but the charged energy between the two of them was off the charts. Makayla kept sending him heated looks as they walked the couple of blocks toward his car. He already tended to be mesmerized by those gorgeous brown eyes and long lashes, but tonight felt like a whole other level. Those looks only became more intense once the two of them were inside the car. She must have decided she didn't want to wait any longer because Makayla wasted no time gripping his length through his jeans.

Reggie bit back a groan. "Chill, Makayla. Don't you want to make it back to my place in one piece?" When she didn't answer, he gritted his teeth. "Just a little bit of space, baby girl. That's all I need."

"Space is overrated," she crooned into his neck as she slid her tongue over his pulse point. This time he couldn't stop the groan that came from his throat. Her hand made its way back to his jeans, only this time, she took the time to undo the button and zipper. Reggie did what he could to focus on the road, but she certainly wasn't making it easy for him. Not when her hand was reaching into his briefs and gripping the hardest part of him.

"Pay attention, baby. Wouldn't want to have an accident, would we?" she taunted.

He thought to answer her but didn't have much of a chance when her thumb ran over the tip of his dick, collecting precum as it went. "Fuck, Makayla," he moaned. "It's like that?"

She let out a giggle. Damn, he loved that sound. Really, he loved every sound she made.

"Haven't you learned yet? I always get what I want." She gave him two pumps, making his hips buck and his foot jerk against the gas pedal.

This time when Makayla laughed, it was full and throaty. She gave his neck one more nibble before pulling her hand out of his pants. She sucked his precum off her thumb and sat back in her seat. "But dying for the dick isn't my idea of a good time," she conceded.

Even though he missed the feel of her hand wrapped around him, Reggie had to admit that he could breathe a little easier knowing that he wasn't about to kill the both of them just for an orgasm. He noticed movement out of the corner of his eye and turned to look at her.

Maybe I spoke too soon, he thought to himself as he did a double-take. Makayla leaned against the door, legs open and inviting.

"Baby girl...what do you think you're doing?" His eyes were back on the road as he tried to control himself.

"Misbehaving."

That was an understatement. The way she looked as she caressed her leg with the same hand that had just been stroking him should've been criminal. Out of the corner of his eye, he could see Makayla hike up her skirt and drag her fingertip along the soft spot between her thighs. Fuck, he wanted to taste her. To worship her. To pull this fucking car over and devour her until she screamed that she couldn't take any-more. Since he couldn't do that, he steeled his resolve and decided that it didn't have to mean that he was left out entirely.

"Don't," Reggie said before she could do anything else. His hardened tone made her stop in her tracks.

"If anyone is going to play with that pretty little pussy, baby, it's going to be me." He took his eyes off the road for just a moment to look over at her. "Now, be a good girl and slide a little closer for me."

For a moment, Makayla looked as if she were going to ignore his request just to torture him. Instead, she did as she was told, sliding across the seat to close the distance. He reached out his right hand, trailing his fingers along her thigh slowly. Reggie wanted her frustrated and on edge. When his fingers finally reached their destination, he slid her panties to the side and swiped his finger down the center of her, drawing a light gasp from her. "Wet and needy," he mumbled.

He took his time parting her lips, moving so slowly that Makayla angled her hips just the right way, trying to force him to make contact with her heat. "So impatient, too," he said with a chuckle.

"Say what you want," she said with a panting breath. "Just make sure you do it while you give me what *I* want."

Denying her was so tempting. Once he got a look at the lust in her eyes, he knew he had no choice but to give her exactly what she needed. Reggie pushed a finger into her and relished the sound of her moan as it was sucked into her warm, wet center.

"I can't wait to have you wrapped around my dick," he said with a groan as he stroked a finger in and out of her slowly. One of her hands gripped the edge of her seat while the other grabbed hold of his wrist, willing him to keep his hand right where it was. The knuckles on his other hand strained as he gripped the steering wheel even tighter. His dick weighed heavily against his thigh, solid as a brick. He gave a silent thanks that she'd left his pants unzipped; otherwise, this would be a hell of an uncomfortable ride. Since he couldn't stroke himself, he gave himself over to stroking her, adding another finger and picking up the pace.

Makayla moaned and whined, her pussy dripping and making a mess of his seat. Her delicious scent filled the car and made Reggie's mouth water. Fuck, he needed to get her back to his place and now. Although his condo was closer to the karaoke bar than hers had been, the trip seemed to be taking forever. He was damn near ecstatic when his building finally came into view. Reggie sped down the street, quickly pulling into the garage and making his way up a few ramps to his reserved space, all the while moving his fingers in and out of Makayla, slowly torturing her. She tried to force him to pick up his pace, but he wouldn't be rushed. As much as he wanted to make her come, he wanted to be able to give her his full attention when he did it.

Once he'd finally pulled into his space, Reggie made quick work of his seatbelt and turned to look at Makayla. Her eyes were closed, face contorted in pleasure. She looked fucking amazing with her chest heaving, legs spread, skirt flared out around her waist and panties pushed to the side. He curled his fingers until they pressed against that spot that made her squirm, causing her breath to catch in her throat.

"Look at me," he said, his voice thick with lust. She whimpered as her hips met each stroke of his fingers. She was lost in the pleasure he was giving her, but he wanted more from her. "Look at me, baby girl. Don't make me say it again."

Makayla finally managed to open her eyes, and the heat behind her gaze punched straight through his chest. "That's a good girl," he said. As uncomfortable as it was, he leaned over the center console. He'd never been as grateful for his spacious truck as he was at that moment. He placed his arms under her thighs and tilted her up until his face was positioned exactly where he wanted it to be.

"Fuck, you smell good," he muttered before diving in face first. The moment he tasted her on his tongue, he didn't care that they were only a few steps from making it into his condo. Didn't care about the mess she was making beneath her. Couldn't find one fuck to give about how fucking uncomfortable his hardened dick was at the moment. The only thing that mattered was tasting her and drawing more of those delicious moans from her lips. He refused to let up, thrusting his fingers into her faster, curling them just right every time he started to pull out. He never took his eyes off of her as he lapped at her clit, and he was happy to see that she was watching everything he was doing to her. Reggie wanted his face to be what she saw when her orgasm hit her.

Right on cue, her walls began to clench around his fingers. Both of her hands pushed against the fogged-up window as she ground her pussy into his face. Reggie wasted no time sending her over the edge, giving her exactly what they were both looking for. He gave her clit a hard suck and was rewarded with the sound of her screaming his name. It was the greatest thing he'd ever heard.

By the time he pulled himself from between her legs, his beard was covered in her scent, and he could taste her on his lips. Reggie gave her shaking legs a squeeze as he pulled his fingers out of her and sucked the taste of her from them.

"Let's go, baby girl. I'm nowhere near done with you."

CHAPTER 20

Makayla

When Makayla woke the next morning, it took a minute for her to find her bearings. Between Reggie damn near sucking her soul out of her body in his truck and then fucking her within an inch of her life in his condo, she could barely think straight. That was the only reasonable explanation for why she now found herself naked and sore in Reggie's bed instead of her own. What she didn't have an explanation for was why she was in his bed alone. That certainly wasn't how she'd fallen asleep.

She stretched and sat up, taking a moment to observe her surroundings. The blackout curtains were pulled, giving the illusion that the sun wasn't up, though her phone said it was well into morning. A small light coming from the walk-in closet lit the room well enough that she could see his room was pretty much immaculate. The only things not in their place were the scattered blanket and sheets on the bed. Makayla didn't keep a dirty house, but her room tended to reflect whatever level of stress she was experiencing in life. If Reggie was anything like her, then the state of his room meant he was basically living carefree. She had to admit that she was more than just a bit jealous of that possibility.

Makayla climbed out of bed and bit her bottom lip. A little snooping never hurt anyone, right? Right. With that logic, she made her way over to his dresser to take a good look. After hesitating for a second, she picked up one of his bottles of cologne and spritzed it once on her wrist. She instantly recognized it as what she had figured out was his signature scent. It reminded her of the mahogany teakwood candle from one of her favorite stores. Makayla couldn't help but laugh. Anytime one of her sisters or friends asked her what she expected a grown man to smell like, that was her go-to answer. Good to know that the universe had been listening.

After putting the cologne back and taking a look at the other items that were on display, she made her way toward his closet. She noticed that her clothes, which she knew for sure had been scattered every which way on the floor last night, were now in a neat pile on his clothes hamper. Interesting.

Reggie's closet gave a great look into his personal taste in clothes. His outfits ranged from casual everyday attire to some very debonair choices that made her wonder just how good he looked in a suit. If it was anything like what she was currently picturing in her mind, then there was no way that she'd survive the wedding.

As Makayla turned and stepped out of the closet, she ran into a very solid wall. A wall that just so happened to have a voice.

"Caught ya snooping."

Instead of being embarrassed at being caught red-handed, Makayla simply shrugged as his hands settled on her bare ass. "You call it snooping. I call it being curious."

"Isn't there a saying about how curiosity killed the cat?" he asked with a raised eyebrow.

"Mmmm, there is, but if the cat could survive last night, then I'm sure she can handle just about anything."

There was a brief pause before Reggie's laughter filled the room. "Yo, I can't believe you just said that," he said, tears pricking the edges of his eyes.

"It was a bit much, wasn't it?" Makayla admitted through her own laughter as she pressed her face into his chest.

"Just a little, baby girl. I promise I won't hold it against you, though. I mean, how can I when you're standing here in my arms looking this damn good?"

Makayla smirked up at him. He was probably right. With the way his eyes were drinking in her naked form right now, she could probably get away with just about anything. "So, what you're saying is, I'm that girl," she said, pushing herself up on the tips of her toes just enough to allow her lips to graze his.

"Absolutely," he murmured before capturing her mouth. There was no trace of lightness in this kiss, only urgency and hunger. She was quickly losing control of the situation and she couldn't bring herself to care. Not when he was caressing her tongue with his just the way she liked. Not when the little nips he treated her lips to were so distracting. Certainly not when one of his hands had a bruising grip on her bare ass and the other one was moving toward her pussy.

Makayla gave him no resistance when two of his fingers parted her lower lips and began mirroring every motion his tongue was making during their kiss. She moaned, bringing her own hands to the back of his neck, her grip on him tightening as she wrapped a leg around his waist. Reggie groaned and pushed her against the frame of the closet door. He used the new position to spread her just a bit wider as he trailed kisses along her jawline and neck. His teeth nipped at her pulse point as he rubbed her clit between his pointer and middle fingers.

"Fuck, Reggie," Makayla whined, rolling her hips in hope of

getting more of that delicious friction. She wanted more. She *needed* more. "Please," she gasped.

"Please what, baby? Say it out loud," Reggie whispered against her skin. His head drifted lower, allowing him to capture one of her nipples in his mouth. Her back arched off the doorway, and she made a keening noise that she hardly recognized as her own. He always seemed to want her begging, and as much as she hated to admit it, the thought scorched her through and through.

Makayla couldn't find the words to answer. She was too distracted by the feel of his tongue gliding over her nipple and the quick, slippery strokes that his fingers were pressing against her sensitive spot. Her orgasm hit her with such force that she was left gasping for breath, shuddering and shaking in Reggie's grip. Even as it subsided, his fingers never stopped moving, threatening to send her over the edge again. As amazing as this felt, it wasn't all she wanted.

"I need you," Makayla finally managed to get out through gritted teeth as her body gave another involuntary shudder. She slid one of her hands into his basketball shorts, pleasantly surprised to see that he hadn't stopped to put on briefs this morning. Wrapping her fingers around his thick shaft, Makayla used her other hand to push his shorts down just far enough to free his erection.

"Show me how much you need it, Makayla." Reggie pressed his forehead to hers, his breathing just as labored as her own.

"Go ahead. Put it in." The growl in his words sent a shot of adrenaline through her. He brought his fingers in front of her face, giving her a clear view of the mess she'd made. Without hesitation, she sucked his fingers into her mouth, using her tongue to clean every inch of herself off of them as she lined his shaft up with her entrance. She fought the urge to close her eyes. Makayla wanted to be front and center when his eyes reflected just how gone she had him.

Luckily, neither of them needed to wait long. She moaned around his fingers as Reggie pushed into her. His eyes snapped shut, and Makayla felt his knees nearly buckle. Bracing himself against the door frame, Reggie pulled his fingers from her mouth and wrapped his arm around her waist trying to steady them both. She could feel his warm breath against the crook of her neck. Her own hands found their place, one at the nape of his neck and the other gripping his shoulder as he steadied them. They fit together perfectly.

Makayla would've paid money to get a look at them from a different view. They were barely holding it together, nothing but each other and the frame supporting them. She didn't even care that she was only in her bare skin while Reggie was still clothed in his tank top with his shorts barely past his knees.

"Fucking heaven," Reggie groaned into her skin as he began to pull out of her. The motion drew a protesting whine from her throat. That whine instantly changed into a high-pitched moan the minute he slammed back into her.

With each stroke, Reggie's fingers dug deeper into her hips. The force of his grip was bound to leave an imprint. Just the thought of walking around with his fingerprints embedded in her skin for the next few days had Makayla's pussy clenching. Reggie cursed as a shudder ran through them both. Whatever he said next was practically unintelligible. He wasn't alone. Makayla couldn't seem to form a single coherent thought. Not when she was so full, and he was hitting spots inside her that she hadn't even known existed. Her nails dug into Reggie's skin, and he hissed in response as he raised her hips to meet each thrust. The quiet of the room captured the few words he managed to get out.

Fucking perfect. So wet. Warm as fuck. All words said into her skin, each one punctuated with another hard thrust until he was practically pistoning in and out of her. And still, Makayla found herself wanting more. Moaning and begging, just the way he liked her.

"Reggie. Fuuuuuck," she whimpered as he nibbled just above her collarbone. "I'm so fucking close," she moaned.

"Don't worry, baby. Don't I always take care of this pretty pussy?"

His cocky words ghosted over her skin, and she couldn't find the strength to snap back. She was just on the edge of coming, every muscle in her body tensing in response. Reggie's hand found its way between them, and as soon as his thumb touched her clit, her walls began to clench around his dick.

"*Reggie. Reggie. Reggie.*" His name was like a prayer on her lips, and yet Makayla felt as though she was the one being worshiped. Their moans carried around the room. She'd never thought she'd love the sound of a man sliding into her wetness this much, but goddamn, it sounded fucking amazing.

Screams began to fall from Makayla's lips, and Reggie quickly silenced them with a hungry kiss. He kissed her as if he were starving and she was the only thing that would satisfy him. The moment he sucked on her tongue, it was over for Makayla. Her legs shook as the wave crashed over her, and she soaked his thick shaft.

Reggie pulled away from her with his own grunt, barely making it in time before his own release came. With one thumb still stroking her clit and his other hand stroking his dick, he kept Makayla's pleasure going, tears pricking the edges of her eyes as his cum landed on both her pussy and stomach. He kept going until she let out a sob and frantically pushed his hand away.

Reggie didn't seem to mind, instead pulling her to him as he kissed her longingly. Maybe she didn't need a break after all. Despite her legs being a shaking mess and being covered in his cum and hers, Makayla was ready to convince herself that she could go just one more round. She was going to suggest just that when Reggie smacked her ass. The impact drew a squeal and a side-eye from her.

"Go shower," he said before placing a quick kiss on her fore-head. "I'll go make breakfast."

As Reggie pulled his shorts up, Makayla couldn't find the energy to argue. Hell, it was enough of a task trying to stand. So, after stealing another kiss, she made her way to the bathroom without a fuss.

And that's exactly what good dick will do to you, she thought in a voice that sounded suspiciously like Jasmine.

CHAPTER 21

Makayla

Makayla stayed in the shower so long that the hot water almost gave up on her. That hadn't been the plan, especially since her stomach had started growling right after she'd used the bathroom and brushed her teeth, but as soon as that water pressure hit her back, she knew she was a goner.

Every ache that she'd gained from their escapades seemed to melt away. It wasn't until the water started to cool down that she realized she may have fucked up Reggie's chances of taking his own refreshing shower. Feeling a little guilty, she turned off the water, grabbed her towel, and stepped out into the muggy bathroom air. When she walked into the bedroom, Makayla found a pair of boxers and one of Reggie's t-shirts waiting for her.

Girl, get a fucking grip, she chastised herself once she realized she was smiling uncontrollably.

The reprimand didn't do much to bring down her mood, but it did make her move a bit faster. She grabbed her phone from the charger, conveniently ignoring the fact that she hadn't been the one to place it there. Nope, no need to analyze that little piece of information. After shooting off a text message to Jasmine and her sisters to confirm that yes, she was alive despite the dicking of a lifetime, she made her way through the condo, following the smell of something pretty damn delicious.

Makayla found Reggie in the kitchen, his back to her in a fresh pair of sweatpants and a t-shirt. How did those strong shoulders of his look even better from the back? What that man looked like in just a simple t-shirt should be a crime, and watching him move expertly through his kitchen should not have been as big of a turn-on as it was. That was especially true considering Makayla considered cooking a basic life skill that every person should master, if possible. Being a man damn sure didn't excuse you from that requirement. She couldn't stand a man who didn't know how to properly cook and feed himself, much less the people around him. Still, watching how comfortable he seemed now in combination with how good whatever he was making smelled? Damn if she didn't want to give him a round of applause.

Is this the type of shit that had Miss Deniece singing about a mediocre man? Makayla thought with a smirk as she recalled her song from the night before.

"That's twice now that I've caught you staring at me. You know, being a bonafide creep is not attractive at all," Reggie said, raising his voice so it carried behind him without having to turn around.

"Are you sure about that?" she teased.

Reggie turned around, and Makayla instantly felt heat rush through her body at his probing gaze.

"I stand corrected. You do, in fact, make that shit look fucking amazing."

She didn't hesitate to roll her eyes at him. That didn't stop her from walking into his open arms and accepting the kiss he had ready and waiting for her. He pressed his face into her neck.

"Oh, I'm already well aware."

Makayla also happened to be very aware of the oversized inhale he'd just taken. She began to squirm in his grasp as his big hands gave her ass a squeeze.

"You good there?" she asked, attempting to control her own breathing.

It took a minute, but Reggie finally groaned as he removed himself from the crook of her neck and pecked her lips before pulling away completely. "Just trying to figure out who told you to come down here smelling like me and looking good as fuck in my clothes."

"You did the minute you let me spend the night and told me to use that amazing shower of yours. Which, side note, I may or may not have used up all your hot water." Reggie chuckled in response. "It's not my fault that shit is so good! Your water pressure is next level."

"Oh, it is, huh? Did you have fun in there?" he asked, raising an eyebrow.

"It is. And no, I did not do what you're thinking, so get your mind out of the gutter!" Makayla said, smacking his arm.

Reggie laughed that full-bodied laugh of his and shook his head. "I'm just playing, baby girl. Don't worry about it. I got in a quick shower, too."

"Oh, so I don't need to feel bad then? Great."

"Let's be honest, baby girl, you didn't feel bad anyway," he teased.

"Yeah, well, you were in need of a little payback for that shit you started last night in the car."

"I'm pretty sure you started that, not me," Reggie said, giving her a pointed look.

Considering how the night turned out, Makayla made no attempt to look even the least bit embarrassed or ashamed. When she wanted something, she went for it, and last night, she'd done exactly that. Reggie just chuckled and shook his head as he turned back toward the stove.

"That smells amazing," she said, wrapping her arms around his waist as he stirred whatever was in the pan.

"Home-fried potatoes with onions, peppers, and chorizo. Should go pretty well with the omelets, bacon, and French toast."

Makayla nodded, somewhat impressed. "Ok, look at you!"

"You know, just a little something-something," he said.

"Need me to do anything?"

Reggie shook his head. "Nah, babe, you're good. Just have a seat over at the island and let me finish working my magic. It'll be ready soon."

Makayla nodded, not needing to be told twice. Just before she took a seat, she had a thought. "Can I use your laptop for a minute? I need to check my work email and…"

Before she could even finish, he was waving her off.

"Of course. It's out in the living room on the coffee table."

Makayla quickly went to grab the laptop and brought it back to the kitchen so she could check her email while Reggie finished up breakfast. She wasn't even sure how much time had gone by when he placed a plate in front of her. What she did know was that she was starving. At least that was what her stomach told her when a rumble echoed through the kitchen.

"Right on time," Reggie said, shooting her a wink before moving to make his own plate.

She chuckled before closing the laptop and sliding it away from her. "Yeah, yeah, yeah. Don't get too cocky just yet. Let's see if this lives up to the taste test because if not, this will be the first and last time I stay over."

So now you want to stay over on a regular basis? That nagging voice said. She ignored it as best she could.

"I'm not worried," Reggie said, though the look he shot her as she took her first bite said otherwise. He was, in fact, very nervous, and damn if Makayla didn't think the shit was adorable as hell.

Any doubt in Reggie's mind had to have disappeared almost immediately because as soon as she took that first bite, Makayla let out an otherworldly moan. She looked over at him, and the smile on his face made her narrow her eyes.

"How the fuck are you real?" Makayla asked, causing Reggie to chuckle. "No, seriously. Are you sure there's not a wife and a few babies hiding around here somewhere because what the fuck?"

That only made Reggie laugh even harder. "I told you. My nana did not play when it came to teaching me how to take care of myself and anyone I came in contact with. Not to mention, you can't travel as much as I do and not pick up a few things along the way."

"Mmhmm, I guess," she conceded. "That still doesn't answer my second question."

"No, Makayla, I don't have a secret family running around somewhere. I promise."

"I guess I'll just have to take your word for it." She took another bite of food, too invested in what was on her plate to challenge or tease him anymore.

The two ate in silence for a few minutes before Reggie cleared his throat. "So, I was thinking, I don't have much planned for today. Maybe get a bit of writing done, watch a few movies. I was wondering if maybe…you'd want to keep me company."

Makayla froze mid-bite of French toast. She could somewhat see him out of the corner of her eye, and he was looking right at her.

"Well, umm… I mean, I was going to head home and get some work done. After checking those emails, I definitely need to approve some layouts and articles for the next edition."

"Okay, so do it here," he said with a shrug. "We can work and chill. I promise not to distract you too much." The wink he shot her said otherwise.

Despite his playful tone, Makayla couldn't help but be a bit nervous as she thought about her answer. Sex, breakfast, and working from home while they relaxed with one another? The entire thing sounded a little too domesticated for her tastes. To be honest, if anyone else had mentioned the same scenario to her, she wouldn't have hesitated to shoot it down. Actually, if this had been anyone else, they wouldn't even be in this situation, to begin with. At most, she would have woken up this morning, thrown her clothes back on, and immediately headed home because sleepovers were not in her repertoire. It was too easy for men to get the wrong idea. Give them enough room to do that, and suddenly, they had you in a relationship without any sort of discussion or agreement. Still...it amazed her that instead of immediately rejecting his proposal like her instincts usually told her, she was actually considering it.

"Does this count as a date?" She chewed on her bottom lip. "I mean, since technically my date was yesterday, would this count as yours?" She wasn't sure what she wanted his answer to be. Maybe this was her weak attempt to keep their boundaries in place.

Reggie shrugged. "No. I mean, I didn't think it would. I actually wanted to test your hand at pool for that. I have this spot I head to with my friends, and they've been wanting to meet you, so..." He let his words trail off. "Do you want it to count?"

Did she? Instead of lying, she decided to tell the truth. "I'm honestly not sure." The silence between them after that response stretched for so long that it teetered right on the edge of awkward.

"I didn't mean to put you on the spot, baby girl," he said, breaking the silence. "Whenever you're ready to head out, I can take you back home."

"No, it's not that," she said quickly before she could second-guess herself. She didn't want to make this moment any more awkward than it already was. "It's just… I don't want to take over your laptop if you need to get some work done too." It was a weak reason, and he clearly knew it.

Reggie looked at her skeptically. "I definitely have more than one machine to work on, baby, so that's not an issue." He put his fork down and turned so that his whole body was facing her. "And even if I didn't, my shit isn't even that pressing, so you'd be good if you needed to use it for a while. Something tells me that's not the only thing that has you hesitating, though."

It took every bit of confidence that Makayla had to turn toward him. She pulled her bottom lip between her teeth, nervous for the first time in a long time to say what she was thinking.

Girl, what is wrong with you? Are you grown or not?

"Listen, I— I'm not used to this." She took a few seconds to find the right words. "This whole situation is starting to feel real cozy and out of my element. I'm not complaining about it, but…" She paused. "But it still makes me a bit nervous, you know? I don't want you to suddenly start thinking that I've changed my mind about what I want out of all this and…"

Reggie stopped her before she could go any further.

"Listen, I know this is a little out of your comfort zone. I get that. And if you really want to go home and have some time to yourself, that's not a problem for me. I don't want to push you into doing anything you don't want to do or something you're not comfortable with." He took her hand in his and pulled her off her chair, nestling her perfectly between his thighs. She brought her arms around his neck and settled in, leaning her body into his.

"But I won't lie and say that I don't love the way this feels. I'm not going to act like I'm not trying to be in your presence for as long as you'll allow me to be. In case it's not clear, I'm feeling the hell out of you, Makayla, and that means I'm willing to take as much or as little of you as you're ready and willing to give me. No bullshit."

Reggie's words sent butterflies fluttering around her stomach. She leaned in, placing a quick and simple kiss on his lips. Instead of hesitating this time, she went with her gut. "I guess staying for a few more hours couldn't hurt."

CHAPTER 22

Reggie

A few more hours turned into almost a full day together, but Reggie was certainly not going to complain. He couldn't even lie, he was nervous as hell asking her if she wanted to spend time with him. Anyone paying even the smallest bit of attention would've realized that everything he'd mentioned to her was shit that real couples did. In that same vein, it'd be ridiculous of him not to remind himself that despite what the outside world thought, they were not an actual couple. Still, having her in his space, wearing his clothes, smelling like his body wash—the entire thing had him overwhelmed in the best ways. Reggie would be lying to himself if he didn't acknowledge he wanted more of this.

Unfortunately, proceed with caution was practically tattooed on Makayla's forehead. He wouldn't necessarily say that she was skittish, but it was clear that this was all new for her. It went against everything she'd told him about herself when they first met. The more time they spent with one another, the easier their vibe became. Sure, they enjoyed one another's company, but the last thing that he wanted to do was make her feel like he was forcing her hand, no matter what their agreement was. So, if Makayla had turned him down and told him to take her home, that's what he would have done. Even if every cell in his body was telling him to hold on tight.

Reggie couldn't help the way his heart skipped a beat as he watched her shoot off email after email while reviewing the templates for each section of the magazine. Makayla was beyond gorgeous when she was concentrating, her plump lower lip tucked between her teeth, brow furrowed, feet tapping to a non-existent beat. Or maybe it was a beat that only she could hear in her head. Either way, while he managed to get some work done, Makayla was a distraction. One he wasn't exactly complaining about.

After arguing with her about not needing to help while he cleaned up the kitchen, he'd finally conceded. They'd double-teamed the dishes, and afterward, Reggie'd set her up in his living room. He made sure Makayla had not only the laptop but also a notebook and a few pens and pencils to write with. When she came out of the kitchen, he saw the way her eyes lit up, and her lips pursed as she tried to avoid letting her smile loose.

The two of them fell into a comfortable silence after that, music playing lightly in the background as they both attempted to get some work done. Makayla was definitely more successful in that area. After a few hours had passed, he'd ordered sushi from one of his favorite spots in the neighborhood so that they could break for a late lunch, at which point Reggie suggested playing Twenty Questions.

"Sir, who said I have twenty questions to ask you?" Makayla said, kissing her teeth.

"I'm sure you can pull something together," Reggie chuckled.

By question five, Makayla looked like she absolutely wanted to throw something at Reggie's head.

"In your poor nana's minivan?!" she half-shrieked.

Reggie shrugged but at least had the decency to look somewhat sheepish about his latest revelation. "I was seventeen! Where else were we supposed to do it?" he asked, which sent Makayla into a fit of laughter.

"I can't believe you just said that. Wow. Losing your virginity in the back of Lovey's minivan. Your ole dirty ass. Was it at least worth it?"

Reggie rubbed the back of his neck, looking even more embarrassed than he had a few seconds ago.

"Woooooow, that poor girl," Makayla said between giggles.

"Listen, there were no complaints from her, okay!"

"She just didn't know any better!"

"Whatever, man. We dated for at least three more months after that. Besides, I think we both know I've more than hit my stride in that department." He shot her a knowing look as he leaned over the coffee table and pulled her into a kiss. Heat flared in his eyes as he pulled away. Her eyes told him that she felt the exact same way. Still, Reggie wanted to avoid everything they did together being centered around them having sex, so he pulled away and reclaimed his seat.

"Okay, what about you then, Ms. Judgmental? What's your first time story?" he asked curiously.

"I was eighteen, home on fall break from college, and Mommy was away on a work trip." Makayla couldn't help the laugh that bubbled up from her lips. "I convinced Kendall to throw a party just so I would have a reason to see the most gorgeous guy from my graduating class." She shook her head. "We'd gone out a few times but hadn't really gotten together since we were going to separate schools. Anyway, like an hour into the party, Lizzie is dancing on the kitchen table after raiding the liquor cabinet, Kendall is trying to keep people from breaking shit, and meanwhile, I'm upstairs in my room with him, and well…you know how it goes."

Reggie nodded because it wasn't hard to figure out where the rest of the story was headed. "So, was it worth it?" he asked, shooting her own question back at her.

"Honestly? A ton of shit got broken, and Lizzie ended up with the hangover from hell. Plus, my mom came home early before we had time to clean anything up, so we all got cussed the fuck out from the top of our heads to the tip of our toes."

That had them both laughing because it wasn't hard to picture Ms. Delilah going off on her daughters after they'd pulled a stunt like that one.

"But…yeah, it was. He was really sweet. Made me feel safe, you know? I mean, it obviously wasn't the best sex of anyone's life, but it still felt…right." She shrugged before taking a sip of her water. "I don't think I would've wanted my first time to be with anyone else.

Reggie just watched her for a while, and when she finally looked back up at him, she rolled her eyes. "You're not going to go all toxic masculinity on me now and demand to know how you measure up in comparison, are you? Ask me whether or not I still think about him? And for the record, yes, I do still think about him, but only because we're actually pretty good friends, and his wife is one of the sweetest people I've ever met."

Reggie chuckled and shook his head. "Nah, nothing like that. Only someone with a fragile ass ego would feel threatened by a nigga you were with fifteen years ago. Honestly, I'm not even worried about how I measure up to whoever you were with before we met. They have nothing to do with what we have going on right now. I'd like to think we're both secure enough to under-stand that that goes both ways."

Makayla nodded, confirming his point.

"So, trust me when I say that was the furthest thing from my mind."

"Okay," she said, tucking her feet underneath her as she got comfortable on the couch. "So, what are you thinking about then?"

"Well…I was just thinking about how beautiful you look when you're telling a story. You get this little twinkle in your eye when you think something is funny or when you're remembering something that makes you feel good. And I'm just wondering if maybe—just maybe—you ever look like that when you're talking about me."

He said it as if it were a statement instead of a question. He didn't want her to feel like she had to have an answer for that. He stood up quickly. "And now I'm thinking that I'm going to clean up this mess, put these laptops away, and convince you to cuddle with me right there on that couch while we watch whatever movie you want."

Before she could respond, he gathered up their trash and did exactly what he said. He hadn't expected any resistance on her part, but that didn't mean he felt any less satisfied when he returned and found that she had already taken care of their work areas. She crooked her finger to signal for him to join her on the couch.

"You just always get your way, don't you?" she asked him as she settled in between his legs, pressing her back to his chest as they both found the most comfortable position they could.

"Only when I'm lucky, and right now…I'm definitely that."

CHAPTER 23

Makayla

"So, this is the famous Makayla," Avery said with a smile as Reggie and Makayla made their way over to the corner pool table. "Girl, I was wondering when he was going to bring you around so we could meet you."

Makayla sent Avery a smile and returned the hug that the other woman gave her. To be honest, she had been more than a bit skeptical when Reggie told her that their date was going to involve her meeting his best friends. Sure, he'd mentioned it in passing last week when they'd spent the day at his house and okay, he'd met her best friend and her family, but that had all been a part of the original plan. Integrating her into his life? Now that was something totally different. Still, she'd been hard-pressed to tell him no. She just hoped agreeing to this didn't blow up in her face.

"I wouldn't blame him for trying to keep me to himself, honestly," she said with a shrug.

"Yeah, well, unfortunately, I don't think I could've gotten away with putting this off any longer," Reggie said, rolling his eyes.

Lucas laughed. "Shit, I don't know why he was trying to hide you, anyway. Then again, this wouldn't be the first time he introduced me to his new girl and I snatched her from right under his nose."

Makayla opened her mouth to shoot a retort his way because hold up, who did this man think he was? The only thing that stopped her was the smile that crossed Reggie's face. They were clearly just teasing each other, so she let it slide, an easy smile appearing on her face as well.

"That was one time in sixth grade, and if I recall, she left both of our asses alone for Dante Moore," Reggie said with a chuckle. "Besides, the real reason I was avoiding this moment is because of the way y'all are always trying to play me to the left. Shit, the way y'all act, you'll probably scare her off. It wouldn't be the first time," he said, giving them both pointed looks.

Avery rolled her eyes. "Listen, like I told you before—if we can scare off any woman you bring around that easily, then she wasn't the one for you in the first place. We can't just let anyone into our group. They have to be able to play on our level."

Avery shot Makayla a look as if she was daring the other woman to challenge her. Makayla just smirked back. She understood completely and had no intention of backing down. "Wanna know something funny? My family said the exact same thing when I told them about him."

"They did?" Reggie looked at her in surprise. She hadn't mentioned that to him.

Makayla nodded. "Sure did. According to them, if you were scared of them, then there's no way you'd be able to handle me. I told them that was shady as hell, but honestly, they probably weren't wrong. And I'm sure your friends aren't either." She shot Avery a wink. "Luckily, it seems that neither one of us scares that easily."

"I guess you have a point. Still seems like they're trying to play us, though," Reggie said with a chuckle.

"Are we trying to play y'all, or do we just know you that well?" Lucas chimed in. Everyone laughed because honestly, it was probably a bit of both. "Anyway, don't expect me to go easy on your ass at this pool table just because your girl is here."

"Bruh, you say that as if you could ever possibly make me look bad with a pool stick. We both know that I am clean as fuck out here," said Reggie as he brushed off his shoulders.

"You say that, and yet, if I recall correctly, you just had to pay me for losing a game double or nothing." Lucas set the rack as Avery and Reggie both grabbed cues. It was clear that Reggie and his friends loved to talk shit, but Makayla didn't mind.

"That's only because you cheated, and you know it," Reggie grumbled as he handed Makayla her pool cue. "Don't let him fool you, baby girl. That man is a sore ass loser and a cheater." He gave her a quick kiss on the forehead, and she smiled despite herself. When the hell did she get so into forehead kisses?

Reggie and Lucas continued to go back and forth while Avery and Makayla chalked their cues.

"Are they always like this?" Makayla asked the other woman.

"Girl, trust me. It can get a whole lot worse. You should've seen the Great Bowling Debacle of 2018. There were flying bowling balls, a broken shoe sole, and over a dozen onion rings involved in that one. Pure chaos."

The two of them burst out laughing, not even noticing that they'd drawn both men's attention.

"What's so funny?" said Reggie, eyeing them suspiciously.

"Oh, nothing. Just giving Makayla a little warning about how immature you grown ass men can be." Avery's tone was deceptively sweet.

"I know you're not over there talking," Lucas groaned in disbelief. "Your ass is worse than both of us combined!"

"No bullshit," Reggie agreed as he walked over and wrapped an arm around Makayla. He placed his finger beneath her chin, tipping her head back to steal a quick kiss from her. She enjoyed how casual it all felt, even though she knew she shouldn't. "Don't believe shit she says. It's all a lie," he whispered against her lips.

"Boy, please! I'm completely innocent," said Avery, shaking her head.

"Yeah, okay, you can play that game all you want, but we all know who really terrorizes everybody in this group. It's certainly not either one of us." Lucas gestured between himself and Reggie as if to reiterate his point.

"I don't know, I'm inclined to believe her. You forget that I know how you get down." Makayla laughed as she stole a second kiss from Reggie.

"Mmmm, you know how I get down, huh?" He placed one kiss and then a second on her lips, each one lingering just a bit longer than the last. She loved it when he did that. Each kiss sent sparks of electricity straight through her body. The way his hand firmly gripped her ass was its own bit of pleasure.

"Alright, damn. Enough of that, please, before my drink comes back up the wrong way," Lucas groaned before giving a fake gag. Reggie shot him the finger, which caused Makayla to giggle.

"The point is, don't listen to either one of these clowns. They both know that *I* am the master of the pool table," Reggie said. He gave Makayla a swat on her ass before setting himself up to make his first shot. "And I have no problem wiping the floor with both of their asses to prove it."

"Hmmm, but the real question is, how will you have time to wipe the floor with them when you'll be too busy getting your ass whooped by me?" Makayla responded, one brow raised in challenge.

Avery and Lucas snickered as Reggie gazed at her with unmistakable heat in his eyes. Her declaration had turned him on just like she'd known it would. She also knew that he wasn't one to back down from a challenge, whether it was inside or outside of the bedroom.

"Let's see if you can back up all that mouth you've got," he said, the innuendo clear in his tone.

Makayla walked over and brushed him aside, bending over as she nestled herself in just the right position so her ass pressed against his dick. She heard him stifle a groan and giggled to herself. "We both know that I have no problem backing up all this mouth." She lined up her cue and took her shot, sinking the exact ball she'd wanted into the side pocket.

"Game on," Reggie said, brushing his lips against her ear.

"Aye, no fucking against the table!" Lucas exclaimed, which, of course, had the group laughing all over again.

For the next two hours, the group laughed, joked, and riled each other up over the pool table. They played against each other before forming teams, Makayla and Avery against Reggie and Lucas. The women had no trouble beating the guys not once but twice, which, of course, caused the guys to blame each other. Makayla could tell, though, that all the bickering was in good spirits. Watching Reggie with his two best friends made it clear to her that they were his family. It wasn't surprising considering that whenever he mentioned them, the admiration in his voice told her how much he loved them. Watching it in real time hit different, though. Reggie looked…at home. He was already laidback and calm, but it was clear that Avery and Lucas had a grounding effect on him.

What was even more interesting was how easily she fell into their vibe. Makayla rarely got flustered around other people, but she also knew that she wasn't everyone's cup of tea. Despite this being the first time they'd met, she felt like she'd known his friends for years. She couldn't help but wonder if that was a testament to how comfortable she was with Reggie.

She watched him laugh with Lucas as they finished off their beers and was so distracted that she didn't even notice when Avery sidled up beside her.

"I was wrong," she said, leaning into Makayla, causing her to jump. "My bad."

"You're fine, girl. I was just lost in thought," Makayla said with a laugh.

"I've heard good dick will do that to you," Avery snickered.

"Trust me, it absolutely does," Makayla said, giving the other woman a nudge and a wink.

"Okay, gross. Damn, girl, you did not have to confirm that!" Avery faked a gag.

"You brought it on yourself, sis," she responded with a laugh. "So, what were you wrong about?"

"You. This." Makayla gave Avery a confused look. "When Reggie first told us about this whole fake dating plan, I have to admit that as much as we joked with him about it, I was not here for it. I worry about him, you know? He's one of my best friends. Has been for years, and well…he's a softy at heart. A romantic."

"I've noticed."

"Yeah, well, sometimes him being such a romantic can… backfire. I've seen him put more effort into relationships than the person he's with, which doesn't lead to anything but him being heartbroken. I just…I didn't want to see that happen again. We finally have him home, and the last thing I want is for anything— or anyone—to send him running again."

Makayla watched Reggie again before turning to Avery. "Yeah, but…" she started, but Avery shook her head.

"No, let me finish. I know that whatever y'all are doing is… well, it may not be serious to you. I don't know if he's more invested than you are in this or not. I just wanted to say that you seem to be good people. I just…I wanted to let you know that I see that. If by the end of this you realize a relationship still isn't what you want, just…let him down easy, ya know?"

Makayla stayed quiet for a minute, reading the sincerity in the other woman's eyes. The protest that had been on her tongue died. "I will. I promise."

"Good. Now let me get over there before these two show their asses any more than they already are."

Makayla shook her head with a laugh as Avery walked over to the pool table. She loved that Reggie was so important to them. Truth be told, she would've had the same conversation with anyone who was dating Jasmine or her sisters. Hell, she had, and none of them had ever been in a situation quite like this one.

While Avery teased Lucas, Reggie made his way over to Makayla. He placed himself between her legs and allowed his hands to fall on either side of her waist.

"What was that about? Looked pretty serious," he said as he gave her hips a light squeeze.

"Nunya business," she teased. He kissed his teeth, and she laughed. "Just having a moment with Avery, is all. She worries about you. It's cute and it makes sense."

"Oh, really?" he asked, kicking up an eyebrow.

"Mmhmm. I've been told I'm quite a handful. I'd be nervous to see you with me too." She slid her arms around his waist and pulled him closer.

Reggie pressed his forehead to hers. "Well, did you let her know I'm happy to take my chances?"

"She knows," Makayla said.

"Good." He placed a kiss on each cheek before moving his lips to her ear. The feel of his warm breath sent shivers down her spine. "Now, how about we take one of those chances back at my place so I can give you your reward for beating my ass on the pool table?"

"Oh, you liked that, huh?" she asked.

"Mmhmm, and I can't wait to show you just how much."

CHAPTER 24

Makayla

"So…" Delilah's voice trailed off as they set up the outdoor snack bar. "How are things with you and Reggie?"

Makayla looked at her mother suspiciously. Her tone was entirely too light and controlled. This wasn't an 'I'm just curious and making conversation' talk. This was more of an 'I'm dying to know the details, but I don't want to send you running' talk.

"We're fine. He should be here soon," she responded in a neutral tone. The last thing she wanted to do was talk to her mother about her relationship. Well, her fake relationship. Then again…was this thing between them still really fake? It'd been three weeks since she'd hung out at the pool hall and met his best friends, which meant they'd been at this for a little over two months now. Three, if you included the few weeks she'd lied about early on to her family. And of course, there was the fact that the more time they spent together, the more the lines were beginning to get…muddled, especially over these last few weeks. She could blame it on the sex, but that'd be a lie. At this point, she just enjoyed his company. Their sleepovers were happening more often these days, whether it was at her house or his and each time she felt herself getting more and more attached. Cuddling on the couch, teasing one another while trying to get work done, listening when one of them was frustrated with how something was going career wise, staying up 'til all hours discussing any and everything imaginable. The truth was Makayla didn't know what the two of them were doing anymore. Of course, she couldn't explain any of that to her mother.

"Just fine? That's it? That's all you have for your old mama?"

"Mommy, please! You're not even old. Besides, I don't know what you want me to tell you." Was there an escape she could make out of this conversation? Because if so, she wanted to make it NOW.

"Hmph. Well, you can start by telling me what exactly he's doing to put that pep in your step. You're basically glowing, and I haven't seen you smile this much in a very long time." Her words made Makayla realize that she was, indeed, smiling. She tried to pull herself under control.

"We're just having a good time, Mama, that's all."

"A good time? Is that what the kids are calling it these days? Because if so, he needs to have a sit-down and explain the details to Percy so I can get some of that for myself."

"Mommy!" Makayla squealed as her cheeks warmed. This was *not* happening right now. Where was a flash flood when you needed it?

"Oh, girl, please! You just said it yourself that I am not old. I damn sure have eyes. Whatever that man is laying down on you is something we all need a piece of," said Delilah with a smirk.

"We are not having this conversation," Makayla said pointedly. Unfortunately, though, she couldn't hide the smile that formed on her lips.

"Mmhmm. I see you're trying to keep all of those goodies to yourself. I can respect that," her mother teased.

Makayla laughed. Any tension she'd been feeling at the

beginning of this conversation was quickly dissipating, thanks to her mother's silliness.

Before she could respond, she heard a familiar laugh that made her heart skip a beat—or two. She looked up toward the gate to the backyard and saw Reggie there, laughing at something that Lizzie was saying. Anyone with a sense of humor knew that Lizzie was not that funny, but she appreciated the effort that Reggie was clearly making, especially since no one else ever really let Lizzie get away with her horrible jokes.

"Whatever he's doing, sweetheart...I hope he keeps it up," her mother said.

Makayla nearly jumped out of her skin. She'd forgotten just that fast that the older woman was there with her. She wasn't sure what her mother had seen on her face, but her skin was suddenly warmer than it had been when they'd been talking about her sex life.

"He looks good on you, baby. You look happy."

With those last words, her mother walked off toward Reggie to greet him with a smile and a hug like he was family. There was an ache inside Makayla that she couldn't quite explain. Did she really seem happier? *Was* she actually happier? And if she did, what would happen once this was all over? Would her family go back to being disappointed in her choices? Hell, would *she* end up being disappointed with her choices? This little arrangement was supposed to make her life easier, not harder.

"You good, baby girl?" Reggie asked. She'd been so lost in her own thoughts that she hadn't even noticed him walking over to her.

Makayla mentally shook herself, trying to clear her mind, and sent him a smile. "Yeah, I'm good. Just trying to get the conversation I had with my mom out of my head." She leaned up to give him a kiss, which he happily accepted.

"Oh, yeah? What conversation was that?" he asked curiously.

"One about our sex life and the pointers she wanted you to give Percy."

The disturbed look on Reggie's face almost had Makayla falling over with laughter. "Trust me, I had the same reaction," she said, threading her fingers through his.

"You didn't tell her that..."

"That you've been blowing my back out and I've been riding you to hell and back like my life depends on it? Of course, I did," she teased. He groaned, and she could only giggle. "I'm just kidding. I kindly told my mama that we were not about to have that conversation, and thankfully, she moved on to say hi to you."

"Yeah, but now I'm thinking about all those looks she and your sisters have been giving me since we showed up to karaoke night, and suddenly, it all makes sense."

As if to illustrate his point, he discreetly gestured to where her family was standing. The group was clearly whispering as they watched the couple. The three of them noticed that they were being watched but didn't even have the decency to look embarrassed about being caught. Her mother and Lizzie only gave her suggestive winks, while Kendall just looked plain agitated. What the hell was that about? The two of them had been doing well since Makayla had gotten here to help set up, but now it looked like her sister was ready to cuss her out. Usually, she wouldn't mind, but she hadn't even done anything this time.

Makayla decided that she wasn't going to let Kendall get under her skin. Not tonight.

"So, what's on the agenda tonight?" Reggie asked as he wrapped his arms around her waist and pulled her into him.

"Which agenda would that be?"

"The 'make sure everyone knows that Makayla has a man and is happy as fuck' agenda. Along with the 'once we make everybody unbelievably jealous, what are we getting into' agenda. Or better yet, where am I getting into you?"

Makayla looked at him like he had three heads. She gave him

a shove as she rolled her eyes. "Oh my gosh, I swear you are the worst."

"I'm pretty sure that's not what you'll be saying later, but I'll let it slide for now." His hands traveled down until they gripped her ass, and she had to stifle a moan. "Mmhmm, that's what I thought."

"Okay, you two, okay, enough of all that. Grab your stuff and let's get this movie night going," Kendall said, brushing by them.

Reggie looked at Makayla and raised an eyebrow. She couldn't do anything but shrug. She had no idea what had crawled up her sister's ass today, but she was hoping that her husband would be able to fix it quickly. Speaking of which...

"I thought we were waiting on Greg," Makayla said, looking around for the man in question.

"No, he's going to be late," Kendall answered. Makayla could've sworn she sensed a hint of bitterness in her sister's voice. "Some of us have adult responsibilities that don't allow us to be at each other's beck and call," the older woman added with an attitude. Her tone almost sent Makayla flying across the yard to snatch her sister up.

In fact, she probably would have if it weren't for Reggie tightening his grip on her hips. "Whoa there, killer. It's not that serious."

"I'm just getting really sick of her slick ass mouth," she responded, elevating her voice to ensure Kendall heard her.

"I know, but the last thing you need to be doing is trying to fight your sister. It's the last big event before the rehearsal dinner, remember? Your mom will beat both of your asses. I would much rather put that mouth to good use later as opposed to having to ice it because your sister popped you in it."

Makayla narrowed her eyes at him.

"I'm not saying she'd win! I'm just saying she'd get in a hit or two," he said defensively.

"Whatever. Bring your ass on here before you don't get shit

but a fat lip from me," she said. Secretly, she appreciated him trying to defuse the situation. She knew that Reggie was right. Her mother would kill her if she showed her ass tonight. When it came to her sister, Makayla tended to have tunnel vision. The last thing she wanted to do was ruin the night entertaining her sister's bullshit.

Instead, Makayla grabbed a large bowl from the table and filled it with kettle corn, chocolate candy, and licorice straws before directing Reggie to grab two cherry colas and a few hard ciders. Once she was satisfied, she walked toward the oversized pergola and grabbed a spot on one of the L-shaped couches. Reggie slid in as well, setting up comfortably behind her so that she would be able to lean back into him while they watched the movie.

Her mother and Percy were movie fanatics. When they were putting together the list of events, it only made sense to include a movie night to round everything out. One of the things the couple did to make sure they kept the romance alive in their relationship was biweekly movie dates. It may have seemed simple, but Delilah always said that she was never more comfortable than when she was cuddled up with a good movie next to Percy. The thought made Makayla smile. As much as she didn't want to admit it, she could see the appeal. The feeling of Reggie's chest at her back provided her with the calm that she needed.

"You never answered my question," Reggie whispered in Makayla's ear as he pulled her in close.

She tried and failed to ignore the shivers that ran down her spine. "What question was that?"

"What's on the agenda?" Makayla could feel the vibrations of his chest throughout her entire body.

She moved slightly, being sure to press herself against him in a way that had his hardness standing at attention. She heard the groan he tried to hide and let out a small laugh. "You'll just have to wait and see."

CHAPTER 25

Reggie

Reggie attempted to hide his excitement as the movie started. When Makayla had mentioned that they were doing a movie night, he hadn't been sure what to expect. The make-your-own snack bar was a very nice touch. It had just about everything that a snack enthusiast could want. He smirked as he looked down at Makayla, who was nestled comfortably in his lap. Her snack combination wasn't exactly something he would pick for himself, but she had been so aggravated by her sister earlier that he was prepared to eat whatever she wanted.

At the thought, he gazed around the backyard. Everyone else's attention was focused on *Brown Sugar*, one of his favorite movies. The only person who seemed to not be paying it any mind was Kendall. Her husband had finally arrived about halfway through the movie, but she wasn't focused on him either. She was too busy staring at the two of them to see what was going on in the film. He wasn't exactly sure what the eldest sister's problem was, but she seemed to be even more agitated tonight than she had been the first night he'd met her.

A protective urge came over Reggie. If Makayla's sister

wanted some sort of show, he was happy to give it to her. Anything to get her off of their backs. He pulled Makayla's hand from the bowl as she grabbed a piece of kettle corn. She looked up at him, just slightly confused.

"Figured I'd get myself a little snack," he said with a wink. Pulling her fingers toward his mouth, he fed himself the kettle corn. Before letting her go, he sucked the salty sweetness from her fingers. He watched as she squirmed, lust flaring in her eyes. Reggie just kissed her fingertips. As he did, he turned to look at Kendall. He sent a wink in her direction, causing her cheeks to flare hot.

That's right. You're caught.

Clearly a bit embarrassed, she quickly turned her attention to the screen. He chuckled to himself. Makayla's questioning eyes watched the entire exchange, and a smile played on her lips.

"Are you messing with my sister?" asked Makayla. She sat up so that the two of them were almost face-to-face.

"Maybe just a little," Reggie said sheepishly. "Seemed like she wanted a bit of a show, so I figured why not give her one? Just something slight." He shrugged as he pulled her closer. He didn't want his voice to carry over the movie. Unfortunately, it seemed as though her sister had other plans.

"Some of us are trying to watch the movie, you know," Kendall called in an agitated voice.

Reggie fought the urge to kiss his teeth. He expected Makayla to have some sort of retort, but instead, she just grabbed his hand and stood from the couch.

"Then excuse us while we take this somewhere private," she retorted before leading him toward the front of the house where she grabbed a seat on the porch swing.

"Needed a break?" he asked as he leaned against the porch railing.

"Yeah. *Brown Sugar* is cute and all, but it's no *Juice*."

Reggie just shook his head as he chuckled. "Somehow, I don't think that's the sort of vibe your mom is going for leading up to her wedding."

"Of course, you'd say that. Didn't you tell me *Brown Sugar* is one of your favorite movies?"

"Sure did. Dope soundtrack, iconic lines, classic friends-to-lovers vibe. How can you not love it? It's a staple."

"Hmm, maybe so, but with the way my sister is acting, a movie with an ass-whooping might've been more appropriate."

"Sure, killer. Whatever you say."

Reggie watched her, the porch light giving her a glow. "Can I ask you a question?" Makayla nodded. "Why do you let her get to you?"

His eyes tracked the way her brow furrowed, and she began to nibble on her bottom lip. He could tell that she was deep in thought, trying to come up with the right words to explain.

"Kendall has always been a bit...high-strung. And that's the nice way of putting it." She sighed and sat back in her seat, letting it swing lightly. "But lately, it's gotten worse. We've never really seen eye-to-eye on things, but for the last six months, it's like everything I do just pisses her off. I love my big sister, but damn, she can be a pain in the ass sometimes. It's like she just looks for things to nitpick about. At first, I thought that she was mad about this," Makayla gestured between the two of them, "because you were Lizzie's pick and not hers."

"Nah, I think it's something more than that," said Reggie, thinking back on the looks she had been giving him ever since he'd gotten there. "What about her and her husband? Greg, right?"

"She and Greg have been together since high school. The quintessential perfect couple. I had the same thought, but honestly, he practically worships the ground that Kendall walks on, so I can't imagine there being trouble in that department."

Reggie wanted to disagree. He may not have spent much time with the couple, but it was clear to him that something was off. The two of them had barely touched one another since ole boy had shown up tonight. Now that he thought about it, the last few times they'd gotten together for wedding events, the couple hadn't acted like any married couple that he was used to interacting with. He'd bet money that something was going on there, but it wasn't really his business. His only concern was the woman sitting right in front of him.

"Now, can I ask *you* a question?" asked Makayla, clearly ready to change the subject.

"Yes, you do have weird ass taste in movie snacks."

The two of them laughed as Reggie moved to take a seat next to her on the swing. He pulled her feet into his lap, fingers gliding lightly up and down her calf.

"Hardy-har-har, you jerk." She rolled her eyes and allowed herself to get comfortable. "That wasn't going to be my question, but you are on the right track. What about romantic movies has you so drawn to them?"

A groan escaped Reggie's lips. "Don't tell me you're about to hit me with a little toxic masculinity and say it's not manly enough." It certainly wouldn't be the first time he'd heard that.

Makayla immediately shook her head. "No, that's not why I'm asking because frankly, that type of thinking is bullshit. That's like saying someone who's extremely feminine can't be into slasher films. Doesn't make a whole lot of sense."

"Oh, trust me, I completely agree. That doesn't stop people from saying it, though."

"You're right. I'm sorry you have to deal with that type of shit. It definitely wasn't my intention to sound like them," she said, shaking her head. "I just… I guess I'm just curious because as cute as they are, those movies have just always seemed so unrealistic to me. What happens when the credits run? Are we supposed to just believe that these two people are going to live happily ever after when the camera shuts off? It just always seemed so far-fetched to me."

Reggie considered her question. He could understand where she was coming from, especially understanding her the way that he did. After giving it a bit more thought, he finally decided on the answer.

"Honest answer? I didn't have my parents, but having my grandmother give me as much love as she did, I knew that it wasn't the sort of thing that was in short supply. Even if I never experienced that great love story for myself, it just seemed too bleak to think that that sort of thing didn't exist. I guess romantic movies just offer up that great hope. The hope that there's something bigger out there for all of us. The idea that there's this one soulmate, this one person who will love you, flaws and all...it reminds me of her." Reggie looked into her eyes and shrugged. "The world can't function without love, right?"

The silence stretched between them as she took in his words. Before he had time to react, Makayla was pulling her feet from his lap and leaning toward him. The kiss she placed on his lips wasn't heated or full of lust. It was soft, sweet, and tasted faintly like chocolate. Reggie was surprised but certainly not unappreciative. After pulling away, she laid her head on his shoulder and cuddled up beside him.

This, he decided, was much better than any movie.

CHAPTER 26

Makayla

"You two looked pretty cozy out there on the porch," Lizzie whispered conspiratorially as she and Makayla walked through the patio doors and into the house.

"I'm surprised you even noticed with the way you and Alonzo are attached at the hip tonight," Makayla laughed.

"Well, it's pretty hard to miss," Kendall grumbled.

Makayla raised her eyebrow but chose to ignore that comment. After the conversation with Reggie earlier, she was determined not to let her older sister get on her nerves. She turned back to Lizzie. "Maybe we're just trying to keep up with you two."

"As if you could," Kendall snorted, and it took everything in Makayla not to drop the trays she was carrying.

"Don't start, Kendall," Lizzie said nervously. As the baby sister, she was always left trying to defuse the situation between Makayla and Kendall. It had been like that since they were kids.

"I'm just saying, it takes a lot more to be an actual couple than a few cute dates and screwing each other's brains out."

Kendall's tone was unmistakably malicious. This time, Makayla took the bait.

"You know, maybe if you and Greg did a little more screwing, you could get that fucking chip off your shoulder. How about you focus on your in-house dick and stop worrying about mine?"

Kendall's anger flashed behind her eyes. Was it possible that Makayla had taken things a step too far? Maybe, but damn, could she get at least one night of reprieve from her sister's judgment?

"Come on, y'all, please," Lizzie said with an exhausted sigh. She looked at Kendall. "We're having a good night. Let's not do the most here."

"Fine," Kendall snapped before storming off.

Makayla just shook her head in disbelief.

"M&M, can you please just…disengage?" Lizzie asked.

"I didn't even want to engage in the first place, Zi! I've literally been minding my business all night."

Lizzie sighed, and the two of them cleaned up in silence. Pretty soon, they heard Percy, Reggie, and Delilah walking into the house having a spirited debate. Their voices carried through to the kitchen before suddenly going silent. Makayla didn't even have to wonder if they could feel the tension in the air. It was obvious by the way they cautiously walked into the kitchen.

"Well, at least I don't have to wonder why your sister is out in the backyard practically barking at everyone while she cleans up," their mother said as she took a sip from her wine glass. "So, is anyone going to elaborate on what happened, or…" She let her words drift off as she waited for their response.

Lizzie looked over at Makayla. After taking a deep breath, Makayla said, "It's nothing, mommy. Just normal sister drama."

Her mother gave her a worried expression but decided not to push the issue. Makayla was grateful. "Anyway, what are y'all so chatty about? You look like you're scheming." She grabbed what was left of her glass of wine and drained it.

Thankfully, the change of subject seemed to work. Unfortunately, Makayla figured out quickly that it was also the wrong
thing to begin discussing. The sheepish look on Reggie's face
while he rubbed the back of his neck was her first clue.

"Oooooh, nothing too big. Just wondering when the next set
of wedding bells will be ringing for this family," her mother said
as she gave Makayla a mischievous grin.

Makayla damn near choked on her drink.

"What?!" she practically shrieked while Lizzie burst into
laughter. "Mommy, I— We haven't—" She stopped and tried to
collect her thoughts. "We haven't been dating long enough for
you to start planning a wedding." She hoped her voice didn't
sound as strangled to them as it did to her. "It's only been a few
months."

"Oh, who says there's a minimum amount of time you have
to be together before you get married? When you meet that
perfect person, you just know. Or better yet," she paused as she
gestured toward Reggie, "your mother knows." She let out a
cackle, clearly thinking she was funnier than she actually was.

Everyone else laughed along with her. Reggie even gave his
own chuckle, though he clearly picked up on how uncomfortable
Makayla was. She couldn't bring herself to play this game with
them, though. Not with the queasy feeling that had settled in the
pit of her stomach.

"You don't have to look so appalled at the thought of forever
with me, you know," Reggie said, pulling Makayla's body into his.
She hadn't even noticed that he'd crossed the room to stand in
front of her. She felt tense against him but couldn't bring herself
to relax. "She's just joking," he said, clearly trying to calm her
down.

He leaned down as the rest of the group carried on with their
conversation and made their way outside to gather more of the
trash. "You look ready to bolt right out that door."

"I just...why would she say that?" Makayla was trying to get her voice under control, but she was beginning to feel just a little bit frantic. "And why are you encouraging her?" she asked, taking a light swing at his shoulder.

Reggie winced. "Baby, she's just being a mom. She's getting married, and everybody is all caught up in this cute couple shit. I mean, it's a little wild that she said it, and it definitely caught me off guard outside. But what do you want me to say? 'Hell no, Ms. Delilah, what the fuck I look like trying to wife your daughter?'" He cocked an eyebrow at her.

"I guess not," Makayla grumbled.

"Exactly. Better to let her have her fun and carry on." He placed a soft kiss on her forehead. "Besides, I'm not saying that I'm trying to get married or anything, but more time with you? Why would I turn that down?" He gave her what he must've thought was a reassuring wink before heading back outside.

Makayla felt the weak smile that spread across her face as she began to follow him outside. But she couldn't ignore the way her entire body felt like it was under quicksand. What the fuck had she gotten herself into here? And whatever it was, was it too late to get the hell out?

CHAPTER 27

Makayla

Makayla was quiet the entire ride home, too consumed by her thoughts to say a word. All of her instincts were practically screaming at her to push Reggie away. This was beginning to feel too real. They were too close. Things were too intense. Could she really keep this charade going, even for just one more week, knowing how close she felt to the edge? At some point, things had changed between them. They'd crossed a line, and she didn't know how to go back. Wouldn't it be best for everyone involved if she stopped this now before she made things even worse?

You don't think they've gone too far already? that all-too-familiar voice asked. She shook her head in an attempt to silence it.

Makayla had been so lost in her own thoughts that she hadn't even realized they'd pulled up in front of her house until Reggie's hand gave her knee a light squeeze.

"Everything okay?" he asked her, a concerned look crossing his face.

She swallowed her thoughts and gave a weak nod. "Yeah. Just

tired, I think." She hoped the small smile on her face was convincing enough.

"You sure?" he asked. "I know that was a lot back there..." His words trailed off as he looked unsure of how to broach the topic. "I can head home if you want."

Was that what she wanted? It was probably what *should* happen. After the awkward as hell conversation they'd had at the end of the night, the last thing she wanted to do was blur the lines even more or talk about what her mother had said. And it hadn't just been her mother. As they cleaned up after movie night, everyone had made little comments about how cute they were together. How she'd never looked happier. How pretty soon, it would finally be her turn to tie the knot. The shit had made her uncomfortable as hell, and she was pretty sure that was why Reggie was offering to leave. Truthfully, though, him leaving was the last thing she wanted right now.

"No," she said before she could stop herself. "You don't have to leave. It's okay." She leaned over, placing a small kiss on his lips before opening her door, suddenly very eager to get out of the confined space of his truck.

She hadn't missed the skeptical look on his face, but something in her chest loosened when she heard the driver's side door open and shut behind her. His footsteps followed her up the steps and into the house.

They moved in silence, sliding their shoes off and locking everything up. She moved toward the kitchen, hoping a glass of water would calm her down. As soon as she heard Reggie's footsteps heading up the stairs, though, she realized water wasn't going to work. Maybe she should have told him that she wanted some space. He would have understood. Wouldn't have pushed against it.

But you know damn well that's not what you want, the voice said again.

It may not have been what she wanted, but maybe it was what she needed if she was going to clear her mind.

Or maybe you could just let Reggie do that himself.

She made a frustrated groan and damn near slammed the glass down on the counter. After taking three deep breaths, she finally got herself together and headed upstairs. Reggie was already in her room. He was on his phone, sitting in the chair near the corner.

"Everything okay?" she asked, pulling her lip between her teeth.

He looked up at her and nodded. "Yeah, just shooting off some emails real quick." Makayla nodded but didn't say anything else. He must have felt her eyes on him because he met her gaze. "If you want to talk about…"

She shook her head. "No, I'm good. I'm going to grab a shower." Her voice was soft as she watched a slew of emotions cross his face. He looked as if he wanted to say something, but before he could answer, she walked past him and into her bathroom. Once she shut the door behind her, she was able to breathe a little easier, knowing she'd put some distance between them.

Makayla rested her head on the door and closed her eyes, taking one deep breath and then another. Seeing Reggie so comfortable with her family and now in her home, looking like he belonged in both…it choked her up. She was feeling things that she couldn't explain, and she *hated* not understanding what she was feeling.

God, what the hell was she doing? Exactly how deep into this shit had she fallen, and when had that happened? One minute, she was just trying to come up with what seemed like a simple ass plan for a halfway simple problem. The next, she was… What exactly *was* she doing? Was she starting to fall for Reggie? Because that certainly had not been part of the plan. Falling was never a good idea, whether it was falling down a flight of stairs or falling in…

"Don't even say it," she whispered to herself.

Makayla stalked over to the shower, stripped out of her clothes, and climbed under the steaming hot water. As soon as slightly-less-than-scalding water hit her skin, she began to relax. There was a running joke on social media that women preferred their water to be the same temperature as the flames of hell, and right now, she couldn't exactly contradict that notion.

Makayla grabbed her washcloth, added what was probably an excessive amount of body wash to it, and then slowly began to wash the day from her skin. Would this shower get rid of the thoughts Lizzie had left in her mind? The argument she and Kendall had? The look of happiness her mother had worn as she kissed Reggie and Makayla goodbye tonight? Would it wash away her confusion about what the hell she should do right now? The longer this carried on, the more torn she was about how happy this situation was making her and how fucked up it would be when everything came to a screeching halt.

She jumped as strong fingers brushed across her shoulder and cold air kissed her nipples, making them pebble immediately.

"Mind if I join you?" a strong voice asked.

Makayla shook her head softly as Reggie climbed into the shower fully and closed the door behind him. Instead of turning to face him, she kept her back to him, afraid of what he might see in her face if he looked too closely.

As she allowed the water to wash the soap away, Reggie guided his hands along her body, starting at her shoulders and following the flow of the water as it cascaded further down. As his fingers ghosted over her flesh, she couldn't help the whimper that escaped her lips. She leaned into him, her back molding to the hard parts of him as the water drenched them both.

Reggie gently took the washcloth from her. "Let me," he whispered into her ear.

She didn't protest, and she couldn't be sure if it was because she didn't want to or she just didn't have the energy. It didn't matter because the way Reggie began to reverently wash her body loosened her muscles and her tongue. It was evident by the content sighs she released over and over again as he slowly washed every inch of her. There was nothing overtly sexual about his movements, even though she could feel him hard and ready against her. He wasn't demanding, forceful, or asking anything of her. It was clear that her needs and making sure that she was okay were all that mattered right now. The thought that he was running the washcloth between her breasts not because he wanted something from her but because he wanted to take care of her—that was what had her pussy practically weeping for him. That was the reason her desire was coating the inside of her thighs and she was trying to press her body closer to him.

Makayla rubbed her thighs together in an attempt to relieve the pressure that seemed to be building within her. Reggie's hand glided across her stomach, pulling her closer to him until his dick was nestled directly between her ass. "You're so fucking beautiful, do you know that?" he whispered into her ear as his hand made its way down between her legs. It seemed to fit perfectly between her thighs. By now, the washcloth was gone, though she couldn't be sure where. The only thing she could focus on was the feel of him cupping her bare pussy as he caressed her breast, fingers simultaneously tracing the opening of her lips and her nipple.

"Please," she whimpered as her hips rolled in hopes of forcing his fingers right where she wanted them. He was toying with her, and as much as she loved the buildup, here—now—she needed something. Anything. The very thing his fingers were promising to give her.

"Please what, baby? You know I love it when you beg." His teeth nipped at her earlobe as he pinched her nipple just a little bit harder. "Please play with this pretty pussy?" His tongue snaked out and found its way to her neck. "Please show you just how much I need to feel you?" He gave her nipple a rough tug, making her gasp. She felt the pull directly in her clit. "Just say the word, and I'll do whatever it is you need me to do."

"Make me come. Please," she pleaded. She'd never begged so much in her life, but it was becoming more and more familiar as she carried on with Reggie. Her feelings weren't the only thing out of control. Her need for him was through the roof. He had a hold on her, and she didn't want him to let go.

Makayla wrapped her arm around the back of her head until her hand was gripping the back of his neck.

"Anything you want, baby," Reggie said as he nestled his lips in the crook of her neck. He licked and sucked what seemed to be his favorite spot at the same moment that his fingers pressed on her hardened bud, sending jolts of electricity through her entire body.

Moans fell from her lips, mixing with the sound of the water hitting their skin and the shower floor. Shower sex had never been her thing, something else that clearly didn't matter when it came to the man who had just buried two fingers into her pussy as his thumb continued to stroke her clit.

"Fuuuuuck." Makayla rolled her hips to meet the thrusts of his fingers. Reggie leaned them both back, pressing against the shower wall in an attempt to keep them both upright. Her legs had already begun to shake. Makayla was careening straight toward bliss, and the insistent stroke of his fingers as they pushed into her wetness, filling her up, only drove her closer to the edge. God, she wanted to feel him thrusting into her, and not just with his fingers. Every inch of Reggie was skilled in pleasing her, and she loved that about him.

"Fuck, I wanna keep you. Can I keep you, baby?" he groaned as she clenched around his fingers, his name falling like a devout prayer from her lips.

She couldn't answer. Or maybe she was too afraid to answer, afraid of what she'd commit herself to as wave after wave of pleasure hit her. Reggie bit her neck and pressed down on her clit, rubbing relentlessly and sending her straight into another orgasm.

"Fuck! Yes…God, yes, Reggie," she moaned.

"You're mine for the taking, isn't that right?" he said, his hips thrusting into her as his dick, slick from the shower, slid between her cheeks, making him groan.

"I'm yours," she repeated back to him, and God help her, Makayla meant it.

Her nails dug into the back of his neck as she came down from the wave of pleasure, her breath coming in pants. He grunted, his hips giving another involuntary thrust as if begging to gain entrance. She turned and looked at him, her eyes hooded and her body languid and satisfied as she wrapped her hand around his length. Just the feel of him there made her want him even more. They both groaned as she swiped the tip of him over her clit.

Reggie's body crowded hers as he backed her against the opposite shower wall, both hands framing either side of her. All that could be heard over the sound of the water was their panting. Makayla watched Reggie close his eyes as she moved him up and down her slit, coating him with the evidence of her need. She notched him at her entrance, just the tip of him pressed against her heat, and his eyes opened, flashing.

"I should…we should get a condom."

His voice was thick, and the words practically came out as a growl. Makayla knew that he was right. They'd used protection every time since that morning in his closet. This was reckless. It was irresponsible. They were playing with fire when it would only take a few steps to get what they needed from the other room.

Yet what left her mouth wasn't, "Ok." No, instead, "We…we don't have to," slipped out instead. She was lightheaded and hot, and damn it, she just wanted to feel him inside of her.

A question filled Reggie's eyes. *The* question. "Are you sure?" he asked.

Precum leaked from his tip, mixing with her own orgasm. Every sensible thought in her head was screaming for her to slow this down, back him up, and reevaluate before she fell in too deep, but she already knew it was too late.

"I'm sure," Makayla whispered as she wrapped one leg around his waist, not only pulling his body in closer but sliding his dick into her. They groaned in unison. One of Reggie's hands came down to grip her hip and hold her steady as he slowly pushed into her. He watched the place where they were joined, and she couldn't help but watch him. Was he really this beautiful, or was that her body talking? Did the sight of him, so enraptured by her, really make her heart skip a beat, or was that just the sensation of her pussy walls gripping him for dear life?

She didn't have time to contemplate the answer to her questions because suddenly, he was fully seated between her thighs, teeth gritted, jaw clenched. She'd never felt so full.

"God," she gasped, her head falling back against the dripping tile.

Her hips rolled of their own accord, and he let loose a grunt. "Shit. Wait, baby girl. Ju—just give me a second."

She could hear the strain in his voice as his fingers tightened around her hips, threatening to leave a bruise. Makayla was even more turned on as she realized the power she had over him, so much so that moved again, tightening her walls against his thickness and sending a guttural "Fuck!" flying from Reggie's lips.

He looked at her, pleading—though she couldn't be sure if it was a plea for her to stop or keep going. In the end, she decided to do what felt best. The steady motion of her hips pressed her clit right against his pelvis, causing the most delicious friction she'd ever felt. Just the right tilt had him angling against her g-spot. She didn't even attempt to stop the soft words of praise that began falling from her lips.

"More…" she begged. She needed him to move, to give her his own thrusts, but he refused. "You feel so good baby. I need more." Her hands gripped her shoulders as she gave her hips a slow whine. "*Pleeease*. I want it so fucking bad."

Instead of giving her what she wanted, he pressed his chest to hers as she continued to ride his dick as best she could. The way he had them positioned forced her to move at a deliciously slow pace. He wasn't in a hurry, and he clearly wanted to make sure that she wasn't either. Makayla wrapped her arms around Reggie's neck, and he picked her up, his hands holding either leg as he continued to press her against the shower wall.

"I want you, Makayla," he said, whispering the words against her skin as he gave her one single slow thrust.

"Reggie," she whimpered.

"Do you want me?" he asked, his lips moving to hover over hers.

"Yes," she gasped as he pushed into her again, all too soon pulling out before delivering another lazy thrust.

"Tell me. Let me hear you say it." She could feel his eyes on her, and as much as she wanted to fight it, she couldn't. She opened her eyes to meet his gaze, and the emotions she saw there almost strangled the life out of her.

"I want you," she whispered, wishing she could keep the truth and vulnerability out of her words.

His lips devoured hers as he fucked into her, picking up the pace just enough to satisfy them both. The sex the two of them had before had been amazing on so many levels, but this…this was different. They weren't just fucking. Makayla could feel it in her bones. It felt as if his dick was touching her soul. Maybe that was why she continued to repeat the words he'd asked for, saying them over and over again with each thrust until she was sure they both couldn't deny the truth.

She gripped the back of his neck for dear life as they kissed, their mouths just as hungry for each other as every other part of their bodies. Soon Reggie's slow strokes picked up speed, and her legs began to tremble.

"Show me how much you want me, Makayla," Reggie said, his eyes staring straight into hers as her ankles locked behind him. "Come on this dick." He reached a hand between them, his thumb pressing down on her bundle of nerves. "Let me feel you come."

She didn't need any more direction than that. Not when his words, his dick, and his fingers were all demanding the same thing from her. Her thighs shook, and she moaned uncontrollably from the force of her orgasm.

"Shiiiit," Reggie groaned as his strokes stuttered. He leaned into her for support, his own pleasure hitting him as her walls sucked him in deeper and refused to let him go. The feel of his cum hitting her walls only prolonged her own pleasure, after-shocks running through her entire body.

The two of them stood there, clutching one another and breathing heavily for what seemed like hours. Makayla could feel the evidence of what they'd done begin to drip down her thigh. Reggie placed soft, whisper-light kisses along her skin, and when they finally pulled apart and washed one another clean, all Makayla could think was that it was too late. She was already way too far gone.

CHAPTER 28

Reggie

Despite the fact that Reggie had a ridiculous amount of work to catch up on, he couldn't seem to focus. He was supposed to be finishing up an article on the new trend of restaurateurs making the leap from food trucks to brick-and-mortar locations. Instead, the only thing his mind could seem to focus on was Makayla. The look on her face when she whimpered. The way she moaned his name in his ear. The absolute terror that seemed to come over her when her mother brought up marriage the other night after the outdoor movie. It was all just playing on a loop.

He knew that her mother hadn't meant anything by it. Well, that wasn't completely true. Her mother was absolutely hoping that their relationship—or at least the one that she knew of—would lead to something more serious. To be honest, he found himself hoping the same thing. If her behavior before the comment was any indication, Makayla seemed to want the same thing. Despite how they'd started this arrangement of theirs, this wasn't just as simple as pretending for her family. He'd hoped that Makayla would just be able to laugh off her mother's joke and move along, but the moment he saw her reaction, he knew she would start to freak out.

She'd been tense and uncomfortable after that. The entire drive back to her house, it had been obvious that she was having trouble getting out of her own head. He'd honestly expected her to send him home after dropping her off. Once she'd invited him in and they'd made love—that was the only way he could describe it—Reggie had thought that Makayla was beginning to come to terms with what they were feeling for each other. Then they'd woken up, and she'd mumbled something about deadlines before sending him packing. He'd taken it in stride, of course. This was a lot to process, and Reggie was willing to give her as much time as she needed. The only problem was that it was now a full week later, and he barely heard from her. Every message he'd sent had gotten one word responses or gone completely ignored.

It made him nervous. For the last couple months, the two of them had been talking damn near every day. Not to mention the amount of time they'd started spending together had become constant as well. It was starting to feel like they'd suddenly taken ten steps back.

A buzzer sounded through his condo, pulling Reggie from his thoughts. A small part of him hoped that it was Makayla popping in to surprise him. Maybe let him know that he was worried for nothing.

Not fucking likely, he thought, heading toward the door.

"Yo."

"It's me, let me up," Lucas's voice said through the speaker.

The last thing he wanted to deal with was his best friend getting into his business right now, but turning Lucas away wasn't an option. He'd already been dodging the man's calls.

Almost as much as Makayla has been dodging you.

He pushed the irritating thought out of his head and buzzed Lucas in before unlocking the door. Reggie contemplated heading back to his office but considering he hadn't been getting any work done anyway, he grabbed a beer from the fridge and took a seat on the couch. Just as SportsCenter appeared on his flat screen, Lucas came walking through the door.

"Oh, so your ass is alive, huh? I guess I can tell Avery to call off the search team."

Instead of responding, Reggie simply took a sip of his beer. Maybe if he ignored his friend long enough, he would get the hint and just leave. Clearly, luck was not on his side because instead, Lucas walked over and smacked him upside the head.

"What the fuck is your problem?" Reggie grunted as his head snapped toward Lucas.

"So what, I gotta beat your ass now to get a reaction out of you? Come on, bruh, what's wrong with you? Tell Big Poppa."

Despite himself, Reggie couldn't help the choked laughter he let out. "I told you I am not calling you that, Luke. *Nobody* is calling your ass that."

"That's because y'all are a bunch of haters," he responded, sucking his teeth.

Reggie just shook his head and watched the highlights from last night's Stallions' football game. The two men sat in silence for a few minutes, both waiting for the other to finally break. Lucas was first.

"So, are you going to tell me what has you in such a pissy mood, or are you going to make me guess?"

Reggie acted as if he hadn't said anything. After another minute, Lucas sighed. "Ok, shouldn't be too hard to figure out. I'm thinking whatever is bugging you happens to be about five-eight, stacked, works for a killer magazine, and is a total pool shark." When Reggie didn't respond, Lucas went on. "Oh, and did I mention she has lips that look like they could su—"

Before he could finish the sentence, Reggie had him out of his seat and hemmed up by his collar. "Just kidding! I swear," said Lucas as he threw his hands up in surrender.

Reggie set him down and rolled his eyes. "You are such a jackass."

"Yeah, well, I've been told it's one of my best qualities."

"By who?" Reggie said incredulously.

"Not your ungrateful ass, that's for sure," Lucas snorted. Once he made himself comfortable, he looked at his best friend, a serious expression on his face. "What's going on, man? Talk to me."

The urge to brush Lucas off was almost immediate, but Reggie knew it wouldn't do any good. Maybe what he needed to do was talk to someone about this. Even though the other man tended to joke more often than not, Reggie knew that if anyone was willing to hear him out and give him their honest thoughts, it was Lucas.

"It's this whole thing with Makayla."

"She finally wised up and cut your ass loose?"

His tone was joking, but Reggie was not in the mood. He shot Lucas what could only be described as a death glare.

"Ok, no more joke time. Got it."

A sigh left Reggie's lips. "She's been avoiding me all week. I figured that things would get dodgy after movie night at her mother's house. Her sister was on her ass for most of the night, and then her mom made this offhand comment about us getting married."

"Wait, what?" Lucas said, suddenly sitting up straight.

"Yeah, I know. I don't think she was a hundred percent serious, but Makayla did not take the comment well. We went back to her place after, and honestly, considering what we did that night, I thought we were good, but I guess her mom's comment freaked her out more than she let on."

"Do you think that's all that freaked her out, or could it have something to do with whatever it is y'all...did?"

That was what Reggie had been worried about. He'd been trying to avoid thinking about the things they'd both said while he was inside of her, but that wasn't really possible. And there wasn't really much he could do about it now. Even if he could take back everything that had been said, he knew that he wouldn't.

"I think...I think that it was both." The weight of Lucas's gaze was almost too much for him. It made him so antsy that he jumped up and began pacing in front of the couch. "I may or may not have asked if I could keep her."

A mumbled "Shit..." came from Lucas's side of the room.

"And that may or may not have been followed by me telling her I wanted her. Like...really wanted her. And..." he cleared his throat, "me asking whether or not she really wanted me, too."

Lucas let out a string of curses. "Okay...and she said what exactly?"

"Yes, to both." Reggie finally stopped pacing and turned to face his friend. "And I think it freaked her the fuck out because she meant that shit."

"Did you?"

"Of course, I did," Reggie said, throwing his hands up. "I wouldn't just say that shit for no damn reason. I'm feeling the fuck out of her, Luke."

"So, try telling her that. I mean while you're not fucking her. It may go over better that way."

Reggie let out a groan. "I've been trying. I've been calling and texting her, trying to get her to just talk to me. I can't fix anything if she doesn't talk to me." Lucas went to say something, but Reggie wasn't finished. "I mean, shit, I know this is scary for her. It's the last thing she wanted. But I thought...I thought..."

"You thought because of how much time y'all have been spending together, when she realized you were falling for her, she wouldn't think it was such a bad thing," Lucas finished for him.

Reggie sighed as he finally took his seat again. "Yeah. That's exactly what I thought."

Lucas nodded in understanding. "I get it, man. I do. And y'all are cute as fuck together, there's no denying that. But take a minute and think about this. Making this shit real between y'all literally goes against the whole reason she started this arrangement in the first place. I know you mean well, and I know you're feeling her. We both know you're an all-or-nothing type of guy. Sometimes that shit can be overwhelming if the other person already feels off-balance."

Reggie could only let out a grunt because he knew what Lucas was saying was true. As much as he meant what he'd said to Makayla, he couldn't deny that he had laid it on a bit thick. All the walls were down, feelings exposed, not even the barrier of protection between them. Even he could admit that it was all a bit much. Maybe if they hadn't been in the heat of the moment, he would've approached things a little differently, but once again, he'd led with his feelings, and it had gotten him in trouble. Shit, this whole arrangement had been him leading with his feelings, hadn't it?

"You can't force her to talk to you, Reg. My guess, though, is you won't have to. One way or another, she's going to let you know what's next. You just have to be a little patient and wait for her to come to you."

Reggie nodded in agreement. Everything he'd said made sense. Makayla's biggest thing in the past had been the fact that her partners had tried to suffocate her with their expectations. That was the last thing he wanted to do. Besides, she couldn't avoid him forever. The rehearsal dinner was the day after tomorrow, and he had no intention of missing it.

"Come on, man," Lucas said, hands slapping his knees as he stood. "Go change so we can head out to the rec center. You're not going to get anything done here. Plus, having me whoop your ass in a little one-on-one will get your mind off of all this shit."

"Do you ever stop talking trash?" Reggie asked with a chuckle.

"Of course not. What fun would that be?"

CHAPTER 29

Makayla

Can't wait to see you tonight. Might be a few minutes late, but trust me, I'll be there.

Makayla had been staring at that text message all day. For a little over a week now, she'd been avoiding Reggie like the plague. She'd found every excuse in the book on why she was too busy to see him or just ignored him completely. That night in her shower felt like emotional overload. She'd told that man that she wanted him and meant it. Told him that he could keep her. Hell, she had let the man come inside her with no fucking condom, and that was some shit she never did. She couldn't even remember the last time she'd had unprotected sex and yet somehow she'd been down that road twice with Reggie. This man had her so far gone that her head was spinning. Her world was turning upside down, and she did not like it. At all.

So, in true Makayla fashion, she'd played the avoidance game and thrown herself back into her work. She'd had little to no conversation with Reggie over the last ten days. At first, it'd been easier than she'd expected. She'd had plenty to do to keep her mind occupied—from staff meetings to mockup reviews, work had been her comfort.

Around day four, however, things had started to get a bit shaky. She found herself checking her phone more, wanting to know what Reggie thought about something she'd seen or bounce ideas off of him. She hadn't even realized how much she'd begun to look forward to their daily chats and interactions. Everything about this terrified her because this was *not* how this was supposed to go.

What had really thrown her for a loop was when Reggie's messages and calls had stopped on day seven. She'd gotten nervous, wondering if she had pushed too much. When she'd gotten the text from him this morning, a part of her had been relieved to know he was coming, but on the other end of that, she was confused as hell. Maybe she was overreacting. Maybe things didn't have to be this stressful and complicated. She enjoyed Reggie's company, his conversation was great, and the sex was amazing. Did she have to make it more difficult than that?

She'd resolved to get over any weirdness. Tonight was the rehearsal dinner, and soon, the wedding would be here, and this entire ordeal would be over.

But what does that mean for you and Reggie?

That was the question that plagued her as she fidgeted with her golden-toned jumpsuit. It was the same color as the brides-maid dresses they'd decided on. Her mother had wanted them to coordinate their outfits tonight with the color they'd wear the day of the wedding. She stood at the bar as she waited for her drink to arrive, so close to chewing a hole in her bottom lip, but she couldn't seem to stop herself.

"You look fucking amazing," a husky voice whispered in her

ear. Her eyes closed as she arched toward the voice. Over a week apart, and he still had the same effect on her.

Makayla opened her eyes, attempting to get control over herself as she turned to face Reggie. "You clean up pretty well yourself."

That was quite the understatement. In his tapered navy slacks and crisp white button-up, he looked practically edible. Reggie pulled her into a hug, and she didn't know whether to run for the hills or melt into him.

"Yeah, well, we can't have me out here looking like I don't have any home training. My grandmother would have my neck. Besides," he pulled her in close, "can't have people wondering whose date showed up looking raggedy, right?"

He chuckled, and while she found herself laughing with him, the word 'date' had her looking for her drink once again.

Get a fucking grip, she chastised herself.

Right on time, the bartender handed over her whiskey and Coke. Makayla tried to sip slow and steady, very aware that Reggie was watching her. Did he expect her to say something about that fateful Sunday night? Because if she had any power over the situation, they would *not* be talking about that tonight.

"Listen, about what happened. What I said, I—"

"Don't worry about it. We just got caught up in the moment, right?" she said, cutting him off before he could say anything else.

Reggie looked ready to protest but stopped himself. "Yeah. I guess you could say that." He sighed, and the look on his face nearly broke her. "Listen, it's obvious you don't want to talk about it, and I get that. I just wanted to say if I made you uncomfortable in any way, that wasn't my intention. I know intention still doesn't change the outcome, but I just wanted to apologize since things got out of hand."

Makayla wanted to just agree and move on, but she couldn't

just leave him out there on his own. She was an adult, after all, and it wasn't as if he'd forced her into anything.

"It's not just on you. You weren't in that situation by yourself. And I know you didn't mean any harm by it."

"I didn't. Don't get me wrong, I meant every word of what I said," Reggie responded, and the intensity in his eyes had her ready to run from the room. "But I also know where you stand on everything and our situation. I respect that. I just needed you to know that while the sex was amazing, that's not the only reason I said what I said."

Reggie reached out and cupped her chin. "But the ball is in your court, and there's no pressure. I'm good with where we are, and I won't push you for more unless that's what you want. I just wanted you to know that."

Makayla swallowed thickly, unable to form any words that made sense. Scratch that. What she wanted to say technically made sense, but saying it was not an option right now. Truth was, she didn't know what she wanted beyond making it through tonight with her sanity intact. Relationships had never been her strong suit. Finding Reggie didn't change that. She was still the same person she'd always been, and before long, that would begin to weigh on him just like it had weighed on every other man she'd tried to date. She wasn't going to put herself through a bunch of bullshit again just because her feelings told her to.

Reggie's different. This is different.

Neither one of those things could be denied, but that didn't mean that *she* was any different. But maybe the question wasn't whether or not she was a different person. Maybe the question was, did she *want* something different now?

Before she could contemplate the answer to that question, the sound of metal tapping glass rang out through the restaurant. She looked up to see her mother and Percy on stage attempting to get everyone's attention. "Okay, y'all settle down! The old folks have something to say before we get this night started."

Everyone chuckled. Makayla looked up at Reggie, unsure of what to say. "Don't worry about it, baby girl. We're just going with the flow, right?"

"Right." The tension in her shoulders said otherwise, and he clearly noticed. He placed a light kiss on her lips.

"Come on. Chug your drink, grab a champagne, and let's head to our seats before your Mama embarrasses us out here. You know she's wild."

This time, the laugh that left her was genuine. He was right. If the two of them didn't get to their seats soon, Delilah would absolutely be calling them out in front of everyone. She followed his directions and then let Reggie guide her toward their table where her sisters, their husbands, and Jasmine and her date were sitting.

Her mother and Percy waited for everyone to get settled before speaking again. "First of all, we want to thank everyone for joining us here tonight. Y'all could've literally been anywhere else in the world, and yet you're here with us."

"Uh-uh, Auntie! Not you stealing from Hov!" Jasmine yelled from her place at the table, making everyone laugh.

"Girl, hush! No one else even noticed that until you pointed it out!"

"Yes, we did," Makayla and her sisters chimed in, which only led to more laughter.

Their mother huffed as if she was aggravated, but Percy only chuckled. "Okay, okay. Y'all leave my woman alone," he said, placing a peck on her cheek.

"Thank you, baby," Delilah said, beaming. "Anyway, as I was saying before I was rudely interrupted," she shot a pointed look at her daughters, "we really appreciate everyone coming to celebrate with us. If you let Percy tell it, this has been a long time coming, and to be honest, he's right."

"Aww, shucks, y'all heard that, right? I've got witnesses!" Percy said.

Everyone laughed as Delilah rolled her eyes. "You better savor it because that's the last time I'll be saying that. Now hush so I can finish."

Makayla couldn't help but laugh a bit harder. Her mother and Percy were a mess no matter where they were. She knew that her mother was only partially joking, though. It would probably be a very long time before she admitted that Percy was right about something again.

"You all know that life and love haven't always been kind to me or my girls." Delilah turned her eyes toward her daughters, and Makayla couldn't help the pang that shot through her chest as she noticed the sad smile that didn't quite reach her mother's eyes.

"So, when this fine gentleman walked into that karaoke bar and into my life, the last thing I was looking to do was start dating again and open myself up to more heartbreak. But..." She swung her gaze toward Percy, who was looking at her as if she was the only woman on Earth. "But I also knew that I couldn't let the past dictate how I spend my future. I had to take the bull by the horns and believe that love was meant for me just as much as it was meant for anyone else." She wrapped her arm around Percy's neck as he leaned down and whispered in her ear. The way that Delilah lit up sent an indescribable feeling through Makayla. She didn't know if she'd ever had that reaction to a man.

Was that how she looked when she was with Reggie?

Of course not. No matter what he says, whatever you have going on could never compare to them.

"And Lord knows I'm so glad I did because after he finished getting on my nerves," she said with a laugh, "he captured my heart." Tears were shining in Delilah's eyes now.

"And I haven't let it go since," Percy said, which only made the tears her mother had been holding begin to fall.

"No, you haven't." She leaned over and placed a kiss on his

lips. "And I must say I don't have not one complaint." Her eyes turned back to the crowd and seemed to find Makayla instantly. It took everything in her not to squirm under her mother's gaze.

"My only wish is that this love that we share is spread to everyone here, especially each one of my girls. And I think...I think I can finally say that that wish is coming true."

Makayla ducked her head, and she could only hope that it looked like she was embarrassed or overcome with emotion. In reality, she felt like she was going to be sick. Her mother had just made a speech about finding love and happiness, ending it by saying that all of her daughters had managed to find love too. How could she ever tell her mother that that wasn't true? The truth was that she was a complete fraud. The realization that her mother was going to be heartbroken when she discovered the truth damn near sent Makayla flying from the room.

Reggie reached over to give her hand a squeeze, and she looked at him briefly. Part of her was happy to have someone else to focus on, her mother's words hitting a bit too close to home. The other part of her wanted to pull away from him. He was part of the problem. How could she pretend to be happy with him for the rest of the night, knowing it was a lie?

But it's not a lie, that voice said again.

Of course, it was! No matter how much fun the two of them had been having, no matter what it looked like from the outside or from Reggie's point of view, this arrangement always had an expiration date. She wasn't cut out for love. There was no point in pretending otherwise.

But what about Reggie? Doesn't he get a say in this?

Makayla swallowed and went through the motions of commemorating her mother's toast while she battled with herself.

Did Reggie get a say in this? Sure, he'd agreed to it, and yes, this had turned into something neither of them had expected, but exactly how far was either one of them ready to go with this? The truth was that she could never be the long-term girlfriend that he was looking for. He deserved someone who was going to turn their life upside down for him. Someone who wouldn't hesitate to pick up his calls even if they were busy with work. Someone who wouldn't break dates or make excuses for why they were too busy to get together. It wouldn't take long for him to figure that out, would it? Sure, he'd been understanding throughout this whole arrangement, but this wasn't normal relationship behavior for Makayla. What happened when she went back to her usual self, too busy to make time for him or their relationship because she needed to focus on her career? He would leave, or she would end things because there was no way he could truly understand that her career was what made her happy and what would always come first. So why drag this out any longer than necessary? They'd already involved their family and friends in enough of the lie, and prolonging the inevitable would only make things worse.

As Makayla tipped back her champagne glass, she steeled herself with resolve. She had to end things with Reggie. The only question was when and how. The wedding was in a few days. Should she end things with Reggie now and save them both the hassle of him having to come to the wedding on Saturday? Did she wait and just end things after the wedding as planned? All of her questions were making her head swim. She had no idea what she was going to do or if she'd be ready to deal with the fallout of her decision.

Makayla couldn't think of anything else for the rest of the night. She danced, ate, and laughed at all the right moments, but the entire time, there was only one thing on her mind. She could tell by Reggie's face that she wasn't doing the best job of hiding her anxiety, but he didn't press her on what was wrong. She was grateful for that.

As the night wound down, she was glad that this time, she'd driven herself. As Reggie walked her to her car at the end of the night, she held onto his hand, relishing the way it seemed to fit perfectly with hers.

"Are we good?" he asked, staring down at her.

She nodded. "We're good."

He nodded, a smirk playing on his lips. "So, does that mean you'll be following me home, or is it the other way around?"

She gave him a smile and hoped it didn't look as weak as it felt. "I'm exhausted. I think I'm just going to head home. I have to head into work early tomorrow, and since Friday is a spa day, I'll have a lot to do, so…" She let her words trail off.

"Soooo, you don't need the very nice distraction I had planned for you. Got it." Reggie leaned down and pressed his lips to hers. She opened up just enough for his tongue to find hers. She loved the way this man tasted, the way his body felt against her. That only lent itself to confusing her even more. Still, Makayla deepened the kiss, gripping his neck like it was the last time she'd get the chance.

When they finally pulled away from each other, breathing labored, she could barely stand to look him in the eyes. "I'll call you," she whispered against his lips.

Reggie placed one more soft kiss on her mouth. "I'll be waiting."

Makayla spent the entire ride home agonizing over what to do. Every time she settled on a decision, she found herself retracting it.

This isn't what you signed up for. Just stick to the agreement and cut him loose once it's all over. He'll understand.

What sense does that make when everything is going this well? What about your family? Did you really think that you could bring him in like this and no one would ask questions once it was over?

Screw the family, what about you? Are you really going to be able to go back to acting like none of this ever happened?

"No," she said aloud. And it was the truth. It wouldn't be easy to forget about Reggie and everything they'd shared. But she also knew that deciding on the alternative and continuing this relationship could only end one way: with her being hurt and both of them being disappointed.

By the time she made it into her house, she'd made up her mind. She had to stop whatever this was in its tracks. End things and cut her losses before it got any more out of hand than it already had. There were only a few days left until the wedding. What was the harm in letting things go now? Why put off the inevitable? This relationship always had an expiration date so maybe it was best for both of them if she just moved it up a bit and gave him an out now. Either he'd take it or he wouldn't. Either way, she had to be clear that once the wedding was over, so were they.

She pulled out her phone and took a deep breath, steeling her resolve and typing out the message.

> Reggie, first I need you to know that these last few months have been… amazing. Truly. I'd be lying if I said that they were anything but.

She erased that message because, what the hell was that? Emotional was not the way to go with this. She tried to find the words a few more times, each attempt more difficult than the previous one. Finally, she settled on what to say.

Thanks again for coming tonight. I know that both this wedding and I have already taken up way too much of your time, so if you want, we can consider tonight the last hurrah. You're obviously still welcome to come Saturday, but you've officially held up your end of the bargain. You're a free man starting now, if you want to be.

After pressing send, she tried to convince herself that this was all for the best. So then, why, she thought as she pressed send, did it feel as though her chest was going to cave in?

CHAPTER 30

Reggie

"So, what exactly is the plan here?" Avery asked Reggie. She'd followed him into his spare bedroom and proceeded to stare at him as he checked his reflection in the closet mirror.

Reggie could feel the woman's eyes on him. The skepticism was loud and clear in her voice. "What do you mean?" he asked.

"She means," Lucas said, walking into the room and leaning against the mirror, beer in hand, "are you actually still going to this wedding on Saturday?"

"Why wouldn't I?" Reggie asked. He was purposely avoiding both of his friends' eyes in the mirror. He could feel their judgment whether they meant him to or not, and he was not even going to give life to what he knew they were both thinking right now.

"Are you serious right now? Is he serious, or is he fucking with us?" Avery asked incredulously.

A muscle in Reggie's jaw ticked. He didn't need this right now. They may mean well, but he did not need them to tell him he was making a mistake. The little voice in his head was telling him that enough for everyone in the room.

"I agreed to go to the wedding as her date. Why the fuck would I back out now?"

"Ummm, I don't know. Maybe because homegirl basically sent you a big fuck you last night?" Avery's voice took on that high-pitched quality it gained whenever she felt like no one was listening to her. Reggie was listening. He just didn't want to hear what she had to say.

"I think what our dear pixie-sized friend is trying to say," Lucas said, stepping closer to the mirror, "is that yes, that's what y'all talked about originally, but things have changed now. Or at least, it seems to us that they've changed."

Reggie wondered if Lucas was aware that Avery was shooting him a death glare for that pixie comment. He tried to focus on that instead of what was actually being said.

Apparently, Avery wasn't having any of that. She walked over to where he stood and punched Reggie in the shoulder. "Yo, Avery, really?" he said in an annoyed tone as he turned around to face her. "Why are you being so childish?"

"Because you're being an asshole," she snapped back. "You said it yourself that she's been avoiding you since before the rehearsal dinner. And then on top of that, instead of telling you to your face that whatever y'all have been doing is over, she waits until she gets home to send you a damn text message. How does that translate into anything other than I'm done with you?"

"She clearly said in the message that I'm still welcome to come to the wedding." It was a weak argument, but one that he was trying to cling to.

"We all know that she only said that because she didn't want to seem like a complete bitch," Avery said, rolling her eyes.

"Avery, chill," Lucas and Reggie both said at the same time.

"You can be mad all you want, but what you're not going to do is be disrespectful," Reggie added.

The truth was that Reggie didn't know what to think after seeing that text Makayla sent after the rehearsal dinner.

> Thanks again for coming tonight. I know that both this wedding and I have already taken up way too much of your time, so if you want, we can consider tonight the last hurrah. You're obviously still welcome to come Saturday, but you've officially held up your end of the bargain. You're a free man starting now, if you want to be.

The minute he'd gotten that message, he'd called her. Actually, he'd called her a total of four times back-to-back last night before she finally turned her phone off. Today, he'd resorted to leaving voicemails and sending her text messages. Anything to get her to acknowledge him and just talk to him about what the fuck was going on. No such luck.

Mentally, he was kicking his own ass for pretending like he hadn't seen this coming. Though he'd gone to the rehearsal dinner and she'd had a smile on her face the entire night, he'd known that things still weren't quite right between them. Every instinct in his body had told him that she was going to push him away. He'd convinced himself that he was just overreacting, imagining things. Hell, he'd hoped that at the very least, she would have talked to him about whatever she was scared of so that they could work it out. Apparently, that was too much to ask for.

It didn't matter, though. He wasn't going to go back on his word and skip out on the wedding. And he wasn't about to let her go without making it clear how he felt. His grandmother had always told him to fight for what he wanted, so that was exactly what he was going to do.

"You're right. I don't know whether she really wants me there or not, but I'm going because it's what I promised to do. And I want—no, I *need* to see her. If she doesn't want me at the wedding, she can tell me that when I get there. If she really wants to end things, she can tell me that to my face. If she never wants to see me again…" He paused as he straightened his lapel.

"If she never wants to see me again, well then… I'll respect her wishes. Either way, I made a commitment and I'm going to see it through because that's what *I* want to do."

The silence between the three of them seemed to stretch on forever. Reggie could tell that both Lucas and Avery were still skeptical.

"So, what happens if she says this shit really is over? What if she meant what she said in the text message? Are you going to be able to handle that?" Lucas finally asked.

Reggie didn't even want to think about that. The moment he'd read that text, he'd felt his heart breaking. Maybe he wasn't supposed to admit shit like that, but fuck it. These last few months had been nothing short of amazing, despite how corny it sounded. He'd never expected to fall for Makayla this hard and this fast. Everything about her intoxicated him. His grandmother had always said Reggie loved with his entire being. As usual, she'd been right.

He couldn't help the chuckle that escaped him at the thought. Even though his feelings scared the shit out of him, he was determined not to hide from them. He'd been running for a long time. Running from the death of his grandmother. Running from what happened in Costa Rica. Running from the possibility of losing someone he loved all over again. He couldn't keep letting the past dictate how he moved.

"Hello, Earth to Reggie," Lucas said, snapping his fingers in front of his face.

Reggie slid his jacket from his arms and tossed it onto the bed. "I don't know. Shit, what do you want me to say? I feel like I'm wading through quicksand right now. I don't have any answers, y'all. I just know that I have to try."

Running his hand over his face, he took a seat on the bed. "I think she could be the one, y'all. I just…need the space and time to explore that."

"Damn." Lucas shook his head and clapped his hand on Reggie's shoulder.

"Exactly. And as wild as that sounds, it would be even wilder for me to let her slip through my fingers without even trying to hold on."

Lucas nodded, understanding exactly what his friend was saying. "Well, for what it's worth, man, I hope she doesn't throw you out on your ass Saturday. Especially since I won't be there to see it if she does."

"Boy, shut up!" shouted Avery as she tossed a pillow at his head. "You always running your mouth."

Shaking her head, she turned to look at Reggie. "Listen, I can't say that I'm overly excited about this whole thing. I don't appreciate her taking the coward's way out and sending you that raggedy ass text message, but…" Her words trailed off as a smile spread across her face. "She makes you happy, Reg. What type of friends would we be if we stood in the way of that?"

Avery wrapped her arms around Reggie and pulled him into a hug. "But Lucas is right. If she throws you out on your ass, make sure someone catches it on camera."

A laugh bubbled up from Reggie's chest. He was thankful for both of his friends doing what they could to lighten the moment. He needed it because truth be told, Reggie was scared shitless. Scared that Makayla would reject him. Scared that she really wasn't feeling the same things that he was. Scared that he'd lost one of the best people to ever walk into his life. And more than anything, scared that there was nothing he could do about it.

CHAPTER 31

Makayla

"Okay, tell me what's wrong," said Jasmine with a sigh as she sat down and looked across at Makayla. Makayla shrugged, making a move to get another spoonful of cookie dough ice cream, but Jasmine snatched it away from her.

"Hey!" Makayla whined.

"Spit it out, sis. You've been moping all day, to the point where you even left work early. It's obvious something happened after the rehearsal dinner last night. I've been here for almost three hours, and you've been avoiding this shit the whole time. As much as I love you, I do not have another three hours to wait on your ass. So please, *SPIT. IT. OUT!*"

Instead of saying anything, Makayla simply handed Jasmine her phone to show her the message she'd sent to Reggie the night before.

"Ok…" Jasmine said, clearly confused.

This girl was really about to make Makayla say it. She kissed her teeth as she tipped her head back to look at the ceiling. After a few seconds, she finally let it out. "I let Reggie off the hook and ended things."

She waited for the other woman to say something—anything —but she was met with silence. After a few moments, Makayla looked over at her best friend. The only thing Jasmine seemed to have for her was a raised eyebrow.

"What?" Makayla asked, now just as confused as the other woman had been.

"Ummm…" Jasmine started. "What exactly is there to 'end' with Reggie?"

"Girl!" Makayla snatched her ice cream back and rolled her eyes.

"I'm just asking! Last I heard, y'all were in a fake ass relationship and happened to be spending some very real time together while doing so extremely real fucking. So, I say again, what exactly are you ending?"

"The whole thing!" she said, throwing up her arms. "The hanging out, the sex, the extra ass feelings. I signed up for a fake ass boyfriend, not all this extra shit." Makayla gave an exasperated sigh. Saying all of that aloud made everything feel that much more real. She hated the strangled feeling that appeared in her chest at her words.

"So, what you're saying is, you wanted a fake boyfriend but fucked around and tripped into some real ass feelings."

Makayla shot daggers at her best friend but finally caved. "Yes," she mumbled.

"Mmhmm…"

The two of them went silent. Makayla watched as her best friend seemed to be contemplating something. Jasmine rarely held her tongue on anything, so she wasn't sure why she seemed to be doing exactly that.

"Okay, so…straight, no chaser?" Jasmine asked, looking at Makayla.

"Always," she answered without hesitation.

Jasmine sat up, put the container of ice cream down on the coffee table, and leaned toward her best friend. "This is bullshit."

Makayla's head snapped back as if the other woman had smacked her. Even though she probably could've guessed what Jasmine was going to say, that didn't make hearing it any less shocking.

"If what you really wanted to do was end whatever the two of y'all have been doing, you would have called him or met him face-to-face and told him thanks, but no thanks. Hell, you just saw the man last night! You could've easily let him know then that this arrangement wasn't working out anymore. Instead, you took the childish way out and sent him a text message. And if these missed calls and messages are any indication, you proceeded to ignore him when he tried to talk to you about your decision."

Makayla felt the heat rising in her cheeks because that was exactly what happened. Instead of facing him, she'd ignored his calls and tried to focus on something—anything— else.

After taking a breath, Jasmine continued. "Listen, sis, we've been friends for more than half of our lives at this point, so I think I have a good handle on you as a person, right? Which makes me feel like I'm qualified to say that you have a pretty fucked up view of love and relationships. You treat them both like they're the plague, and the only reasoning that I can come up with is that you're scared of love."

"Umm...excuse me?" Makayla said, taken aback. Jasmine nodded. "Scared? That's your diagnosis?"

"Yep. After all these years, it's the only thing that actually makes sense. You've always had this...this really weird hang-up about relationships. Or I guess, better yet, *your* relationships."

Makayla was in shock. Or hearing her wrong. Or both. That was the only explanation for what was happening right now. "No," she said finally, shaking her head. "You're wrong."

"Okay," Jasmine said with a head tilt. "Then explain to me

exactly why you catching feelings for Reggie is such a bad idea. What's your actual reason for ending whatever y'all had going on?"

Makayla let out a frustrated sigh. "I don't have time for this shit. I have plans. Expectations. Goals! I do not have time to try and placate a man's ego because I have to cancel a date for work, or I don't have time to be available whenever he wants me to be. Chasing after a man is not on my agenda."

"I'm pretty sure if anyone is doing the chasing in this situation, it's Reggie, not you," Jasmine cut in.

"That's not the point!" huffed Makayla. "The point is long-term relationships just don't work for me. I don't have time for them. You know this!"

"Noooo, actually, I don't know that for sure. I just know what you tell me."

Makayla looked at her friend in disbelief. "You cannot be serious right now."

Jasmine shrugged. "I'm just saying. I know we talk about your busy schedule, and I know we joke about how you're anti-relationship or whatever, but honestly…" She paused. "I think that the real reason you don't do long-term relationships is because they terrify you."

Makayla scoffed and crossed her arms. "And what exactly would I be terrified of?"

"I don't know, bitch, maybe being vulnerable!" Jasmine threw her hands up as she stood from her chair.

"Be honest, girl, opening up isn't exactly one of your strengths. Hell, it took you forever to get to the point where you opened up to me, and sometimes it feels like you still hold back. You've never been an emotional person, and that's fine. You don't have to cry every ten minutes, but sis, you also can't hold everything in! Half the time, I have to beg you to tell me when something is bothering you. You're so busy trying to make everyone think you can do everything on your own that I think you've forgotten that everyone needs a little help sometimes. It's not a weakness to want someone who understands you or have someone take care of you."

Makayla didn't say anything because she didn't actually know what to say. She could admit that getting in touch with her emotions wasn't her specialty. It wasn't unheard of for her to keep shit to herself more often than not. In her mind, everyone else already had their own shit going on. Why add to their load?

Jasmine made her way over to the couch and sat next to Makayla. She looked at her best friend, a sad smile on her lips. "I'm not saying I don't believe you when you say you're happy single or that your job is important to you. I know both of those things are very true. I've never given you shit about being single like your family because if you're happy being single, then I'm happy for you." She let out a sigh. "But what I need you to know is, finding someone who makes you happy doesn't automatically mean you've been lying this whole time or that you have to change who you are."

"I get that, Jas. I hear what you're saying. But how do I make time for that person without compromising who I am?"

A laugh escaped Jasmine. "Are you serious, M&M? You always make time for the things and people you want to make time for. You may cancel sometimes, but so what? When it comes down to it, you always make sure there's room in your schedule for me, your sisters, and your mom. I can't even remember the last time you missed a karaoke night or one of our mini spa days. You damn sure make time to get dick when you want it. So, I think it's safe to say that if you really found someone you cared about and could see yourself with long-term, you'd make time for them too. Case in point...you've made plenty of time for your dates with Reggie lately."

The logic was there, but Makayla's instinct told her to resist everything that she was saying. It couldn't possibly be that easy. She said as much to Jasmine.

"If that's really all it took, sis, then Nick and I wouldn't have fallen apart the way we did," Makayla pointed out.

"Girl, please. First of all, that was doomed to fail from the beginning because that man had a fragile ego. That's exactly why his whole nice guy routine fell apart at the end. You put in the work and the effort with Nick. He just didn't appreciate it because it didn't look the way that *he* thought it should."

A lump formed in Makayla's throat. Hadn't Reggie basically told her the same thing when she'd mentioned this to him?

"Second, Nick was three years ago. So, because something didn't work out years ago, that means you stop trying? Now you know better than that."

"Okay, but—"

"But nothing," Jasmine said, holding up her hand. "Has Reggie ever given you the indication that he doesn't understand the demands of your job? Or that he doesn't get how important work is to you? Has he at any point said something that made you feel like he would want you and your needs to take a back seat if y'all got serious?"

Makayla shook her head. In fact, she was pretty sure he'd told her the exact opposite of everything that her best friend had just said. In truth, wasn't his job just as demanding as hers? But still, there was a part of her that worried that when this wedding business was finished, and everything returned back to normal, the understanding Reggie would suddenly disappear.

So maybe you are just as scared as Jasmine said you were.

"I'm going to assume your silence means you know that I am, once again, all-seeing and all-knowing."

Makayla suddenly wished that looks could kill, so she'd be down a best friend right now.

"So now that we've dispelled the myth that you don't have time for a relationship, do you have an actual reason for why you called things off with Reggie?"

Makayla opened her mouth to respond but froze. Everything

she wanted to say was basically more of the same. *What. The. Fuck.* Was this real life right now? The realization that Jasmine was right must have settled on her face because her best friend, amazing person that she was, pulled Makayla into her arms. As soon as she felt Jasmine's arms wrap around her, the tears started to flow from her eyes. The intense feeling punched her right in the chest, making her breath catch in her throat.

"Shit, Jas," she said between sobs. "Why didn't you call my ass out sooner? You might've saved us both a lot of trouble."

"Honestly? You're sort of skittish. I always thought if I brought it up before you were ready, you'd take off like a cornered animal or something. Your fight or flight response is top-tier."

"Oh, screw you," Makayla said, her words caught between a laugh and a sob.

Jasmine laughed with her as she pulled away, still rubbing her shoulder. Makayla leaned into her, not quite ready to let go.

"Seriously, though, for a while there, I thought you knew and just didn't want to talk about it. Then it was sort of like, 'okay, M&M's smart, so she'll figure this out, right?' But now it's just sort of clear that if I don't point it out, you're just going to keep talking out your ass and embarrassing us both."

Makayla kissed her teeth and shoved her best friend.

"Okay, okay. What I meant to say is that I realized that if I want you to actually be your best self, then I have to sort of help you out along the way. I mean, can't blame you for burying this shit so deep. I know what you saw your mom and Lizzie go through. They're both just now finding their happily ever afters, so how could that shit not freak you out?"

Makayla knew Jasmine was right. She was happy for her mother and Percy, but she still couldn't wrap her mind around the fact that her mother was willing to put her heart on the line again after losing love not once but twice. It was the same with Lizzie. She'd watched her little sister have her heart broken time

after time after time. How did she not end up utterly devastated? How did she have the courage to keep trying? Makayla
just couldn't understand it. And as for Kendall... Makayla
couldn't help but wonder how her sister kept her relationship
going with Greg after all these years. How could she measure
up to that?

"Listen, I'm not saying all this because I'm trying to drag you.
I'm not even saying all this because I think that Reggie is the end
all be all and you should get down on your knees and propose to
him tomorrow. All I'm saying is, why take yourself out of the
game before it even really starts, sis?" She pulled away so that
Makayla was forced to look up at her.

"I may not know a whole lot, but what I do know is that man
looks at you like the world shines out of your coochie, okay?"

Makayla let out a laugh as she shook her head.

"It's true! And honestly, I've never seen you this comfortable
with anyone like...ever. Or this happy. So why lose all of that just
because you're a little..."

Makayla shot her a look.

"Okay, a lot scared. Talk to Reggie like an adult. He'll understand. And if he doesn't, well, then...eventually, if you want to,
you'll find someone who will."

Jasmine leaned over and pulled Makayla into one last hug
before standing up. "Now, as much as I hate to leave you here
with your melted ice cream and my pure genius insight, I have to
go because some of us don't have the luxury of a spa day
tomorrow."

"Just blow up my world and head out, huh?" Makayla said
with an eye roll.

"You're very welcome. Don't worry, I know how to let myself
out." Jasmine blew her a kiss before heading out the door and
locking up behind her, leaving Makayla to her thoughts.

Instead of getting up to put away the ice cream or heading to
her room, Makayla stretched out on her couch and grabbed the

remote. She needed to find something, anything to get her mind off of her conversation with Jasmine.

As much as she hated to admit it to herself, her best friend had read her from top to bottom. Whether Makayla acknowledged it or not, relationships scared the shit out of her. Keeping things light and fun had always worked for her in the past. It let her keep just enough distance between herself and her partners because if things stayed casual, then no one got hurt, right? There was no way that she could be left in a position to not only lose the other person but herself as well.

Hell, after the whole thing with Nick, she swore she'd never put herself in that position again. Was love really worth all of that risk? The possibility of heartache, the tears, the extra work. Was any one person worth all of that? And if she finally decided that someone—that Reggie—was worth taking that leap, would he think she was just as worthy? Maybe that was what this all came down to. The last thing she wanted to do was tie her worth to another person. When you really thought about it, though, was it any worse than tying her worth to her career? That's what she'd been doing all this time. She may have avoided serious relationships, but that energy clearly had to be focused somewhere else, and from where she was sitting, it had all gone into work.

Did she love her job? Hell yes. That certainly hadn't changed. But did she really have to choose? And if she did give in and decide to give the real thing a try, did that mean her family had been right all this time and that she'd been missing out on something? Did it mean that, despite all her protesting, she really hadn't been happy single?

Makayla groaned because holy hell, if this is what her brain was going to be like from now on, maybe she should say screw it and forget the whole thing.

"Girl, grow up," she said to herself aloud.

When she finally stopped flipping through the channels, she couldn't help but laugh at what she'd landed on. Was the universe attempting to kick her ass or just kick her off a cliff? The sound of Taye Diggs celebrating his "divooorce" rang through her soundbar. *Brown Sugar*. Of course.

Despite herself, she settled in on the couch, her thoughts drifting back and forth between the movie in front of her, Reggie, and her conversation with Jasmine. As much as Makayla wanted to deny it, she had something with Reggie. They may not be the perfect verse over the perfect beat like Sidney and Dre, but maybe that was okay. Maybe what they had was still worth exploring, and all she needed to do was be brave enough to take that chance.

CHAPTER 32

Makayla

Makayla found herself wishing that she'd stayed the fuck in bed. Whose idea was it for Delilah's daughters to take her out for a relaxing spa day the afternoon before the wedding?

It was your idea, remember?

Of course, it was. Makayla mentally kicked herself for putting this together. From the moment the group had met up for brunch at the spa's restaurant, today had been the day from hell. She was still conflicted about what to do about Reggie and the hangover she had from two and a half bottles of wine on a halfway empty stomach had not done her any good.

Any reprieve she'd hoped to get today went out the window as soon as Kendall showed up with her nasty attitude and foul ass mood. It'd started out small, with Kendall pointing out Makayla's hangover. She'd brushed that off because it was the least of her worries. Unfortunately, her sister could never leave well enough alone.

"I can't believe they're making us do our services separately. I knew I should've taken the lead on the spa," Kendall huffed as she crossed her legs.

"Oh, Kenny, it's not even that big a deal. So some of us have to wait. It's not like we have anything else to do," Lizzie said, shooting a nervous look at Makayla.

Makayla rolled her eyes and sat back in the chair, grabbing a flute of champagne and taking a long sip. She'd nearly drained the whole glass. Just a few more hours, and she'd be free.

Until tomorrow, that is.

Right. Of course. How could she forget? She had no idea whether or not she'd actually have a date tomorrow. Even though, she'd opened the door for it, Reggie not being there would do nothing but bring a slew of questions from everyone, including Kend—

"You know, if all you're going to do is drink, you could've stayed home. I mean, damn, we're in public, it's the middle of the day, and you're getting drunk," the older woman scoffed.

"I'm going to need to be drunk to get through this day with you."

"Oh, shit," slipped from Lizzie's lips as Kendall jumped out of her seat.

"Excuse me? What the fuck did you just say?"

The door to their private lounge opened as the spa concierge came in with her assistant. Before either woman could tell them what was next on the schedule, Makayla looked up at her sister.

"I said, I'll need to be drunk to get through today with you and your fucked up attitude."

"*I've* got the fucked up attitude? Me? You're the one who showed up hungover and couldn't even be bothered to make sure the spa services were set up correctly. I mean, damn, Makayla, all that fucking time you spend on that so-called complicated ass job of yours, and you can't even get this shit right?"

"Actually, ladies—" The concierge didn't get the opportunity to finish her sentence.

Makayla stood. "Oh, please, Kendall! You've been acting like a bitch since you showed up this morning. Pouting because your massage won't happen at the same time as Mommy's? You're that hard up? I mean, shit, maybe if you weren't getting on everyone's fucking nerves so bad lately, you could've asked your husband for a damn massage. Maybe it's not too late. Though I can't imagine he'd want to touch such a frigid bitch these days."

The fire behind Kendall's eyes let Makayla know she'd struck a chord.

"M&M!" Lizzie hissed.

It was a low blow, and part of her felt guilty, but damn, could her sister give her a fucking break?

"Fuck you, Makayla! At least I can keep a man. You can barely—"

"That's enough!" Delilah's words were so loud both spa attendants and her daughters nearly jumped out of their skin. "I am sick and tired of you two bickering like children! You're two grown ass women. It's time you start acting like it."

Delilah turned to the spa attendants. "Ladies, could we please have the room?" Both women scurried out without a word, clearly wanting to get as far away from the group as possible.

"You two have always gone back and forth, but it's gone too far."

"But—" Makayla started, but her mother cut her off with a look.

"But nothing! I'm supposed to be getting ready for the happiest day of my life. Instead, I'm sitting here playing referee for two very grown women who can't get their shit together for just a few hours. Look at you. Sitting up here arguing over petty shit. I'm tired! *I. Am. Tired.* I refuse to do this shit with y'all anymore."

Both Makayla and Kendall at least had the decency to look ashamed. Makayla knew that her mother was right. They were supposed to be here making this day special, and instead, the two women had made it all about them and their own drama.

"Now, I don't know what issue you two have with each other, but you better get it worked out here and now." Delilah stood up from her seat, tightened her robe, and moved toward the door. "Lizzie, let's go."

"Mommy, are you…" Lizzie started, but her mother held up her hand.

"I said let's go!"

Lizzie stood up quickly and met her mother at the door. Makayla and Kendall were left standing in the middle of the room, jaws nearly on the ground. Their mother looked back and forth between the two of them and shook her head.

"I love you. Both of you, but if you don't get this in order, I promise you, neither one of you will be welcome at my wedding." They looked at her, shocked. "And let's be clear, you can try me if you want to. You'll find out who your mama really is. Fix it. *Now!*"

With those final words, Delilah and Lizzie left the room. Makayla couldn't do anything except shake her head. She was really fucking this up, wasn't she? This was not how she'd planned for this day to go.

After a few moments of silence, she turned to her sister. "I'm so tired of this."

Kendall kissed her teeth. "And what exactly is it that you're tired of?" she asked with an attitude.

"This! The arguing, the bickering, the goddamn nitpicking that you seem so inclined to do whenever we're in the same room lately. I don't understand what your problem is with me, Kendall, but it's getting very old."

When Kendall didn't answer, Makayla walked toward her. "Kendall, we've always been close."

Kendall shot her a look, and Makayla rolled her eyes.

"Yeah, ok, we tend to go at each other a bit, but that's what sisters do! This is different, though. It's like lately, you find some-thing wrong with just about everything I say and do. Not to mention you seem to love throwing the fact that I'm the only single person in this family in my face every chance you get."

"That's because you have no problem reminding us that you're the only single one. You can't deny that you think it makes you better than the rest of us."

"I have never said that." Makayla hadn't…had she?

"You don't have to. It's in the way you act like you're so busy all the damn time. How many times have you scoffed at the fact that I stay home with the kids while you're at work? You act like I don't do anything but sit on my ass all day sipping tea." Kendall cleared her throat and began to mimic the other woman.

"Kendall, I'm busy at work, what do you want? Kendall, I don't have time for your bullshit, some of us have a job to do. Kendall, please, you know you have plenty of time to help mama with the wedding. I'm swamped at work."

She shook her head. "Just because I don't go into an office every day doesn't mean I don't have my own shit going on. It's like being married with kids is beneath you. How do you think that makes me feel? Pretty damn shitty."

Makayla shook her head. Had she really said those things? Okay, sure, maybe she'd done it a few times, but it wasn't a lie. She was busy at work. "Kendall, I don't say those things because I think you're beneath me. I'm literally just telling you what's going on in my life! Of course, being a stay-at-home mom is work, but you make it seem so easy." She scoffed. "I would never knock you for taking care of Greg and the kids. You know I love them and you."

Kendall rolled her eyes as she took a step away from Makayla. "My God, M&M, you've been doing it for so long that you don't even realize it. You literally make a face every time I bring them up like you can't even bring yourself to imagine living my life."

"Because I can't!" Makayla yelled.

The hurt look on her sister's face gave Makayla pause. She took a deep breath, moved a bit closer to close the distance, and tried again. "That…that didn't come out the way I meant it." She softened her tone.

"What I meant to say is I can't imagine living your life, Kendall, not because it's so horrible or tragic but because… because your life just seems so damn perfect. I just…I don't know how you do it because I'm pretty sure I could never measure up."

"What do you mean?" A confused expression crossed Kendall's face.

Makayla took a deep breath. *Here goes nothing.*

"I mean, dedicating your life to loving someone else. I don't know how you do it because the thought is terrifying to me. You and Greg have been together forever. It's like the perfect love story. You're living your happily ever after damn near effortlessly. I could never do that. Hell, I can't even commit to a man for more than a few weeks, let alone a lifetime. No way in hell could I open myself up to loving someone so…completely. I could never do what you do or have the life that you have."

Makayla's revelation sucked all of the air out of the room. The silence started to press in on them. No matter what Kendall thought of her, Makayla meant every word of what she'd said. She'd always been amazed and a bit envious of the fact that Kendall found the love of her life so young and seemed to have it all figured out. She was an amazing wife and a damn good mother. She knew taking on both roles full-time couldn't be easy, and yet, her sister was consistently killing the game.

"Kendall, you have a husband that absolutely adores the ground you walk on. You don't ever have to worry about whether or not you're capable of love or being loved because you already have it." Tears pricked the edges of her eyes.

"Don't get me wrong, I love my life and my job. And for the most part, yes, being single has been my choice, and I don't regret that. But if I'm being honest, I've always been a little jealous of how safe your relationship with Greg has always been. I don't think I've ever felt like I could just let go and feel secure that the other person would be there to catch me. The whole concept just terrifies me, and that's never seemed to be a problem for you. I just wish I could have that sort of confidence." Makayla cringed at her admission and the truth behind her words.

"I am legitimately terrified of the possibility that it just isn't meant to happen for me because the truth is I do want that type of love with someone. I'm just not sure if it's possible. What if I never get that part of my happy ending?" Her last words came out as a whisper, her voice thick from the tears that were beginning to fall.

She wrapped her arms around herself and turned away from her sister. "God, this is so fucking embarrassing," she said with a halfhearted laugh.

Makayla was making her way toward the door when she heard Kendall say something under her breath. "Huh?" she asked, turning around.

"I said we're separated. Greg and I have been separated for eight months." Kendall let out a breath and looked up at the ceiling.

What had she just said? "Holy shit."

"I know."

"Holy. Shit."

"I. Know," Kendall responded with a miserable laugh.

"But I thought you and Greg…" Makayla moved toward her sister, unable to even finish her sentence.

"Yeah, everyone thought me and Greg…" Kendall said with a shrug. "And I wasn't exactly about to correct anyone."

"Eight months?" Makayla asked as she took a seat on one of the ottomans.

Kendall nodded, taking a seat on the ottoman next to her. "Since January. Right after New Year's. And before you ask, no, neither one of us is cheating. We just…we've been drifting apart, I guess. I think he's gotten complacent, and I just feel sort of… lost."

Makayla reached over and took her sister's hand, giving it a squeeze. Kendall wiped away a few tears. "Greg's wrapped up in work, and even though I know he loves me, it feels like he's taking me for granted. The kids are growing up and don't need me as much as they did before. It literally feels like I'm stuck, and everyone else is just sort of…moving on without me."

"Do you regret it? Getting married so young?" Makayla hoped her sister wouldn't be offended by the question.

"What? No," Kendall said quickly, shaking her head. "I love my husband, and I love my babies. I just…I think I built my life around being a mother and a wife and forgot to build a life for myself outside of those things. I've lost myself, and I don't know how to get me back."

Makayla didn't know when they both started crying, but she grabbed them a few tissues. She pulled her sister into a hug as she continued.

"I guess that's where all my animosity has been coming from. Every time I turn around, you're talking about how great your job is, the way you're dominating shit at work, hell, all the bomb ass dick that you're out here getting with your single ass," Kendall said, teasing Makayla.

"Trust me, Ken, as much as I love me some bomb ass dick, sometimes it's not all it's cracked up to be," she said with a shake of her head. She pulled her bottom lip between her teeth. "Do mom and Lizzie know?" she asked.

Kendall shook her head. "No. Greg and I agreed not to tell anybody until we figure this all out. We're both still living at home but sleeping in separate rooms. We've started seeing a marriage counselor, but I just don't know where to go from here."

Makayla nodded. "But counseling is good, sis. It means you're both willing to work on things, right?"

Kendall nodded. "I know. The therapist thinks I should take some time to figure out what I want to do outside the home. You know…focus on me while we work on the marriage too." She shrugged. Makayla could tell that there was more she wasn't saying, but she didn't want to push her too much.

"It just sucks because I'm supposed to have this great life, and meanwhile, I've basically failed at the one thing that I set out to do. It doesn't help when your younger sister clearly hasn't failed at anything in her life. I guess… I just don't want you to think any less of me."

Guilt washed over Makayla. "Sissy, I never ever wanted to make you feel that way. I think you're an incredible wife, mother, and sister, even if you do get on my nerves sometimes," she teased. "And trust me when I say I'm not as perfect as you seem to think."

Before her sister could respond, her own confession came rushing to the surface. "Now is probably a good time to tell you that Reggie and I aren't actually dating," she said, eyes closed.

When she peeked at her sister, she could see Kendall looking at her with narrowed eyes. "Are you fucking with me right now?"

Makayla shook her head. The laugh she let out sounded bitter even to her own ears. "Nope. We went out that first time, it was great, I gave him my usual spiel of not having time for a relationship, and we went our separate ways. When I told y'all we were dating that day in the bridal shop, I hadn't actually spoken to him since the date."

"So you lied?!" Kendall squealed.

"I took one look at the smug expression on your face when you brought up the whole couples activity thing, then saw the disappointed look on Mommy's face, and I just…I panicked. I panicked, and next thing I knew, I was telling you that we were dating. I still don't know how I managed to convince him to go along with the whole idea. I just knew that I couldn't face any of you after telling that lie. I would rather have him think I was a fucking mess than come clean."

Makayla didn't know what she expected, but it certainly wasn't for her sister to burst out laughing. "Oh, I'm so glad you find this shit so funny."

"I'm so sorry, sissy. It's just…a fake boyfriend? For somebody who can't stand romantic movies, you sure pulled that plan right out of one."

"I know, I know," Makayla groaned. "And now I've gotten myself caught up because he wants this thing to be real."

"Well, do you want it to be real too?" asked Kendall cautiously.

Makayla felt as if she'd swallowed a lump as she nodded. "I think so."

Kendall seemed even more confused. "Ok, so what's the problem? As much as it might've pained me to say this an hour ago, the man seems pretty perfect to me. And y'all are pretty freaking cute together."

"That *is* the problem! He seems so sure about us, and I don't understand how! How do people make this type of shit work? It terrifies me. I just don't know if I can do this. I mean, hell, you're a damn near-perfect wife, and your marriage is in trouble! No offense."

Kendall nodded her head. "None taken. And I get that you're scared, but let me ask you this: does he make you happy?"

"Yes." Her answer came without even a bit of hesitation.

"Okay, so then take a word of advice from your big sis. Go for it. Yes, relationships are hard. They take a lot of work and don't let anyone ever tell you any different. No matter what anyone says, no one's relationship is perfect, but they don't have to be. Putting yourself out there requires a huge leap of faith, and I know that can be scary as hell, but when that other person is willing to take that leap with you…it's worth it. Do you think he's ready and willing?"

Makayla thought about it. She knew how she felt, and Reggie had no problem letting her know how he felt. She was the one that was putting the brakes on everything and hesitating every step of the way. But...was he really as invested as he said he was? Could she really trust that?

"I don't know."

Kendall nodded like she understood. "Okay. Just remember that you're worth it, whether he knows it or not. I'm not saying you have to have the answer right now, but don't throw away the possibility of something good just because you're scared. Mommy raised us better than that." She nudged Makayla's shoulder.

Makayla nodded. She knew her sister was right.

Twenty minutes later, when Delilah and Lizzie walked in, they found Makayla and Kendall laughing up a storm. "Umm... so is it safe to say that y'all have figured your shit out?" Lizzie asked, cautiously walking toward them.

Both women nodded. "Yeah, we figured it out. I think we understand each other a little better now."

"Good, because the next time either one of you pulls some shit like that, I swear I'm putting y'all over my damn knee. You are never too old for an ass-whooping," Delilah said with a hmph.

"We're sorry, Mama," they both said, standing up to pull her into a hug.

"Yeah, you better be!" she said, swatting at them before returning their hugs.

They pulled Lizzie into the hug with them, all four women loving on one another the way they were supposed to. Makayla finally felt like things were going to be okay. Now she just had to figure out what the hell she was going to do about Reggie. Kendall and Jasmine had both told her not to let her fear get the best of her. When it all came down to it, though, could she take that leap of faith and trust Reggie to catch her?

CHAPTER 33

Makayla

This was it. The day of the wedding was finally here, and damn if Makayla didn't wish she had just a few more days. All morning, she'd been running around attempting to ensure that the wedding planner had everything in order. She'd been so busy that she didn't have time to sit with her own thoughts. She'd done enough of that the night before. She welcomed the stress of the day because it gave her a much-needed break. Now that things were slowing down, though, it was suddenly hitting her that she really might be at this wedding alone.

Makayla hadn't spoken to Reggie since the wedding rehearsal. Part of her had hoped that he would call or text her, if only to give her an inkling of what he planned to do. Of course, she wasn't surprised when neither happened. She'd dug her own grave on this one. When he'd wanted to talk, she'd ignored him. Why wouldn't he go radio silent?

She peeked through the doors of the historic mansion to the outdoor ceremony space. Guests were arriving and taking their seats, but there was one guest in particular that she was looking for.

He's not going to be here.

She knew the voice was right, but that didn't stop her from hoping. She closed the door, urging herself to get it together. No matter what, today was not about her. She'd figure out how to fix things with Reggie tomorrow, but today... Today was about her mother and Percy.

As everyone took their places for the wedding processional, she watched Kendall's eyes track Greg as he made his way through the outdoor space. Now that she knew what was going on, she noticed the tense way he moved. He hadn't even kissed Kendall on the cheek before going to take his seat. How long had she missed the signs that her sister's marriage wasn't what it appeared to be? It made her sad, knowing what her sister was going through. She wanted nothing more than to try and fix it for her, but she knew that this was something that Kendall and Greg needed to work out for themselves.

So instead, Makayla took her place behind her sister, lightly grabbed her hand, and gave it a squeeze. Kendall turned around and gave Makayla a soft smile.

"You look gorgeous, sis," Makayla said, returning her smile.

Kendall gave Makayla's hand a squeeze of her own. "Had to bring my A-game."

"Only game we know how to play." The two of them laughed at their joke.

"Okay, maybe Mommy needs to lock y'all in a room together more often," Lizzie said as she took her place behind Makayla.

"Hush," Kendall hissed, though Makayla could've sworn she saw the laughter in her older sister's eyes.

"Places, everyone!" the wedding planner called, moving to the front of the group.

"Let's get this show on the road. I've made this man wait long enough. Any more waiting and he might change his mind."

Delilah sidled up behind the group, clutching her bouquet for dear life.

"Trust me, Mommy, he's not going anywhere." All anyone had to do was take one look at Percy to know that he was in it for life with Delilah.

"Thank you, baby," Delilah said. "And I'm sure Mr. Reggie isn't going anywhere any time soon either."

The pit of Makayla's stomach felt as if it were filled with lead. "I wouldn't be so sure about that, mama," she said in a voice just above a whisper.

"M&M, anyone could see that man looks at you like you're the moon to his stars."

She couldn't do this anymore. This was probably the worst time she could choose to tell her mother the truth, but Makayla couldn't hold it in anymore. Not when her mother was looking at her with that glow and happiness set behind her eyes.

"Mommy, I have to tell you something."

Delilah kicked up an eyebrow but didn't say a word.

"Reggie and I... Well, we—" Makayla took a breath. "We were never really dating. He only agreed to be my date after I lied to you all about it. He...he was doing me a favor. Nothing more, nothing less."

"Nothing more, nothing less, huh?" Delilah said with a smirk. "So, you weren't bussin' it down for that man on a semi-regular basis?"

"Mommy!" Makayla hissed. She looked around to see if anyone heard, but her sisters were too busy fussing over one another's hair to pay attention, and everyone else was outside.

"Please, baby, we are both grown, okay?" She gave her daughter a pointed look, and Makayla couldn't help the blush that followed.

"Fine! That's not the point. We were never serious. It...it was all a lie." There, she'd said it.

Makayla waited for her mother's anger, confusion, or any sort of outburst. Instead, the only thing that seemed to shine in her mother's eyes was amusement. "You know, it never fails to amaze me how you girls think that I can't see straight through you." She let out a laugh at Makayla's bewildered look. "Baby, I already knew that you two weren't dating when you brought him to the paint and sip."

The bouquet in Makayla's hand nearly hit the floor. "You can't be serious."

"Of course, I am! You may have had your sisters fooled, but from the moment you told us you two were dating, I had my suspicions. I mean, come on, baby, you practically looked sick when your sister announced the idea for the wedding activities. And let's be honest, you and Jasmine never could whisper." She winked. "I heard both of you going on and on about your little arrangement over the snack table."

Makayla let out a small groan. "And you let me make a fool of myself the entire time? Mommy, that's just mean!"

"*Mean?* Little girl, you are a whole adult. I was not about to blow up your spot. To be honest, I wasn't sure you'd keep up the charade for this long. And then, every time I saw you two together, it seemed less and less like an act. If you ask me, it may have started out as a lie, but it turned into a very real relationship, whether you realized it or not."

Delilah took a step closer to Makayla, placing her hand on her cheek. "Baby, the way you light up when you talk about work is the same way you light up when that man is around. I know I've been a bit much when it comes to trying to set you up, but it's only because I wanted you to have someone to share your happiness with. I didn't want you to have to struggle the way that I did. I am so grateful for Percy, and I know that he came into my life at the time he was supposed to, but it took a long time to get here. If I could prevent you from having to wait as long as I did...well, I had to try, didn't I?"

Makayla hadn't realized she was crying until her mother

wiped away a stray tear. "It just always felt like you were saying I wasn't good enough because I was alone."

"Awww, baby." Delilah pulled the other woman into a hug and held her tight. "Don't you ever let anyone make you feel less than. Your life is so full of joy and love, I know that. I just… I put my insecurities onto you, and I shouldn't have. I am so sorry that I ever made you feel that way."

She hadn't expected an apology, but Makayla realized that it was exactly what she'd needed after all this time. She'd known that her mother had the best intentions. Still, it was good to hear that. It was something she'd needed to hear.

"And just because your relationship with Reggie wasn't what you expected doesn't make it any less real."

Makayla had begun shaking her head before Delilah had even finished her sentence. "I messed it up, Mommy. I ruined it. I pushed him away, and now I don't even know how to fix it."

"What do you mean, you don't know how to fix it?" Delilah said, pulling away so that she could see Makayla's face. She pushed a stray braid from the woman's face and kissed her teeth. "Anything worth having is worth fighting for. Didn't I teach y'all that?" Makayla nodded. "You damn right I did. So fight. You say you messed up? Then talk to him and fix it. Any man who looks at you the way he does deserves a chance."

"I don't even know how. What the hell would I even say? To be honest, I'm the last person that he probably wants to see." Makayla really wished that the pressure behind her eyes would stop. Any more crying and her eyes would be red and swollen in the wedding photos.

"Now see, wait a minute. Last time I checked, I didn't raise a quitter. If you don't go after what you want, baby, then no one else will." She wiped away Makayla's stray tears. "Now, I suggest you get your ass into high gear and go find your man."

"But the wedding—"

"Can be pushed back just a little at the bride's request. Trust me, they'll survive." She turned Makayla around toward the front door. "Now get your ass out of here and hurry back."

Makayla let out a laugh and shook her head. "You're the best, mommy."

"Tell me something I don't know."

With a newfound sense of determination, Makayla took a deep breath and headed to grab her car keys from the bridal suite. She could hear the frantic words of the wedding planner wondering where she was going and hoped that her mother really could manage to get this thing pushed back just a bit. Then again, when Delilah set her mind toward doing something, nothing on earth could stop her.

Keys in hand, Makayla made her way outside to her car. She glanced down at her cell phone. If she hurried, she could make it to Reggie's place in about twenty minutes, assuming she didn't get pulled over for speeding along the way.

Her anxiety was through the roof as she threw her car into gear and pulled out of her space. She was so lost in thought that she completely missed the familiar truck passing her in the parking lot until a honk pulled her out of her stupor. Makayla turned, ready to lay out whoever was fucking up her plan, only to see Reggie looking at her as if she had two heads.

They both rushed to roll down their windows.

"Ummm...I've heard of runaway brides, but never a runaway bridesmaid," he said, leaning out of his window.

Instead of responding, Makayla put her car in park and scrambled out. Reggie did the same, meeting her in the space between.

"What are you doing here?" she asked, shocked.

"I know you may not want me here," he said sheepishly. The uncertainty in his eyes was cute. If Makayla's heart hadn't already melted, this certainly would've done the trick. Rubbing the back of his neck, he watched her intently. "But, where else would I be?" Reggie asked.

"I thought…" She struggled to finish her sentence. "I just assumed that after my message, after what I said, you wouldn't be here."

That look of uncertainty seemed to grow. Reggie shook his head. "I'm sorry, baby girl. If you want me to leave, I will. I realize this was totally out of pocket and that I probably should've stayed away, but I just… I figured today would be a lot for you. I didn't want you to have to go through this alone. I guess I may have overstepped. I'm sorry."

Reggie made a move to get back into his truck.

"Ask me where I was going!" Makayla said quickly.

Reggie turned, confused. "Huh?"

"Ask me where I was going," she said again, this time more sure of herself.

The tension in Reggie's shoulders seemed to dissipate just a little. "Where were you going?"

Makayla closed the gap between them, wringing her hands together. "Well, after getting my ass handed to me by my mother for screwing up royally, I was on my way to find you."

"Why?" he asked, a small smile slowly spreading across his face.

"Because I realized that even though I had every right to be terrified out of my mind, that didn't mean it was okay not to talk to you about it." Makayla shook her head as she looked down at her hands. Reggie lifted her chin, forcing her gaze to his.

"Everything about the time we've spent together has been scary and fucking unexpected. But it's also been fun, exhilarating, and…unexpected."

Reggie chuckled. "You said that one already."

"Yeah, well, it warranted mentioning twice. Now stop interrupting," she playfully snapped.

"You got it," he said, throwing his hands up in surrender.

"Anyway, like I was saying, I guess… I realized that running away never solves anything. And I've never been the type to be scared of taking chances or doing something different. So, this is me telling you that I want to try. I'm scared out of my fucking mind, and I don't know if this will work out, but I want to try… with you."

Reggie stood there for a moment just looking at her. Her skin was starting to feel itchy, and she felt vulnerable and exposed. "If that's not what you want, then—"

His lips stopped whatever she was going to say next. God, she'd missed the taste of him. If the groan that escaped his throat was any indication, he missed the taste of her too.

"No matter how this started out, what I feel for you is very, very real," Reggie whispered against her lips as they pulled away from one another. "I don't know where we're headed. I can't even promise you that this shit will be easy. What I *can* promise you is that I can't picture myself anywhere other than here with you." He pulled her hands into his. "I want to try with you too."

Those were the exact words that Makayla needed to hear. She leaned in to kiss him again, and he swept her up in his arms. Reggie kissed her hungrily, and Makayla accepted without hesitation, just as greedy for it as he was. The two were so lost in the moment that it took a while for them to register another honking car.

Cheeks flushed and chest heaving, Makayla turned and saw Kendall and Lizzie inside the latter's car. Both were trying very hard to hold in their laughter.

"This is all very nice, but we're behind schedule, and the wedding planner's head is about to spin off. Reggie, can you handle parking both of your cars so we can get your lil' boo's makeup touched up?" Kendall called out.

"Yeah, I think I can manage that," he said with a chuckle.

"See you out there?" Makayla whispered before placing another kiss on his lips.

"Of course."

She quickly grabbed her bouquet out of her car and jumped

in with her sisters. Over the next twenty minutes, they quickly did what they could to get her ready for her walk down the aisle.

"Please take your positions," the wedding planner called out, clearly annoyed at the delay.

As the four women found their positions, the smile never left Makayla's face. And when Johnny Gill's "You for Me" played through the garden space, she still couldn't seem to break her smile. Especially not when she saw Reggie watching her from the back row, and he winked as she walked past. Maybe they couldn't promise each other forever like her mother and Percy were doing, but as she stood at the altar and watched her mother glide down the aisle, she knew that they didn't need to. She didn't need that sense of security. Makayla realized the only thing that she truly needed was to know that what they could have was more than worth the risk.

Epilogue

MAKAYLA

"Fuuuck, right there," Makayla moaned. Her head fell back, hitting the shelf behind her. "Ow, shi—" The words caught in her throat as Reggie sucked on her clit with just the right amount of pressure.

Makayla could've sworn she had more willpower than this. She'd fully intended on holding out until the wedding was over. The ceremony was beautiful. Her emotions got the best of her halfway through her mother and Percy's vows, so, of course, she'd started crying. Once the vows were said and sealed with a kiss, the entire wedding procession closed out the ceremony by dancing back down the aisle. It was cheesy, and they'd tried to talk their mom out of it, but Makayla was surprised by how much fun the entire thing was.

Throughout the wedding party pictures, Makayla hadn't seen one trace of Reggie. They had all the time in the world, so she wasn't too worried about it. Then she'd spotted him watching her from the doorway as she took her individual pictures. Maybe it was all the emotion from the wedding, or maybe she'd missed him more than she'd thought, but somehow, she'd gone from posing for the camera to having one leg slung over Reggie's shoulder as he devoured her like she was his last meal.

Reggie was a sight to see, on his knees, half-buried under her bridesmaid dress. That in and of itself was enough to send her over the edge, but the punishing grip he had on her shaking thighs coupled with the flick of his tongue sent that tell-tale shiver through her.

"Reggie, I— I'm gonna…" Her voice quivered, and her hand gripped the top of his head, urging him on. It wasn't long before she was whimpering as she came all over his tongue. God, could anyone hear her on the other side of the door? The reception was in full swing, but there was no telling who was walking by the coat closet. As Reggie stood from his kneeling position and kissed her so that she could taste herself on his tongue, she didn't give one shit about who may or may not have heard what they'd just done.

As their tongues tangled together, Makayla made quick work of his belt and pants.

Reggie groaned as her hand wrapped around his dick and gave it a quick stroke. "Baby, we've got to get back out there. People are going to start looking for us soon."

Honestly, everyone had probably already noticed that Makayla had missed the wedding party introductions to the reception. As long as they made it out before the toasts began, they were perfectly fine.

"Better be quick, then," she said mischievously as she used her other hand to pull a condom out from between her breasts. Reggie snapped back, his face registering surprise. "I may have asked Jasmine to work some magic after you showed up."

Heat flashed between Reggie's eyes as he kissed her greedily. He managed to pull himself back enough to put the condom on while Makayla used the opportunity to shimmy the top of her dress down enough to pull her breasts free. She gave her nipples enough of a twist that a hiss slipped through her teeth.

"Reggie, please," she whined.

"Fuck, you know I love it when you beg," he said as he leaned in, licking and sucking along her neck until he reached her breasts. His tongue grazed her nipple just as he lifted Makayla up and slammed home, drawing a groan from his own lips and a high-pitched keen from hers.

"You feel so good." She gasped with each upward thrust of his hips. Had she really thought that she could let this go? That moment felt so far away now.

As her moans grew louder and louder, Reggie did his best to swallow them with kisses. He silently hoped the closet was far enough away from the reception hall that no one would hear them, or at the very least, he hoped the music would cover their noises. On the other hand, though, as her nails dug into the back of his neck to pull him in closer, he decided that he didn't give a shit.

"Take what you need, baby girl," Reggie whispered against her lips as he stopped pushing into her. He turned them around so that she was no longer knocking into the shelves but instead had her back against the door. "Take it."

She didn't need to be told twice. Using the door and her grip on him as leverage, Makayla rolled her hips, grinding down on Reggie frantically. Every time her clit grazed his pelvis, she let out a curse. She moved faster and faster, her walls clenching around him as her pleasure began to peak. She never wanted to let him go, and apparently, her pussy felt the same way.

As the wave hit her, her rhythm faltered, and Reggie took over, fucking into her until she was a loud, moaning mess. He made no move to silence her, too busy praising her and how good she felt clenching around him. He cursed as he thrust into her, only slowing once his own orgasm took over.

About two minutes after they'd finished, Makayla's legs still wrapped around him as the aftershocks went through her body, a pounding came at the door.

"If you two are done, we're about to start the toasts!"

"Jasmine," Makayla whispered.

"Yep, and we'd appreciate it if you cleaned your nasty asses up before you come back out."

"And that was Kendall," Makayla groaned, though her sister's tone was playful at best.

"Don't worry, baby girl." Reggie kissed her forehead and set her back on the floor. "There's more where that came from."

"Mmmm…" she said as she pulled him in for a kiss. "There better be."

————

REGGIE

Reggie watched Makayla as she took her turn dancing with Percy in the middle of the room. Delilah and Percy had made it a point to ensure that each of them was able to get a moment to dance with all their children and grandchildren after their own first dance. As she threw her head back and laughed at something the older man said, Reggie couldn't help but be mesmerized.

He'd been shocked to see her in her car, barreling toward his, leaving the venue. Even more stunned when he realized that she had been coming to look for him. Hearing that she wanted to be with him as much as he wanted to be with her made everything worth it.

"I'm pretty sure that you can't stare any harder at her than you already are," a voice said beside him.

He turned to see Makayla's brother-in-law, Greg, standing next to him at the bar. Despite having been in each other's presence quite a bit over the last couple of months, Reggie realized that he hadn't actually talked to the other man that much. Nothing beyond casual greetings, to be honest.

"I'm pretty sure you're right." His answer came quickly, and there wasn't an ounce of shame in his words. Makayla was his, and she was gorgeous. How could he not stare?

"Don't worry. I'm definitely not judging you. I remember what that was like." He paused. "Try to hold onto that."

Reggie glanced at the other man and saw him gazing across the room at his wife. There were a lot of emotions there. Sadness, hurt, maybe even a bit of anger. Reggie wondered what that was about but realized it probably wasn't his place to ask. His cryptic words left enough of an impression, though, that he made a mental note to ask Makayla about the couple later.

Greg raised his glass in Reggie's direction before throwing back the shot and setting it back on the bar. He made his way through the crowd, getting lost among the other wedding guests. Reggie didn't know him that well, but he found himself hoping that whatever he was going through, Greg came out alright on the other end.

"Everything okay?" Makayla asked. Reggie had been so busy trying to find Greg in the crowd that he hadn't noticed her walk over to him.

"Yeah, I'm good." He pulled her into a hug and placed a kiss on her forehead. "You looked beautiful out there."

She smirked. "You're already getting more pussy later, baby. No need to lay it on thick."

The laugh that slipped out of him was so loud that the guests nearby turned to stare. "Cute. Real cute."

They both looked to the front of the room as Lizzie called everyone to attention. "Okay, y'all, it's time for the bride to throw the bouquet. That means all non-married folk head out to the dance floor. And yes, I said folk because my mama wants everyone in on this. None of that women-only shit in here, okay?"

The crowd chuckled as they began to follow directions. "Think you should try your luck?" Reggie asked as he gazed down at the woman in his arms. He wouldn't tell her just yet, but he knew love was definitely on the horizon for them, whether she realized it or not.

She snorted. Why did he love that sound so much? "Mmmm...I think not. We'll let the rest of the crowd have their fun with that." She held up a hotel key. "We're going to have our own fun." The glint in her eye told him exactly what she had in mind.

"Won't your mother notice we're gone again?" he asked, though he was already letting her lead him toward the exit so they could find an elevator that led upstairs.

"Probably," she said with a shrug. Makayla turned to him and gave him a wink. "But this will definitely be worth it."

A Final Word

Thank you for taking the time to pick up my debut novel. It means the world to be that you gave Makayla and Reggie's story a chance. It may not be perfect, but it's mine and I hope you were able to see the beauty in it.

If you're able, please find the time to leave a rating and/or review on your favorite platform (Goodreads, Storygraph, etc.). They're the best way to help readers find new favorites and so important when supporting indie authors.

To keep up-to-date on upcoming Lady Marie projects, be sure to sign up for the Spice In Your Life Newsletter, join me on Patreon (Lady Marie Affair), check out my linktree, and follow me on social media @ladymariewrites.

To order a signed copy of any of my physical projects, merch, or web exclusives, please visit the Lady Marie Shop at lady mariewrites.com

Acknowledgments

Let's be honest, I may have managed to get the words on the page, but this book would have never happened without the love and support of my friends and family. There are so many of you who helped me get to this place and I can't even begin to know how to thank or name all of you. While you all played a special role in making this happen, I have to take the time to thank my Sissa (Ashley) and my Mommy. Without the two of you, I wouldn't have had the courage to finally put action behind my dream. You always pushed me, even when I couldn't push myself. And of course, to the best little sister the world could provide, thank you Kennedy for always being my cheerleader.

To RM, Nicole, Bee, Lorryn, and Maliyah, I couldn't ask for a better virtual squad. You had faith in this story long before there was ever a single word on the page. Your encouragement was never ending and you never let me doubt myself, not even for a moment.

Makayla and Reggie took me on quite the journey. What started out as a cute, quick glimpse into a budding relationship, quickly spiraled into an unexpected, fully grown story about two people finding love amongst family pressure and just a bit of chaos. Trust me when I say that I did not expect to give y'all all these words, but Makayla and Reggie basically held me hostage and demanded I give a full experience. I wish I could be mad about it, but they absolutely deserved it. So with that being said, I have to say thank you to the Wordmakers writer's group and

Tasha L. Harrison, who inspired me during the #20kin5Days challenge. This story was born during my very first attempt at this challenge in the fall of 2021 and I haven't looked back since.

To my beta readers – RM (Virtues), Nicole (whopickedthisbook), Rilzy (Adams), A.H. (Cunningham), and Lynell (weekend reader). Thank you for helping me shape this story. This was my first real attempt at finishing a project and I can't even begin to tell you how much I appreciate you being willing to go on this adventure with me. I definitely would not have made it here without your insight, advice, and comments.

To my editor, Kai (AdotKEdits) because I KNOW my aversion to commas and repetitiveness probably drove you up the wall, but you never quit on me. You're amazing and you're stuck with me at this point, so get used to it.

To the authors who came before me and didn't hesitate to offer me advice and encouragement: RM Virtues, Tasha L. Harrison, Brynn Harbon, Katrina Jackson, A.H. Cunningham, Rilzy Adams and Aveda Vice. You've been there, done that, and were always there when I had a question, no matter how big, small, or annoying. Thank you a million times over.

And finally, to the amazing community I've developed on social media and to my readers. Thank you for taking a chance on a first-time author. Thank you for picking up this debut and whether you love it or hate it, I appreciate your time and opinions all the same. Without you all, there wouldn't be a Lady Marie and I wouldn't be here now, living this dream.

Also by Lady Marie

SISTERS & SERENDIPITY SERIES

Worth It (A Fake Dating Novel)

Found Forever (An Established Couple, After the HEA Novella)

SUGARED AND SPICED SERIES

Sugar, Sugar (An Age Gap, Sugar Arrangement Novella)

Sweet Heat (A FFM Age Gap, Sugar Arrangement Novella)

Sugar-Coated Kisses (An Age Gap Insta-love Novella)

Sweet Control (An Age Gap, Sugar Arrangement Novella)

SLEIGH THE NIGHT COLLECTION

After Tonight (A Brother's Best Friend Novella, *Sleigh the Night* Prequel)

Sleigh the Night (A Winter Shorts Collection)

HOLIDAY NOVELLAS AND SHORT STORIES

With Sugar on Top (A Sugared and Spiced NYE Short)

Sinnamon & Golds (A Lick Back Season, Thanksgiving Novella)

Szn's Greetings (A Sinnamon & Golds Christmas Short)

Resolutions (A New Year's Novellette)